RAG DOLL

The stairs creaked beneath my feet. All was dark below, lit only by a thread of moon seeping through the open windows. I did not need a lamp; I knew where I was going. Numbly, I seemed to float to the cupboard, and I opened the drawer. The wooden handle felt cold on my fingers, and the smooth steel of its long blade caught the glint of moonlight and shimmered silver-blue.

Slowly I ran my finger along its edge. It was sharp. Dazedly I stared at it. I remember feeling the cool breeze of night as it gently caught my gown. Mixed with the soft breeze was a whisper. "Slit your throat, Rachel. Slit your throat. Slit it with the knife."

Like a leaden weight, I felt powerless to move or think. The glint of steel mesmerized me and carried me away into the caressing voices.

Then I heard Mama behind me.

"Rachel! Pray, God, what are you doing with that knife? Give that to me! Give it to me this instant!"

Like a rag doll, I stood limply within her grasp, my head bobbing backward and forward as her hands shook my shoulders.

WITCH CHILD

Elizabeth Lloyd

ZEBRA BOOKS
KENSINGTON PUBLISHING CORP.

ZEBRA BOOKS

are published by

Kensington Publishing Corp.
475 Park Avenue South
New York, NY 10016

First printing: December, 1987

Printed in the United States of America

Salem, 19 July 1692

I think I am a witch.

Today I watched Goody Glover hanged. I stood on Witch's Hill, feeling myself a small body swallowed in the crowd of onlookers, and listened to the clop, clop, clop of the horses' hooves and the creaking of the cart wheels which carried Goody Glover up to her gallows. The air felt cool and damp on my cheeks after the morning rain. The branches of the tall, broad, hanging tree before me dripped with the moistness of the early showers. A wheel of the wobbly cart stuck in a muddy rut, and as it stuck, a loud piercing jeer rose from the crowd.

"'Tis the Devil trying to save her!" they cried. "He's trying to keep her from the gallows!"

But the driver overcame the Devil. With a whip of his oxen, he dislodged the wheel, and slowly the wobbly cart continued bumping and jolting its way across the marshes toward our small, barren hill and the sprawling branches which have become our gallows.

Reverend Parris stepped forward; his face was grim and solemn, his figure was clad in a long black waistcoat, and in his stern voice he asked of Goody Glover if she had any last words to offer for her redemption. Goody Glover spat out something mean and caustic. The crowd hissed, angrily. Then, calm as stone, Goody Glover marched defiantly forward, and the henchman with his brown hooded face placed the noose around her neck.

Two black eyes stared out at us. I felt those eyes searching amongst all our faces, coldly and with an accusing glare. Finally I felt them fall on me.

Shuddering, I wondered, "Does everyone feel Goody Glover's eyes on their particular person?" I tried to look away, but I could not. I don't know why I could not. Now I wish I had.

The crowd was still, watching, their breathing silent and intent. Then suddenly, without warning, a loud clang shattered that stillness, the floor beneath the gallows fell open and Goody Glover's body dropped—then stopped with a small jerk. A silent scream filled my mouth, and one hand flew to my throat. Oddly, it burned with the feel of a rope.

Beneath Goody Glover's swaying brown skirts, two long feet twitched. Her head hung at a strange angle. Tiny bubbles of saliva drooled from the corner of her lips. Yet it was not the saliva nor the broken neck nor the twitching feet which so tormented me. It was her eyes—big and wide and bulging. Like a frog in Papa's pond. *And they still stared right at me.*

Though they burned through me like hot coals, my body froze like ice. I shivered. Instantly I willed my hand to fly back down to my side. Terrified, I wondered, "Does Mama notice?" Hastily I pulled my cloak round my shoulders and murmured something about a chill caused by the morning's rain. I think Mama believed me. But my throat still burned so raw, I could scarcely swallow.

When we arrived home, I decided to write all this down and to hide it in a secret place, so that someday, if

When we arrived home, I decided to write all this down and to hide it in a secret place, so that someday, if I am found out, I can tell people about this journal, and they can read it and know I never intended to be an evil person. Mostly I do not think I am evil at all.

Salem, 20 July 1692

Last night was so terrifying I can scarce believe it to describe it. I am dazed. And frightened.

I know not where to begin.

In my sleep she came to me. Goody Glover. I awoke with a start, feeling as if I were being prickled by a thousand pins, and there she was, staring down at me from the rafters. Her mouth was wide and cackling like an evil hen, and drool dribbled from the side of her mouth, down and under her chin. Terrified, I instantly screamed, "Away! Away, you evil witch!"

Frantic, I dove beneath the covers. She followed me. I could hear her cackling laughter. Tears streamed down my cheeks, and my body was all atremble. 'Twas not my tears wetting my face, but her drool!—her drool sliding down from her chin and down around the top of the quilt and onto my cheeks. My whole body shook, and again I cried out in fits and sobs, "Away! Away! Be gone, you evil witch!"

Mercy, in the bed across the chamber, arose, tiptoed over, and touched me. I let out a shrill scream. 'Twas not Mercy's touch, but Goody Glover's long bony fingers reaching out for me, cloying, clutching. An evil grin danced in front of me, and beneath the depths of my quilt, I felt as if I should suffocate.

The whiny little voice of Mercy asked, "Rachel? Rachel? 'Tis a nightmare you're having?"

The chamber rang with deafening cackling as Goody Glover threw back her head in laughter. No longer could I control my limbs; they heaved in violent spasms. I screamed. Again and again I screamed, and I could not stop myself. My lungs felt on the verge of bursting, and I could not catch my breath; yet still the screams flew from my lips.

Mama's voice sounded, and when she pulled the covers back, I sat bolt upright and shrank from her touch. "Don't touch me! Don't touch me!" I screamed.

The full moon outside the windowpane threw back its head in cackling laughter.

Where'er I looked, Goody Glover's face leapt out at me, her scrawny face thrown back in evil laughter. On the washstand, in the looking glass, on the thread of moonlight streaming across the rag rug—everywhere was Goody Glover's vision. Her face rose from the water pitcher, and when her mouth opened and cackled, from its depths leapt out the bulging eyes of a snapped neck.

From my convulsing limbs, the bed heaved, the ropes groaned, and I was certain 'twas Goody Glover shaking my bed, coming to fetch me.

Again Mama reached for me, and this time I fought her, thrashing and sobbing. "Away! Away! Don't touch me!"

Mama's voice was stern and commanding. "Hush, Rachel! Hush!" she said.

Vaguely I remember the light of a candle. Papa set it on the table, and it made soft lights dance in the chamber, casting shadows on the walls, scores of shadows, all evil and terrifying. In each of those shadows danced the wicked face of Goody Glover, cackling, drooling. Long bony fingers—witch's fingers!—reached out for me. Hardly could I scream again so weak was my body. Yet still I found strength, and I thrashed and fought.

Firm hands closed round one of my wrists, and so frantic was I, I thought my pounding heart would explode. From some distant part of my brain, I heard the sound of tearing cloth, then Papa's voice, swift and heavy: "Hold her, Martha, while I tie her to the posts."

As one arm was held tight to a post, I nearly tore the other from its socket trying to release it. But swiftly the other arm, too, was wrenched, jerked, and tied tight, and I screamed at the top of my lungs. My kicking legs heaved the lower half of my body from the bed. One foot met the resistance of Papa's stomach, and I saw him stagger. It was not Papa's stomach. It was the tall, angular stomach of Goody Glover, and it was Goody Glover I kicked across the chamber.

Only when both legs were finally secured, when my sprawled body, tied to all four posts, moved in small heaves, could I faintly recognize the sound of Mama's voice.

Sitting on the bed beside me, Mama removed her nightcap and used it to mop the perspiration from my brow.

"'Tis not perspiration!" I wanted to cry out. "'Tis Goody Glover's drool!"

"Who is it, Rachel?" Mama demanded. "Whom do you see?"

"Goody Glover!" I frantically cried. "'Tis Goody Glover—come to get me!"

Papa's voice, in wonderment, sounded. "I can't believe 'tis happening!" Papa said.

"What does she say?" Mama pressed. "What does Goody Glover speak to you?"

Through muffled sobs, I whimpered, "Nothing!

Nothing, Mama! She says nothing! She . . . she just stares! And . . . and laughs! And she reaches out for me!"

"But *why?*" Mama persisted. "*Why* does she want you?"

"I don't know," I sobbed. "O, Mama! Make her go away! Don't let her take me!"

Slowly my sobs silenced into whimpers, and my body grew limp and exhausted and flushed with fever. Papa laid a cool cloth upon my brow; then he leaned over me, and I saw his forehead creased in disbelief and confusion. Mercy, standing flat against the wall, was white and frightened. Daniel filled the doorway, his hands on his hips, his face purpled with rage. Glaring at me, Daniel declared, "She shall bring shame upon this family!"

Mama's calm voice filled the room, quoting the Bible, and her controlled presence gradually quieted us all as she eased into a soft chant of psalms. In muffled chokes I asked, "P . . . Papa? C . . . could you please bring in another candle? Her . . . her face keeps popping from the shadows."

Papa brought in three, and I felt a little better; so slowly he began to remove the cloth bindings, watching to make certain my fit had subsided. And when finally he released me, Mama's capable hands gathered me up and folded me into her bosom, nestling me like a frightened lamb into her breasts. She paused from her psalms then and, in a stern voice, addressed the chamber.

"We shall speak of this to no one," commanded Mama. "'Tis to be kept secret—only within our family."

With renewed fright, my body shuddered. So I am a terrible secret which everyone must hide. I am indeed to bring shame upon our family, as Daniel predicts! O dear God, pray do not let this really be happening!

I sobbed again, and Mama shook me, ordering, "Rachel, listen to me. You must collect yourself. Hush, now. Be silent while I read."

With one hand she opened the Bible, and Daniel stalked from the room in disgust. Mercy's eyes were wide and frightened, and in them I suddenly saw Goody Glover's, so I squeezed my own eyes shut to make them disappear.

In mesmerizing tones, Mama continued with the Scriptures, and Papa eased himself down upon the foot of the bed, looking oddly lost and ill at ease. For hours Mama read. At some point in those readings, in my exhaustion, I must have fallen into slumber, but when I awoke, Mama was still next to me, sleeping, the Bible open between us.

At morning meal, all was awkward and uneasy. While Mama ladled suppawn from the large black kettle in the hearth, Papa kept his eyes upon his trencher and made stilted conversation. Mercy's face, still white and pinched, cast darting glances at me, her eight-year-old body rigid with fear. I knew she was frightened of me. Daniel—who, at sixteen, felt his word carried as much weight as Papa's—continued to glare at me, still plainly furious, and at one point, he concluded, to no one in particular, that I was a sorry addition to the family; that I had always been a disaster.

Miserable, I waited for Papa to defend me. But Papa was too busy making stilted conversation. And Mama, drawn and weary, merely took her place at the trestle table.

Pray, God, help me! I am only twelve!

Salem, 20 July 1692, aft

I can't stop thinking about *her*. Goody Glover. All day she has rattled round in my brain, and last night haunts me like a fearsome shadow.

During the trial, the jury bade her take off all her clothes, then they searched her for witch's teats. I should die of shame should that ever happen to me. Goody Glover was shamed, too. Yet beneath her flush of shame, out of the corner of her eye, she stared at me in that peculiar way—almost, but not quite as bad as she stared at me at her hanging.

They say she invoked the power of the Devil by stroking poppets with her spittle. Goodman Bishop found some of the poppets stowed beneath Goody Glover's bed. One of them had light brown hair like mine. I don't think anyone has made a connection, though. Lots of girls have light brown hair.

The conviction said Goody Glover gave entertainment to Satan. During the trial she was locked in a small wooden hut on the edge of town so she would not infect anyone else. Then she was convicted. And hanged. The next day. Which was morning last.

So many people testified. Goody Morse told about when she had refused Goody Glover the use of her horse, so Goody Glover had made her house rife with terrifying strange noises. William Seager said Goody Glover had made a strange white cat attack him in the woods. Goody Osborne wept for her poor gone Mr. Osborne, lost when his fishing boat capsized in a freak storm. She said the storm was brought on by Goody Glover because Mr. Osborne admonished her for the loss of his babe when Goody Glover served as Goody Osborne's midwife. What's more, Goody Glover had inflicted the babe with a fit. 'Tis why it died.

Goody Osborne, William Seager, Goodman Bishop and Goody Morse all applauded when Goody Glover's body dropped in the rope. Finally I applauded, too, but my hands were numb.

This morn, after meal, Mama's bread wouldn't rise. Mama set it on the hearth for hours, yet it remained flat as a corncake. I felt ill with fear. Mama sighed and said something about a poor batch of yeast. Pray, God, don't let it be *me!*

Salem, 21 July 1692

I have told Jeremiah about my visions. Now I regret that I did, for his reaction was not as I wished.

He came, today, to show me the musket his father gave him for his birthday. 'Tis a lovely musket, having a long, smooth barrel and a grip of polished mahogany, and eagerly I admired it. Jeremiah was pleased by my admiration. I was glad. I like pleasing Jeremiah.

Jeremiah is fourteen. He is olive of complexion, slender of form, and decidedly handsome—at least so thinks Phebe Edwards who always swishes her skirts and assumes airs to gain his attention whenever Jeremiah is around. But, then, Phebe oft swishes her skirts and assumes airs.

I like Jeremiah because he is very wise and kind. He knows ever so much more than I ever shall; and he is ever so much kinder to people than I can ever be. Jeremiah, I think, is the only person who truly understands me.

In telling about my visions, I think I should have tempered my recounting. Phebe Edwards, undoubtedly, would have tossed her head in that infuriating manner which makes her curls dance, then teasingly murmured over her shoulder, "O Jeremiah, you shall never guess who visited me evening last!" But I? I simply planted my feet and blurted out my story.

Jeremiah was taken aback. His slender face paused in mid-smile, then grew long and concerned; and as my last word was spoken, he instantly bade me hush. Bade me not to give any more thought to it. "Rachel Ward!" he exclaimed. "Should you want to give cause for talk and have others consider you *possessed!*"

I frowned. I climbed upon Papa's split rail fence, which is my favorite place to think, and put my head in my hands to consider the matter. I tried to decide whether possession is really so shocking. After all, lots of girls this summer are possessed. 'Tis preferable indeed to being a *witch!* But then, one oft leads to the other. I suppose that's why Jeremiah is so frightened.

Jeremiah climbed up beside me, put his arm round my shoulders, and made his voice soft and gentle. I like it when he touches me. It makes me feel all tingly inside. He tried to console me with the thought that everyone in the village fears himself possessed. Or else his neighbor is a witch.

I shuddered when he said "witch."

I guess Jeremiah liked his line of thinking. Because he concluded that I was merely impressionable. Those were his very words. He said, "Rachel, how impressionable you are. Your nightly visions are merely bad dreams. Very bad dreams. And are brought on merely by . . . well, by all our rains. Girls your age are always having dreams—why, you've told me so yourself. Many times!"

Morosely I thought about Dorcas Good. Only four, yet hauled off to Boston prison in irons for entertaining Satan. So much for dreams. And girls my age. I decided not to tell Jeremiah about the bread not rising.

Sighing, Jeremiah asked, "What's happening to us—to all of us? Does the Devil intend to constantly give temptation? Is God testing us for our evil ways? Father talks daily of how our jail is bursting to the irons, yet not another sun sets when another neighbor isn't added. Pray, Rachel, do not you be possessed, too. And pray, do not be seeing reality in merely your dreams."

I wondered whom Jeremiah was trying to convince: me or himself. Jeremiah is extremely conservative. He dislikes it immensely when something happens to disrupt the natural order of things.

Sensing my annoyance, he reached down and picked me a daisy. Curtly I told him it had a bug on it. He laughed, brushed the bug off, but still I didn't want it. Nor did I wish to accompany him to watch him shoot his musket, as he suggested.

The nice thing about Jeremiah is that never is he in ill-humor. My sullenness disturbed him not at all. He merely smiled, saying he would see me on the morrow.

After he left, I went round to my chores in the malt house and prayed to God not to make me evil. Then I cursed Jeremiah for being so proper and unbending.

Salem, 21 July 1692, eve

'Tis horrid how she so terrorizes me.

This eve, after meal, Papa bid me fetch his pipe, which he had forgetfully left upon the chopping stump when he had been splitting wood prior to meal. Mama had bid me hasten so as not to delay the commencement of our nightly singing of psalms, and she was quite put out with me for pausing at the well for a sip of water.

"Rachel!" she called from the window. "Do be quick about your task! The Lord awaits our reverence!"

"Aye, Mama," said I, swiftly dropping the ladle back into the bucket which made a dull plop as I lowered it into the well. So peaceful was the dusk, I had hoped to prolong my errand; but Mama, as usual, had somehow guessed my intentions, and I felt her eyes upon me until I quickly turned the corner at the barn.

The chopping block is situated midway betwixt the barn and the forest, and lies about ten paces from the road, such placement being convenient for Papa when the oxen drag tree stumps from the forest and out onto the road toward home. There Papa splits countless cords to feed our hearth.

Seated atop the stump this dusk was a cat, large, orange, and quite plump, and I thought little of him as I hurried across the grass, intent upon not increasing Mama's irritation. Suddenly the cat moved up onto all fours, arched its back and hissed. Beneath it lay Papa's pipe.

"Move, kitty," I ordered as I approached and was startled when it made a small leap toward me, menacingly. Its eyes were glassy green and vicious, and I paused, retreating a step so as to avoid its attack.

I stood a moment, thinking 'twas my imagination, for slowly the plump creature settled back upon its haunches, appearing quite benign. Yet, when I again took a step forward, the creature once more leapt to its feet and spat, and as I attempted to reach for Papa's pipe, it clawed at me.

Instantly I let out a small cry. Long scratches upon my hand reddened with blood and stung like fire. And when I looked up, the creature's mouth was opened into a wide leer, as if laughing at me.

In the distance I heard Mama call, "Rachel! Rachel, do you still dally? Make haste for psalms!"

But I could not make haste. In those glassy green eyes, I alarmingly saw the eyes of Goody Glover. Quickly I shook my head to make her disappear. "'Tis foolish," I told myself. "Why should I fear a cat?"

Yet every time I attempted to approach, a large orange paw snatched out for me, nails vicious and sharp; and as I began moving round the stump to avoid it, the plump creature jumped from its perch and kept me at bay, pacing back and forth betwixt me and my quarry, its back arched, its orange hair on end, its glassy eyes leering. 'Twas as if it played a game with me, moving me farther and farther from the stump, all the while hissing threateningly.

"Rachel!" Mama called impatiently. "Where are you?"

Frightened, I halted, awaiting the cat's next reaction. Slowly it lowered itself onto its haunches and began to slink toward me, hissing; and as I picked up a piece of wood to chase it away, it paused, its green eyes gleaming with challenge, and they were the same eyes that had stared at me from a noose.

"Away! Away!" I instantly screamed. "Begone you vicious witch!" The spitting mouth yawned into a grin and howled, a howl which reached into the depths of my soul and seemed to tear it from my breast. Swiftly the vicious creature leapt at me, clawing at my legs, tearing through my stockings; and as I frantically kicked and screamed, I ran, claws all the while digging into my flesh, an angry hiss harshly erupting into a cackle.

"Begone! Begone!" I screamed as I stumbled to free myself and was nearly driven mad with pain.

Papa's voice said, perplexedly, "Rachel? What on earth . . ."

On the ground I lay, crying, Papa standing over me, and at his sound, the animal instantly released his hold and fled. My stockings were torn to shreds, blood oozing from their tatters, painfully.

"O Papa! Papa!" I wept. "She attacked me! 'Twas Goody Glover!"

"Hush," ordered Papa instantly. "Hush! 'Twas only some stray barn cat! Good heavens, daughter! Look at your legs! Why did you not defend yourself?"

"I tried to, Papa!" I cried. "But she wouldn't let me!"

"Hush!" Papa repeated firmly. "Let us bring you inside so your mother can apply some ointment."

Tenderly he then lifted me up and carried me, and when we reached the house and Papa made a short explanation, Mercy said, wondrously, "Rachel was attacked by a cat?"

Let them all think what they like! I know it was Goody Glover! She was trying to take me!

Salem, 22 July 1692

A very sad thing happened today. Buttermilk died.

Buttermilk was Papa's favorite cow. At noon she fell strangely ill, and Papa found her in the south meadow, lying on her side, heaving. Try as he could, Papa could not help her. Before his very gaze, she just rolled her eyes and died. She was a very gentle cow. Papa said she gave the best milk in the village. We had a small ceremony, Papa dug a grave and we all cried. I had stopped to pet her this morn on my way to the woods to pick sassafras for tea. I wish I hadn't petted her. I hope no one finds out I did.

Mama sat with me all last night. A candle burned on the night table beside us, and Mama read from the Bible while Mercy lay wide-eyed and silent in her bed across the chamber. Mercy is afraid of me.

Salem, 22 July 1692, eve

I feel quite pleased with myself, and this aft was able to distract my mind from my terrifying visions.

At midday, Deliverance Porter came round and bid me come with her to find amusement. I like Deliverance. She is a happy, friendly, amiable sort, who makes life ever so much fun. Also, she brings out the mischief in me, which is what I desperately needed. Removing our shoes, we raced along the river bank until we reached Ann Sibley's house.

Ann Sibley is also nice, but of different character than Deliverance—being shy and quiet, but sweet. With Ann was Abigail Watts—whom I can't much tolerate, being not only homely as a mule, but of equally mulish, disagreeable temperament—and (to my disdain!) Phebe Edwards. So sweet is Ann, she would never turn away a body who comes to call—not even Phebe and Abigail.

I knew I was in for nettlement when I spotted Phebe. Two more distant characters I cannot imagine than Phebe and I, and constantly are we at each other's throats.

The trio was sprawled in stacks of hay in Ann's barn, petting a lamb and daydreaming about the identity of their presumed future weddeds. 'Tis Phebe's favorite topic.

"Mine shall be *very* handsome and fetch me pretty dresses from Boston," announced Phebe, airily, while Deliverance and I settled ourselves amongst them. Our arrival had hardly disturbed Phebe's self-absorption.

I could not restrain myself. Cattily I retorted, "No one in your family has ever *seen* any dress but homespun in their entire lives."

Phebe merely smiled confidently, tossed her curls, and concluded, "I shall be the first."

Hah! thought I. And cows shall dance on the moon, and pigs fiddle! Deliciously I pictured Phebe in the years to come, a frumpy goodwife surrounded by her mewling brood, and scarcely could I wait for that day to arrive to be able to remind her of *this!*

Deliverance, turning to Ann, asked, "And what about you, Ann? Whom shall *your* wedded be? And what shall be his profession?"

Ann blushed. 'Tis no secret Ann has long held an admiration for Deodat Easty—yet so shy is Ann, she cannot even bring herself to speak in his presence. Softly Ann murmured, "I . . . I think he shall be fair of complexion. And perhaps a husbandman."

We all giggled, knowing the description to fit Deodat. Ann flushed again, then questioned Abigail about *her* intended. Such a great show did Abigail make of pondering the question that I listened with vast interest, wondering who would be the poor soul to be stuck (forever, no less!) with one possessing such a disagreeable nature. Finally, Abigail settled on Joshua Snow, and I snorted. Joshua Snow is not only the ugliest boy I have ever laid eyes upon, but a halfwit as well. His father is a cabinetmaker by trade, yet Joshua cannot tell one end of a mallet from the other.

Abigail glared at me with challenge. "And who

might *your* intended be, Rachel?" she demanded.

My eyes narrowed. I had no intention of being caught up in their little web so they could ridicule *me*. Besides, long ago Phebe declared Jeremiah for herself, and I would appear the fool claiming Jeremiah to be mine instead. And what if, in the end, Jeremiah *does* select Phebe over me? Then I'd be the fool indeed!

Aloud, I played for time. "Deliverance hasn't yet given *her* intended," I said.

It didn't work. Laughing, Deliverance said something like: "O nay, you first, Rachel. 'Tis of *you* the question was asked. Besides, everyone knows I shall wed Peter Cook!"

Caught, I flippantly remarked, "How should *I* know my intended? I'm not in possession of some crystal ball."

Deliverance smiled, deliciously. Already I have recorded how she brings out my streak of mischief. So I then announced, "But I shall make one!"

Everyone was ecstatic. In unison, hands clapping, they eagerly asked, "How?"

My mind began racing. Having put myself on the line, I had to be clever. "Well . . ." said I, "bring me the white of an egg and . . . and a clear glass."

Excitedly five bodies raced into Ann's mother's kitchen, then raced back to the barn, the mind in one body (mine!) all the while searching frantically for a procedure. Carefully, with four sets of eager eyes anxiously huddled round me, I cracked open the egg on the side of Ann's mother's prized crystal bowl, then slowly let the egg's white ooze down the side of the glass.

Phebe asked, enthusiastically, "What is to happen, Rachel?" 'Twas the nicest she has ever spoken. I stammered. I was not yet entirely certain of my intentions, but my pride was at stake, and I had to think of *something.*

"Well, er . . . 'tis . . . 'tis to take the shape of the first letter of the name of my intended."

Nothing much was happening, so I swirled the bowl a bit. Suddenly Abigail cried, "Why, 'tis the shape of a 'J'!"

To my utter astonishment, gazing down, and as sure as my shift is laced, a thread of solid color in the egg's white did indeed form a distorted 'J'!

"'Tis for Jeremiah!" cried Deliverance, happily.

Stunned, I could scarce tear my eyes from the white. Then I laughed. What a delicious joke! Fate has indeed intended Jeremiah for *me!*

Phebe sulked. "Piffle. 'Tis probably for Joshua Snow."

Joshua Snow! That halfwit! I would have smothered Phebe with wads of hay, were I not saved by Abigail.

"Joshua is *mine,"* whined Abigail.

In a snit, Phebe grabbed the bowl, tossed the white onto the dirt floor—whereupon the lamb eagerly lapped it up—and, with a flip of her head, decided "'Tis a foolish game, anyway. Whoever heard of an egg serving as a fortune?"

Phebe is such a goose. She never plays by the rules, unless she wins. I feel smug as song for having outsmarted her. But I know 'tis only a matter of time before she retaliates.

Salem, 23 July 1692

At Meeting today, Reverend Parris lectured on the evils of witches, and I listened extra intently, hoping his bellowings would help drive away Goody Glover.

"'Tis a guileful and deceitful age we live in," thundered the booming voice of Reverend Parris from the lecture stand. "Rotten-hearted devils have infested our community and corrupted our unity and peace. Alas, our war against the Devil has raised amongst us great hatred, which ariseth even in the nearest relations. 'Tis that hatred which brings us betrayal and subversion. A great guiltiness I feel in our village. Corruption in the human condition. Amongst us there are those who covet and care for money more than for the Church. But we shall weed them out! There shall be no more pacts with the Devil!"

'Tis as near as I can remember what he lectured, for on and on he did ramble. Mama, beside me in the fourth row on the women's side, nodded piously at appropriate points, and though I tried to concentrate with intentness, my mind wandered constantly.

On my other side sat Goody Bishop, she who is even more devout and Godly than Mama, and whose back was straight as a board and equally as unmoving.

Goody Bishop is keen on spotting witches. Already she has reported three. Nervously I tried to appear pure and serene. I shall have to take care with Goody Bishop.

Daniel and Papa sat opposite, with the men; but Goodman Bishop was absent, he being elected as one of the tithing men to patrol the village for Sabbath breakers. And behind Papa and Daniel, sat Jeremiah and his father. Jeremiah smiled at me when he entered. I smiled back, deciding to forgive him for afternoon last.

So suffocatingly hot was the room, I could scarce catch a breath. The glass in the windows, having long been shattered and with no funds for repair, are boarded in some crazy-quilt fashion, which keeps out not only the birds and the elements, but the air as well. The light was dim. The air was still. Perspiration crept down my back, wetting my shift. Reverend Parris's voice droned on, admonishing us all for the requirement of tithes.

Sometimes it seems Reverend Parris will never tire of demanding money for his Meetinghouse, or for his salary. All, presumably, tied up with the sudden profusion of witches—though 'tis hard for me to understand the connection. I tried to, though—through the heat and the bellows.

My cheeks felt warm and feverish. I fanned myself with my hand. My face went from hot to cool, and my blood felt as if it drained to my toes. My hymnbook, open upon my lap, swam before my eyes. Suddenly, from out of its pages, popped the evil face of Goody Glover. Even in Meeting!

Anxiously my heart began to pound. I squirmed, in fright. Mama frowned and reached over to still me. Mixed with Reverend Parris's booming voice was the cackle of Goody Glover's laughter. I feared to breathe, so terrified was I of exposure.

Reverend Parris led a prayer, but in my frantic state, I could not remember the words. My voice stumbled in distraction. Mama's foot hit mine, sharply. It hurt. Blood rushed from my head. Perspiration dripped. Laughter deafened my ears. My body felt dazed and icy. My stomach shrank into a small pit. And when we rose to sing a psalm, I fainted.

I think the fainting was my salvation, for had I not, I would surely have been discovered. When I came to, I was lying sprawled on the Meetinghouse steps, cradled in Mama's arms and listening to Mama calmly explain to Goody Bishop how I had not eaten my suppawn at morning meal—thus causing my weakness.

I think Goody Bishop believed her. I hope Goody Bishop didn't hear me stumble over my prayers. Goody Glover stumbled over prayers when they tested her for being a witch. 'Twas part of her conviction.

Salem, 24 July 1692, morn

Last eve Mama again sat up with me, reading from the Scriptures, trying to ward away my visions.

"Yea though I walk through the valley of the shadow of death," Mama read, "I shall fear no Evil. For Thou art with me."

Her steady, certain voice comforted me. Papa came in and placed another candle upon the washstand, and one upon the chest, and the whole room was bathed in light, driving away all the fearsome shadows. How I do dread the shadows.

Fitfully did I doze upon Mama's shoulder, waking with jumps and starts to the drifting sound of cackling laughter. Mama would hold me closer then, and I would fix my eyes upon her open page, willing them not to trail toward the rafters.

Sometimes I would see Goody Glover's face moving about in the light of a candle, and I would whimper. Other times, blood would ooze from her snapped neck, and I had to rise and wash the gooey stickiness from my hands.

Mama's voice, in sureness and certainty, moved steadily onward. "The Lord is my shepherd, I shalt not want. He maketh me to lie down beside him in green pastures. . . ."

Daniel came in once, glared, and mumbled something about a dark blot upon the family history. I think he meant me. Mama did not seem to hear, so I pretended not to, as well.

Salem, 24 July 1692, eve

After noonday meal, Jeremiah came to fetch me, and Mama bid me leave of my chores to go with him. Mama likes Jeremiah, which is evident by the pleasant manner in which she treats him. His father's ordinary, being of good profit, I suppose influences Mama's opinion. Mama thinks 'twould be a good match for me. I don't care a pence about the ordinary. I like Jeremiah just because of *him*.

We went to our favorite place, which is on the river's edge shaded by the stand of birch. Having brought our poles, we competed as to whose catch would be the first. I won, displaying a plump, squirming bass. Jeremiah caught the next two; then I one; then Jeremiah one; and so on. So in the end I came up two short, and Jeremiah had beaten me.

I pretended Jeremiah's victory to be due to his greater age and wisdom. Jeremiah likes it when I make him appear as a man, rather than a boy. Truthfully, however, Jeremiah won simply because I gave him the fatter worms.

We did not talk of my visions. Jeremiah did not ask, and I did not mention. I don't think Jeremiah wants to know.

Once, a few months ago, he said he felt all these witch trials to be full of hocus-pocus and terribly unfair. Yet sometime afterward, when I brought up those feelings, Jeremiah vehemently denied them. "I do, of course, wish we had no need for the trials," Jeremiah corrected. "But never have I disagreed that the need exists."

Jeremiah is not one for creating dissension or bucking the tide.

Salem, 25 July 1692

Much excitement was there today over the opening of Papa's new mill. Papa was up hours before the sun, gobbled down his morning meal, left Mercy and I to do the milking and was off in a great flurry with Daniel racing behind. Mercy asked Mama if she could tend another chore instead of assisting me with the milking, she being afraid to be alone with me.

I do hope, for all our sakes, the mill is a great success. 'Twas built with every penny of Papa's inheritance from Grandfather and all of our savings. Papa says we shall have to be frugal until the mill shows its colors, because our till is empty. But if the mill is indeed a success, Papa says 'twill bring us fortune, ever so much more fortune than husbandry.

A lot of our neighbors are jealous of Papa's sudden gain. When the mill was being built, the men used to find all sorts of excuses to come by and inspect, and I saw many leave with their heads down and their shoulders hunched for sadness at their own impoverished situations. Even did I hear a few grumble how "Some people have all the luck."

Goodman Corwin was the worst. His face was pea green. No wonder, since Goodman Corwin seems never able to eke out sufficient existence on his scrubby eighty acres, and 'tis as evident as sun that he'd give his right arm to feed his family of ten with a mill bright and shiny like Papa's.

Mama says we must feel sympathy for families like the Corwins. Mama says 'tis a pity there is no more good land to be had. 'Tis difficult, though, to feel pity for someone who always whines and makes such pathetic failure at what he attempts.

I think 'tis partly because of families like the Corwins that we have such a problem with witches. Everyone is looking for something on which to blame all their discouragements, and there is no better salve for suffering than finding a cause. Once I hinted as much to Papa, but he bade me never, ever to breathe such a thought to another living soul. 'Twould call my attention to the courts, which more and more requires scant doing to be labelled a witch. Such is the case with Goody Knapp, who was arrested afternoon last—with her only crime that of being a spinster.

I do hope the mill brings us fortune. If so, perhaps Papa will rise in stature and be addressed as "Mr." And we shall have sugar with every tea!

Salem, 26 July 1692

This morn, as I went to depart the door to milk the cow, it was there again. The cat.

Stealthily his plump form paced back and forth beside the hitching post, green eyes gleaming and fastened upon the house. 'Twas as if he stalked me, lying in wait. And as I opened the door, he halted, staring at me, orange back bristling, hair upended like a porcupine. With a gasp, I immediately leapt back inside and slammed the door behind me, my heart pounding. Everywhere she reaches for me!

Mama, at the hearth, said, "Rachel? Are you not tending to the milking?"

Nervously I stammered—"I . . . I can't. The . . . the cat's out there"—all the while wondering whether my admission would cause yet more bother, but not knowing an alternative.

Indeed, I was correct. Mama was irritated. Impatiently she said, "Take the broom to shoo him away. Rachel, do try not to be foolish and frightened of a cat."

Too keenly did I recall the horror of the other eve. "Can't I do the milking later?" I pled.

"Would you have the cow throb with pain?" Mama asked.

Better the cow than me, I thought, fearfully. "Couldn't Daniel do it?" I asked.

"Daniel tends the salt licks," Mama reminded.

"When he gets back?" I pled.

"When he returns he must eat so he might hasten to help your father at the mill. Now do be quick about your chores, Rachel. Your father shall be down any moment, and you shan't want to displease him."

Timidly I peered out the window. The menacing orange creature still paced and leered, its tail held high and erect. In his eyes gleamed the eyes of Goody Glover, laughing, mocking me. Taking a deep breath, my hand clutched the broom, and my fingers shook, for I knew 'twas useless to fend her away. "Pray, God," I breathed, "be with me."

Slowly I opened the door, gazing out from a crack, and as I did so, my torturer again halted. His mouth hissed and spat, and his menacing eyes awaited me. Swiftly, I again retreated.

"Mama!" I wailed. "She's going to get me! Pray, don't let her torture me!"

"She?" Mama repeated.

"Goody Glover!" I cried.

"Rachel, this is ridiculous," said Mama, sharply. "Hand me the broom. If you shan't shoo away a cat, then do allow me."

Annoyed, she quickly took the broom from my hand and opened the door. To my great astonishment, the cat had disappeared.

Papa, his tread heavy upon the stairs, asked, "What commotion do I hear?"

"Nothing," said Mama, calmly, and her swift frown

told me to hold my tongue. "Rachel was just going to tend the milking."

"With a broom?" asked Papa quizzically, as Mama hastily shoved the object into my hand while giving me a quick push forward.

"Rachel must sweep the yard when she returns," replied Mama. Woefully I heard the door shut behind me.

Dreading my fate, I nervously glanced this way and that, my hands shaking as if with palsy, and just as I took a step forward, the cat again appeared, from out of nowhere it seemed, and once more blocked my path. I think now he must have been hiding in the shadows, but at the moment, his return was as sudden as the appearance of an apparition.

Back arched, his spitting mouth emitted a low howl, as he had done the other eve, and as he began skulking toward me, I saw not him but her. Goody Glover. Coming to get me.

Screaming, I turned and nearly fell to the ground as I frantically fought my way back inside. "'Tis her!" I screamed. "Don't let her take me!"

Papa glanced up, perplexed. "Who?" he said.

"Goody Glover, Papa! The cat! The cat is Goody Glover! She waits to attack me!"

"Nonsense!" said Papa. His voice was disgusted, whether at the cat, Goody Glover, or me, I do not know. Angrily he grabbed up his musket and tore outside.

I think the cat must have concealed himself again, for in the intervening quiet moments, I knew Papa was searching him out. Then the still morn was shattered by the sudden explosion of a gun, which made my ears ring.

Papa's returning steps were purposeful, and he

appeared wholly satisfied as he resumed his place at the table. "'Tis the end of Goody Glover," he remarked.

I knew 'twas not so. At that very moment, her angular face peered through the curtains, grinning, beckoning, laughing. But I held my tongue.

Salem, 26 July 1692, aft

Now I know why Daniel is so angry with me. Because of Prudence Cory. Today I found out about him and Prudence, and now Daniel is doubly furious.

'Twas when I was running an errand for Mama that I learned it, hearing the murmur of voices coming from the thicket of trees near to where the road crosses the river, which is the short cut I always take. I did not—I repeat, I *did not*—intend to spy. No matter what Daniel thinks. I simply stumbled upon them.

Imagine my surprise! Daniel and Prudence were kissing!

Startled, I stopped still and stared. Daniel sat with his back against a tree, while Prudence, beside him, was all squashed and leaning into his side, and such a mass of entangled arms and legs were they, I thought they looked like two jumbled spiders. Crumpled in a pile of leaves lay Prudence's bonnet. And while Daniel was fervently kissing Prudence's hair, Prudence, eyes closed, nibbled on Daniel's neck like some hungry little rabbit, all the while softly giggling and sighing. So that's what lovers do! 'Tis positively silly, I do think!

I don't know what surprised me most—to see stern Daniel being affectionate, to see prim and proper

Prudence giggling, or knowing both could be thrown in the stocks for such sinful dalliance. And Prudence the daughter of the wealthiest man in the village!

When they spotted me, both sat bolt upright, and if I hadn't been so stunned, I would have laughed at how swiftly they disengaged themselves and scrambled to their feet. Prudence blushed as red as a strawberry. And Daniel, as flustered as I have ever seen him, coughed, shook out his limbs and cleared his throat.

Swiftly he recovered himself. "So now you've taken to spying!" he angrily accused.

"You've burrs on your breeches," I said tartly. I knew I had the advantage.

"I . . . er . . . we were discussing some property of Prudence's father," Daniel said. Prudence meantime was helping him pick off the burrs.

"Really?" I replied. Prudence's father does indeed have property—two lots in town, a wharf, and three sailing vessels, all of which any boy in the village would simply love to acquire as dowry. But property had definitely not been their "discussion."

Boldly I asked, "Does such property include the inveigling of affections? Or misplacement of Prudence's bonnet?"

Prudence flushed scarlet. Nervously she fumbled with her bonnet. Then, straightening her collar, which was all askew, she murmured something about having to meet her father in front of the ordinary where he was having some business discussion with a man from Boston.

Daniel shot me a look full of daggers. I know it was killing him not to be able to retaliate by spouting out my deep dark secret. But he could not. 'Twould be his detriment for certain were Prudence to learn it. After he walked Prudence as far as the road, he instantly wheeled back and ordered me, upon pain of my life, to keep my lips shut.

That really nettled me. I said, "Why don't you simply ask Mr. Cory to officially court his daughter and be done with sneaking off like thieves?" I, of course, knew the question's answer before it was posed.

Daniel harrumphed. "I shall. When I am ready."

"You haven't," I challenged, "because you know Mr. Cory shall refuse. Mr. Cory holds lofty aspirations for his daughter, which reach far loftier than *you!*"

So furious was Daniel, I thought he would explode, and I nearly laughed out loud at how his cheeks swelled. "You've always been a thorn to this family!" he cried. "I'll thank you to keep those thorns from *my* affairs! And you just wait and see how lofty I climb! The day will come when you'll plead at my feet!"

I did not give him the satisfaction of a reply. Smugly I turned, knowing in a bizarre way 'tis *I* who holds Daniel's future. And Daniel knows it.

Salem, 27 July 1692

Goodman Cole was arrested today, charged with being of middle age, never married, having a querulous nature and reading thoughts. His sister is beside herself with grief. How I do hate that word "querulous." Mama once applied it to me, and I had to ask Daniel of its meaning and was immediately regretful, for Daniel, of course, instantly decided he was in agreement with such description. And told me so.

Character and nature seemed to control my thoughts today. This aft, as we sat with our samplers, Deliverance and I engaged in an interesting conversation on the subject, and Deliverance, being of highly amiable nature, says her own type of character bears a weighty burden.

"Always I am afraid people shan't like me," Deliverance confessed. "'Tis so inwardly tiring, always trying so hard to please."

Surprised, I said, "But you always appear so happy. As if you are having such fun. And you are so *friendly.*"

"'Tis just the point," Deliverance explained. "Friendliness comes to me because I fear *not* to be. If I shan't be friendly and fun, no one shall like me. 'Tis so wearying—so very wearying—to be entertaining.

Sometimes I yearn not to see people at all for how drained it makes me."

I turned this curious discovery over in my mind. Then I asked, "But why is it so important that people *like* you? I mean, why do you *care* what people think?"

Deliverance heaved a long sigh. "I wish I knew. If I knew, I could *stop* caring. O Rachel, how I do envy you! You never seem to care a fig what people think! Why, you just plunge right in saying or doing whatever you please, having no burden whatsoever!"

Oddly, I still cannot discern whether Deliverance's compliment was really a compliment at all. I know Daniel would not think it so. Nor would the courts.

Salem, 28 July 1692

My visions continue to torment me.

They came again today at Mama's quilting bee, immediately after Goody Sibley turned to me sending the regards of Ann.

"'Twas Ann's intention to be here," explained Goody Sibley in her bubbly chatter, "but this morn has brought Ann much distress. Her lamb—of which she was so greatly fond—was found dead in the pasture, of unknown causes."

I feel badly about Ann's lamb. I know how much she loved it. I remember how we all played with it the day I led the fortune telling.

"Ouch!" I cried suddenly. I had stuck myself with my needle. Oddly, my whole body suddenly felt as if it were being pricked with needles. Just like that first evening!

In rising panic, I glanced at Mama and grew even more frantic. In her face I saw the face of Goody Glover. Nervously I gulped, squeezing shut my eyes and gritting my teeth.

Goody Bishop looked at me strangely.

Mama ordered, crisply, "Rachel, pray fetch the sugar for the tea."

Mama realized! Gratefully I arose and fled to the

cupboard. Yet when I opened the door, whose face should I then see, but that of Goody Glover, her evil, angular grin peering out at me. Hastily I grabbed the sugar and re-took my position on the stool.

The most peculiar sensations began to overwhelm me. A dozen hands moved in and out of the patchwork, and the hands were the long, bony ones of Goody Glover. A thread of stitches swirled round like snakes, curling toward me, hissing. Blood oozed from the rafters. The blood from Goody Glover's snapped neck.

Frantically I began to chatter. I chattered, non-stop, about anything which I could think: how the rains do linger, how Daniel keeps up with the pasture fences, about the rag rug Mercy is braiding, about the number of eggs our hens have lain. On and on I chattered, ceaselessly. 'Twas the only way I could fight the visions. Everytime I paused for breath, a face loomed out at me. Swiftly I rubbed my hands against my skirt to rid them of their drool. And blood.

The roomful of gaggling hens stilled. Goody Bishop peered over at me, peculiarly. I suppose I, whose tongue is always so stilled and wooden, must have caused surprise with such incessant conversation. I tried not to think of it. Smiling brightly, I continued my babbling, determined to will away those horrid visions. Some of what I said must have made little sense, for from time to time Mercy nervously interrupted with "What Rachel means is . . ."

Hardly did I pause for Mercy's explanation. Eagerly I rambled on, fighting the panic rising in my words.

Finally, and with firm solemnity, Mama ordered, "See to the cows, Rachel. 'Tis time for new salt licks."

Relieved, I jumped up, nearly knocking over the quilting, and fled to the pasture; whereupon I threw myself upon the ground and wept.

Goody Bishop stared after me, suspiciously.

Salem, 28 July 1692, eve

A rather solemn thing has happened. I have become a woman.

This eve, while I was helping Mercy with the dishes, I felt rather strange. As I turned round to place something in the cupboard, Mercy, behind me, gasped, which caused me to pull my skirt round to the place to which Mercy pointed, and there I discovered a large spot of blood. So instantly certain was I that 'twas blood from Goody Glover's snapped neck, that I screamed. A terrified scream. Suddenly blood oozed from the rafters, spilled down my neck, ran along my fingers and filled my hands. So frantic was I, that I immediately dropped a trencher which clattered to the floor with a resounding crash, and I would have run from the room, hands over my ears to drown out the cackle, had not Mama grabbed hold of me to calm me.

Mama shook me vigorously. Her voice was loud and commanding, and the whole family stood agape at the commotion which had erupted. Papa looked stunned; Daniel, angry.

When finally my fears had subsided, Mama shooed everyone away and proceeded to take me upstairs and sit me on the edge of my bed. Then she talked to me quietly. She told me how I mustn't be frightened, that 'tis something of which I should be proud, that it means I am fortunate, for it promises that someday I shall bear a child.

But after I had calmed, I was not at all frightened. I was rather pleased with myself. I felt superior to Phebe and Abigail and all the rest, for they were still children, and I was grown. Inside me, a creeping warmth felt serene and awed. And older.

Then Mama showed me how to tear up cloths to the right size to absorb my womanhood. I must wash the cloths whenever they are changed, Mama instructed, else they will stain. And I must practice discretion, so as not to cause embarrassment to Papa and Daniel. And also, I must be careful not to handle berries when I bleed, for the poison in their leaves might cause me to be sterile.

Perhaps now that I have gained womanhood, I shall also gain wisdom, like Mama. And Goody Glover shall find it futile to plague me.

Salem, 29 July 1692

Jeremiah called today. I wanted to tell him about my new womanhood, but naturally I could not. Instead I told him about my fashioned crystal ball, and of its portention.

Jeremiah laughed. I think he was a little abashed, because he blushed. Then, playfully, he grabbed me by the hand and swung me round in a wide arc, making my skirts fly and my breath come in short gasps through my laughter. 'Tis unlike him to be so playful. Usually he is rather sedate. That is why I know he was embarrassed.

But he did not deny the portention. So now I know Jeremiah has no designs on Phebe! 'Tis *me* Jeremiah wants!

Because I knew not what else to do, and feeling rather awkward about my exciting realization, I raced Jeremiah round to the pasture behind the barn to watch our new colt. Mischief overtook me. Snatching up an old broom which leaned against the barn, I began riding it like a horse, neighing and snorting and gamboling after the colt—who hadn't a clue what to make of all my antics, save for appearing to love them. He gamboled back and forth in front of me as if I were a sister, matching all my neighs with snorts and whinnies.

Jeremiah howled.

I don't think Goody Bishop was much amused by my antics, though. Her small cart appeared round the bend, harnesses jingling, and I saw her pull up to the hitching post in front of the house. She, with spinning wheel in hand, climbing down, had come to visit Mama. Out of the corner of my eye, I watched her stop, stare and frown. 'Tis no wonder what she thought after my yesterday's chatter. I didn't care. I went blithely on with my neighings and gambolings, adoring being the center of Jeremiah's attention.

I don't think Jeremiah saw Goody Bishop, he being doubled in laughter in the shadow of the barn; for if he had, I am certain he would have bade me stop. But he did not bid me. So I didn't.

To blazes with Goody Bishop!

Salem, 30 July 1692

I have made the most startling discovery.

Upon returning from Goody Bishop's house by the path through the woods, having borrowed some candle wicking for Mama, I heard a twig snap behind.

Whom was I to find, but Goodman Glover!

He said he was searching for bees from which to collect honey, but I didn't believe him. I had the oddest sensation he had been following me. Even more oddly, he tried to engage me in conversation. Removing his face-cover of bee's netting, he began explaining how he had come to fashion his strange device.

A short, slight man is Goodman Glover, with shoulders somewhat stooped and with one eye which moves eerily about in its socket. In that one eye, I think, he is blind—though I did not ask because I didn't want to encourage his conversation. 'Twas so disconcerting, half listening to rambles and not knowing on which eye to focus.

My brain rambled with shivering thoughts. I wondered how he felt having had a wife hanged. What was it like, I wondered, being wed to a witch? What did they say to each other? What did he think about her casting of spells? Did they, in fact, cast omens *together?!* My thoughts gave me the creeps.

His voice was soft and low, almost soothing at the beginning.

"A pretty little thing, you are," he told me.

Never in my entire life has anyone even so much as hinted at prettiness in my description. Truthfully, I am rather plain. I hate to admit it, but I was flattered.

He said, "You'll be as handsome as your Mama when you're growed."

Mama, handsome? Momentarily I pondered the idea, then decided Mama was plain, as well. I turned to leave.

"I knowed your Mama when she was young," Goodman Glover said.

Suddenly my attention was rivetted. Halting in my tracks, I thought, "This strange man has known my mother? How—and with what intention? Were they playmates together, tossing horseshoes and romping along the river?" Odd, thinking of Mama as a playful child. Finally I decided his knowledge of Mama had been merely as neighbors.

Curtly I said, "I must return to the candle molding."

He would not allow me to go. Swiftly a small hand caught at my sleeve. As it did so, I felt a queer panic.

A low voice said, "I almost married your Mama. Courted her a summer, I did."

Stunned, my mouth fell open. A small face stared back at me. A face which slowly began to look like a weasel. Liquor reeked on his breath.

I could not help myself. In a breathless voice, I stammered, "You . . . you almost m . . . m . . . married my Mama? But . . . but why did you *not?*"

"Cuz your Papa stole her from me."

My mind raced. What on earth had Mama ever seen in a man as horrid as this? How could Mama ever possibly have allowed him to come courting? And what if Papa hadn't come along? What if . . . ?

With a start, I suddenly realized: "Why, Mama could have been Goody Glover!!!"

One unwavering eye burned into me—not *through* me, but *into* me—as if this man were willing thoughts into my head!

His soft voice now made my hair stand on end.

"You could have been *my* little girl," he said.

At that, he reached out to clutch at me with his other hand, but I shrank back. My heart hammered in my ears as suddenly I tore from his grasp and raced along the path—like the Devil himself was clutching to retrieve me—all the while stumbling over rocks and ruts, frantically scrambling back to my feet, daring not to look behind.

When I reached home, I was sobbing. My dress was torn, and one knee was gashed, bleeding through my stocking.

Dazed, I headed for the malt house and threw myself upon the floor, weeping and frightened. My brain was a blur of faces, all evil and cackling, all mixed together like a horrid stew. Over and over, like a pounding storm, my thoughts kept hammering:

"I might have been Goodman Glover's daughter!! Mama could have been Goody Glover!!"

Salem, 31 July 1692

Last night was the most terrifying ever. Even tying my limbs to the posts could not halt my thrashings and convulsions. Where'er I looked leapt the cackling face of Goody Glover. And this time when she threw back her head in evil laughter, from the depths of her open mouth popped out the weasely face of her husband, his one wavering eye rising in a vapor.

"Mama! Mama!" I screamed. "Don't let her take me!"

"Hush!" Mama commanded. "No one shall take you, Rachel."

No words could soothe me. Papa stood at the end of my bed, and wildly I thought, "At the foot of my bed could have been Goodman Glover! Mama might have been his wife!"

Goody Glover's bony fingers reached from the rafters and clasped the small, stubby fingers of her husband. Then they clasped Mama's. Three figures stood together, then two, then one. My screams rang out as loud as my lungs could allow. And when Mama touched me, I screamed still louder. Everyone was mixed all together into one. Mama. Papa. Goody Glover. The weasely face of her husband.

Mama kept asking, "*Why,* Rachel? *Why* does Goody Glover want you?"

Why? For reasons I could not tell. Does Papa know about Mama and Goodman Glover? Does Papa know Mama herself could have been Goody Glover?! Does Papa know I could have been Goodman Glover's little girl?! Perhaps we could all be witches! Perhaps we all *are!* Perhaps 'twas the very thought Goodman Glover was trying to will from his head into *mine!*

"Mama! Mama!" I screamed. "Make her go away! Don't let her take me! I don't want to be a witch!"

The bindings only increased my terror. My every limb felt clutched within the grasp of Goody Glover. Around me the wandering eye of her husband swirled, staring at me from wherever it roamed, leaping out from the glow of the candles.

So long did my convulsions last, breath could not come when finally my fit was ceased. Spent and exhausted, I lay in my disheveled bed, my sheets soaked as if from drowning, my pillow as wet as rain. From Goody Glover's drool.

Mama was as drained as I. Papa looked confused. Mercy, ashen. And Daniel, looming in the doorway, clearly wished witch's fingers had indeed snatched me from my bed, drawn me out the window and made me disappear from the face of the earth forever.

I wonder what Daniel would say if he knew Mama could have been Goody Glover.

Salem, 1 August 1692

Today was a strange day. Mama bid me to Goody Abbey's on an errand, and I took the long way round, by the road, for fear I might otherwise encounter Goodman Glover. I know not what secret lies betwixt him and Mama, but neither do I wish to learn it from his thin, weasely lips.

Passing the Lawsons', I found a small crowd gathered round the door and soon saw why. Shortly the constable appeared, dragging away a frightened Goody Lawson, her poor wailing husband racing from his fields to plead for his wife's redemption. But his pleas went unanswered. They are wed but a year. His new wife was bound in chains and shoved into a rickety cart with nary a backward glance. 'Tis said she mixed a brew of spiders and toads and cast a spell upon Goodman Turbell, which sent the Turbell horses into fits, and all the result of an argument regarding the Turbell pigs which got into Goody Lawson's kitchen garden. I feel sorry for Goodman Lawson.

At the Meetinghouse, I found a notice tacked to the door. It read:

Two days hence, on 3 August, will begin the trial

of Goodwife Patience Hale. All who have evidence of her entertainment of the Devil appear before the magistrates at dawn on the appointed day.

Goody Abbey, I know, shall be at the trial. Her daughter, Bethshaa, accuses Goody Hale of making her possessed. 'Tis said that when Goody Hale entered the Abbey house, a beam fell upon Bethshaa, and Bethshaa has not been in sound mind since.

I wish I were Bethshaa. Bethshaa is more fortunate than I. Bethshaa can be redeemed by the death of her afflictor. My afflictor already lies dead. The only one left of *my* affliction is me.

Today, when Goody Bayley walked past the Ingersoll house, a chair flew across the room. Will Goody Bayley be next, I wonder?

Today is hot and steamy. I feel sorry for Goody Lawson, Goody Hale and all the others who are crammed into the wooden hut that has become our prison.

Papa says 'twill rain again this aft, as portended by the dark gray clouds on the horizon. One of those clouds looks like Goody Glover. Another, like her weasely husband.

Salem, 2 August 1692

So unhappy am I, I can scarce take delight in Papa's mill and its great success.

Everyone in the village now comes to Papa to grind their grain. "'Tis ever so much easier," declares Goody Bishop, "than grinding it on one's own small stones."

Tonight, at evening meal, Papa was beside himself with joy. On and on he waxed about how many sacks already he has ground. Creaking carts, says Papa, roll up to the mill practically all the day long.

When meal was finished, Papa pushed back his chair, Mama brought him his pipe and Papa bade me come sit beside him on the stool by the hearth, sensing my sadness.

Mama said, "The supper dishes wait for Rachel, Jacob."

I said, not meanly at all, "I prefer to sit with Papa."

Mama did not like my reply. She gave me a swift swat on the backside—which I did not feel at all through my heavy muslin skirt and petticoat—and admonished me for my willfulness. Then Daniel chimed in, glaring. "Rachel needs obedience lessons."

Evilly I made a face and stuck out my tongue. Mercy looked frightened. I suppose she thought I was going

into one of my fits. Already she fears to sit next to me at meals. "Mama," Mercy always whimpers in her whiny voice, "please don't make me sit next to Rachel." I like the power I'm beginning to have over Mercy.

To Daniel, I taunted, "And what of you and Prudence Cory?"

I know 'twas mean of me. Daniel turned purple with fury. Satisfied, I listened as Daniel attempted to explain my remark to the rest of the family, all the while glaring, wondering if I would expose him further. I decided not to. I shall use it as a weapon, doling out little balls of shot piece by piece, as Daniel deserves.

I wonder if 'tis monstrous for a sister not to feel affection for her brother. Since Daniel is only a half-brother, perhaps 'tis forgiven. Once I asked Papa what Daniel's real mother was like, the mother who was Papa's wife before he married Mama, and Papa said merely she was a kindly woman whom Daniel adored. She died when Daniel was five. I guess I should feel sad for Daniel, but I don't. Because he's so bossy. And because Papa treats him as special. Papa has willed Daniel the mill.

Daniel is Papa's favorite. Mercy is Mama's favorite. And I? I am no one's favorite. But I don't care. Someday they shall all be sorry for how I am treated.

When I finished the dishes, Mama announced 'twas time for family prayers. So 'twas prayers and much singing of psalms I had to endure before I could hear more about Papa's day at the mill. Pray, God, do not think by these words that I begrudge your psalms and prayers. 'Tis only that they come so *often*.

"Goodwife Hale's trial is to be tomorrow," Mama remarked.

"Mmm," Papa replied.

Vexed at being overlooked, I interjected, "Who else was at the mill today, Papa?"

"Ah, let's see," Papa said. "There was Goodman Burroughs—has two new mules, Martha. And Hezekiah Abbey brought his wife, Sarah . . ."

"Sarah's to testify tomorrow," Mama said.

"Aye," Papa replied. "The daughter's been possessed by the Witch Hale."

Stubbornly I again interjected: "What were Goodman Burrough's new mules like, Papa?"

Mama said, "'Tis time to practice your stitches, Rachel. Idle hands are the work of the Devil."

I did not want to do my sampler. My stitches are always uneven—not neat and perfect like Mercy's. "But what are Goodman Burrough's new mules like, Papa?" I persisted.

"Hefty, handsome critters," Papa said. "Asked him what he'd take for a trade."

"Rachel, watch your stitches," chided Mama. "Jacob, do you think we ought attend tomorrow's trial? I fear sometimes simply being near witches is an ill omen, yet . . ."

"'Tis not a witch till she's tried," Papa reminded.

"Aye, 'tis so, Jacob. Yet with the evidence . . ."

Witches, witches, witches! If I hear the word one more time, I think I shall scream! I merely wanted to talk to Papa about the mill! Why does no one listen when I speak? Frustrated, I threw down my sampler, put my hands over my ears and fled from the room—up to the bedchamber where I am now writing.

Mama called out after me, "Rachel Ward! Pray, return here this moment!"

But Papa said, "Let her be, Martha. 'Tis the age. 'Tis difficult half betwixt child and grown."

I'm glad Papa took my side. I wonder if Goody Glover would help me cast a spell on Daniel.

Salem, 3 August 1692

'Twas helpful I had been so out of sorts with Mama and Daniel. It gave me determination.

For when Goody Glover came last night, I cried out with all my strength, "Go away! Go away! Be gone, you cackling witch! You shall never take me! I swear it on my life!"

Mama held me and rocked me. Eventually Goody Glover left, though her blood still covered my hands, and all day I have had constantly to wash them.

Daniel is too ecstatic to live with. This aft he officially asked Mr. Cory's permission to court Prudence, and Mr. Cory has agreed. So Daniel prances and preens like some barnyard rooster; and no matter how much he talks about caring for Prudence, I just know 'tis her property he adores, and he is picturing himself lord and master over a wharf, two town lots and three ships.

Daniel finally went to Mr. Cory, I think, because he feared I would eventually tell about his and Prudence's "discussion"—which I probably would have. How I would have loved to have watched Daniel in the stocks!

Mr. Cory, I think, then agreed to the courtship because of the successes of Papa's mill, about which everyone is now remarking. I've noticed how Daniel is taking great interest in Papa's books, and I'd like to tell Papa that Daniel does so out of his own interest, not Papa's. But Papa probably wouldn't believe me.

Salem, 3 August 1692, eve

The most delicious thing has happened!

This eve, after evening meal, when I was feeling so disgusted about Daniel's prancing and preening, Jeremiah came round to ask if I would like to accompany him to search out a deer. Cradled in his arm was his new musket. With it he said he had found quite good fortune, and to be certain, I did not refuse the venture.

I do so adore accompanying Jeremiah on any purpose or on no purpose whatsoever. I so admire him, and today was a perfect example of the reason.

We set out through the woods, taking no particular path, but rather winding our way amidst the trees and heading toward a place in the river where a small tributary branches off and settles into a pond. "'Tis where the deer come to drink just before dusk," Jeremiah told me.

When we reached our destination, Jeremiah bid me silence, and we sat upon a log to wait.

"Shall it be long?" I asked. I was impatient, and for some reason my insides were bouncing with exuberance, which is quite unusual for me.

Jeremiah, too, was eager, and he smiled at me, his

dark, smooth complexion creased in gentle humor and anticipation. How I hungered to talk with him, to exchange all the little trivialities of the day, to tell him about Prudence and Daniel and all my exasperation. Yet I held my tongue, for I knew if I spoke our mission would be spoiled, and Jeremiah would be disappointed.

How still everything was about us. Leaves rustled softly over our heads as a warm, early evening breeze drifted in from the sea. A goldfinch ferreted amongst the bed of dried pine needles at our feet, searching for supper, I suppose. The lowering sun made our private world dim, yet light enough to see, and comfortably cozy. I thought about Goodman Glover. I wondered if he lurked somewhere about us. I thought how 'twas the first time I had ventured so far within the forest since my ghastly encounter, yet I was not at all fearful. I am never fearful with Jeremiah. Merely being with him makes me feel secure.

Quietly Jeremiah opened his powder horn and poured a trickle into the barrel of his musket, then tamped it down. "Hold this," he said, softly, as he got out his pouch of shot, and I did so gladly. Frequently have I gone with Papa when he hunted for our table, but never have I felt so excited as I did today with Jeremiah. Perhaps 'twas a premonition of what was to follow.

The slightest snap of a twig signalled that our quest was soon to be discovered. Beside me, Jeremiah scarcely breathed. His brown eyes danced, and lightly he touched my arm, winking, then motioned my gaze in the direction of the pond.

More twigs crackled, then ahead of us, emerging from the depths of the forest, stood a stag, so magnificent I nearly gasped. Twelve points sat atop his majestic head. Twelve points! I thought, "How green

Papa will be with envy!"

That magnificent animal stood poised not thirty footsteps from us; yet so concealed were we by the trees, and so motionless were our forms, that his large head glanced keenly about, and he saw us not at all. Slowly, gracefully, his smooth neck lowered, and he began to drink. Beside me Jeremiah raised his musket. For a moment I was torn. The beauty of the stag so took my breath away that I yearned to cry out, "Let him live!" Yet another part of me desperately wanted Jeremiah to triumph. That part of me feared the trees, or Jeremiah's youth, would cause him to miss, and I did not want him to miss. I wanted him to win. I wanted him to succeed.

Suddenly our silence exploded with the shattering of a musket. The stag fell. His magnificent body shuddered in one last plea for life, then lay beautifully still.

"I got him!" Jeremiah shouted. He leapt to his feet. "Do you see, Rachel? Right through the breast and the heart!"

How excited Jeremiah was! Exuberant, he hugged me and led me in a quick little dance, then grabbed my hand and hastened me toward the stag. "I must dress him immediately," he said. "'Tis almost dark. My father shall wonder what's happened to me! And yours, too! O Rachel! What luck you have brought me! Twelve points, and meat enough for a month, perhaps two!"

Betwixt his excited jabberings, it occurred to me that Jeremiah was surprised by his own proficiency, that he had not expected to down such a prize. Yet I was not at all surprised. I always expect Jeremiah to shine at everything he attempts. I was proud of him. Eagerly I told him so and squeezed his hand.

That was when it happened.

I am not certain about the exact procession of events, for what happened occurred so quickly that I think we were both somewhat startled. 'Twas right after I squeezed his hand, when I thought once more he intended to hug me, but instead, his head bent down and . . . he kissed me!

He kissed me! Jeremiah kissed me!

To be sure, 'twas a swift, small kiss. Not at all like the absorbed entanglings of Daniel and Prudence. And after Jeremiah did it, he blushed a little and ducked his head. And I think I blushed, too. My blood felt all warm and tingly, and my eyes were probably as wide as Mama's trenchers. But then Jeremiah glanced back down at me, his smile shy yet sparkling, and he kissed me again. Our noses bumped, awkwardly, and foolishly we both turned our heads in the same direction; but finally one of us got it right, and our lips once more touched—a warm, lingering touch.

Playfully Jeremiah placed his finger upon my nose and gently squished it. "You're nice," he said. His eyes looked right into mine.

"You're nice, too," I replied. Eerily my voice seemed to come not from my mouth, but from someone else's. I was numb. I had no feeling, yet I felt every movement of the breeze around me. A thousand sensations filled me.

Purposefully Jeremiah then took his knife from his belt and began to dress the deer, and all the while he worked, he spoke to me. As I helped him, I spoke in return, and I, who can never seem to find my tongue, was suddenly as glib as a chipmunk. But best of all, everything I said was right! Nothing was wrong! Jeremiah laughed at my teasings! He was amused by my jestings! And I felt the cleverest person alive! Yet now I have not a clue as to what I said, for I cannot recall a single word.

Giddily I knelt so my arm would touch against his, hoping my touching would seem an accident and that it would prompt him to kiss again. Which he did. Thrice more as he worked. And after each, we giggled and blushed.

How happy I am! All the way home, and even still, I feel as if I am floating. How jealous Phebe shall be! I can scarce wait to tell Ann, knowing Ann shall tell the others!

And so, dearest journal, today I have received my first kiss. I, who have always been so plain and who have always so yearned for the admiring glances that seem destined to be directed continually toward people like Deliverance and Phebe, finally feel pretty. How fortunate I am to have someone like Jeremiah. How I do adore him!

Salem, 4 August 1692

I have told Ann about Jeremiah.

Although I recorded evening last that I had indeed intended to tell, by this morn I had changed my mind. I wanted to savor my delicious secret and keep it private so it would not tarnish, as if the revealing might make it ordinary. 'Tis not at all ordinary. And I do so want my listener to be as thrilled as I. 'Tis why I chose Ann with whom to confide.

Scarce could I sleep last night for my thoughts of Jeremiah. Dreamily I envisioned some chance encounter whereby Ann, Deliverance and Phebe would all be present, and whereby Jeremiah would suddenly appear, smile gently at me and remark upon something only he and I had shared. Then, laughing, we would stroll off together hand in hand, and everyone whom I intended to know would not have to be told; they would see!

Still another dream was of Jeremiah joyously telling Deodat and all the boys. They in turn would eagerly relate everything to Ann and the others, and Ann would excitedly search me out and breathe, "Rachel! Why did you not tell me!" How dramatic it would be!

How frustrating to have such lovely dreams constantly interrupted by Goody Glover's cackle. Laughing hysterically, Goody Glover made fun of me! Pray, God, shall I never be rid of her fiendish presence!

So it was that despite my intentions to remain coy and mysterious, when Ann arrived this morn on an errand for her mother, I could not find restraint. Elated at the knowledge that I am liked, and eager to demonstrate that I am liked, I quickly took Ann back round by the barn and told her.

Excitedly I blurted, "Ann, you shall never guess what! Jeremiah has kissed me!"

Breathless, I waited for her reaction. A small lump in my stomach suddenly lurched. With trust I had opened a sliver of my heart and displayed it for vision; I prayed Ann would not chop that sliver to pieces. I need not have worried.

Sweetly, sincerely, Ann smiled and cooed, "O Rachel! Do tell every last detail! Shall he now come courting, do you think? Has he asked you to be his intended?"

"Not yet," I laughed with a full heart that is O so confident of Jeremiah's affection. "But next week I shall turn thrice and ten, and then we shall see! O Ann! I am so happy! Please be happy for me!"

"I am Rachel! I am!" she laughed. "Now do tell me everything that happened!"

I am glad I told Ann. My secret has not at all tarnished, but instead has increased in reality. My telling, and Ann's reaction, renewed my excitement and made me yearn for Jeremiah's presence. My heart now feels as large as today's bright blue sky, swelling so inside me that I sense it shall burst!

I wonder if Jeremiah now dreams of *me?*

Salem, 4 August 1692, aft

I did something I should not have. I fashioned a crystal ball to ward away Goody Glover. Let it be recorded that I did so only out of frustration for how terrorized she makes me. *I did not at all intend to be engaging in witchery.*

I did it when Mama was in the kitchen garden, Mercy was carding and Daniel had followed Papa to the mill. Sneaking out Mama's glass sugar bowl, I proceeded to pour the sugar into a wooden noggin, then race to the barn, bowl hidden in my apron, and scramble up to the loft.

Then I waited. Staring into the rafters, I knew any moment she would appear. I wanted her blood. 'Twas her blood that would make it work.

But she did not appear. Beneath me, a pig nosed into a pile of hay, looking for some tasty morsel. Squawking came from the chicken house. But all else was silent. No cackling laughter.

Frustrated, I challenged her. "Come out! Come out, you evil witch! Show your face, so I can be rid of you! All I need is a drop of your blood!"

I must have frightened her. From somewhere down in the depths of Hell, she must have known what was to happen. The Devil probably told her.

The longer I waited, the more frustrated I became. I could wait no longer. If *her* blood would not appear, why not *mine?* Could not mine work to wash away hers? Swiftly I climbed down the ladder, grabbed hold of Papa's scythe, gulped, took a deep breath, and ran it across my finger. It stung. I think I whimpered. But too near my goal was I to stop. A red trickle of blood ran down my hand, and cradling my finger in my palm so I would not lose my precious quarry, hastily I climbed back to the loft.

Victoriously, I announced, "Aha, you evil witch! I shall get you now! I shall rid your blood with mine, and you shall be gone from me forever!"

I listened, waiting for cackling laughter. Nothing. Silence.

Carefully I placed the tip of my finger against the edge of the sugar bowl. A drop of blood trickled down its side. 'Twas not enough, I decided. Squeezing my finger to make more, another drop, then another, trickled into the bowl. My finger ached.

I waited, watching to see what would happen. Lifting the bowl, I swirled it.

"Tell me," I asked my fortune telling device, "how am I to rid myself of Goody Glover?"

My drops of blood made a tiny pool. Slowly they formed a small "S".

"S?" Wracking my brain, at first I thought 'twas "Satan." For an instant, I thought it meant I was to be taken! So horrified was I, I almost dropped the bowl.

Then I realized. "S" means "secret". I must find out the secret 'twixt Mama and Goodman Glover! In the secret lies my salvation!

Suddenly I heard the whiny voice of Mercy. "Rachel? Rachel, are you in here? Mama needs . . . O there you are! What on earth are you doing up there?

We've been looking for you high and low. Mama needs someone to take the quilt to Goody Bishop, and . . ."

Halfway up the ladder was Mercy, and I, in a panic, sat on the bowl to conceal it.

"Why, Rachel!" gasped Mercy. "What on earth is wrong? Why do you look so . . . so strange? And . . . and why are you sitting up here? Your . . . your face looks . . . er . . ." Her voice trailed off as she suddenly halted on the top rung, in terror.

I could not help myself. Instantly I threw back my head, opened my mouth and screamed out at the top of my lungs: "Eayah!"

I had meant it mostly as a diversion but also as sport because Mercy was so terrified. Quick as a wink, Mercy scrambled down the ladder, nearly toppling to the floor, and ran from the barn screaming, "Mama! Mama! Come quick! Rachel is having another of her fits!"

The diversion didn't work. I had hoped it would provide time to conceal the bowl until later when I could retrieve it and replace the sugar. But I couldn't. Mama and Mercy both found it—along with the small pool of blood—and Mama was horrified.

"Rachel Ward!" exclaimed Mama, aghast. "Get you into the house this instant! And Mercy—back to your carding! Is there no end to your nonsense, daughter?!"

Salem, 4 August 1692, eve

Jeremiah came this aft. I did not tell him about my crystal ball, for fear I would cause him anger.

He helped me gather herbs for tea, and although I was thrilled by his presence, I was bothered, too, that I could not discuss the one subject which so disturbs me. 'Tis odd how quickly moods do waver. This morn, so exuberant was I that I would have thrown myself toward Jeremiah and gaily pled with him to romp off to the pasture. Yet this aft, I was so deeply troubled by my visions and by Mama's reaction to my attempt to dispel them that I could scarce muster an ability to entertain. I felt as dull as lead. I wondered what Jeremiah could ever see in me.

Jeremiah picked a clump of sassafras and handed it to me. He said, softly, "I thought about you last eve."

My heart lurched. I hoped I wouldn't say something foolish. "I thought about you, too," I replied.

Suddenly I wished he would leave. I wished he had never come. My confidence had vanished, and I wanted to be alone with my memories. All my life I have spoken openly to Jeremiah as a friend, yet this aft suddenly everything seemed all changed. I could not think of a single word to speak. All that churned round in my brain was Goody Glover. Her face appeared in the ground before me, and I shuddered.

Taking my hand, Jeremiah said, "I'm glad you are my friend."

I did not feel like a friend. I felt like some colorless little toad whom Jeremiah would suddenly and clearly recognize as such, then flee. Pray, God, why have you blessed me with such a wooden tongue? And such burdensome visions? Why could you not have endowed me with cleverness and a heart as light as Phebe's?

"Are you all right?" Jeremiah asked. His olive face creased with concern.

"Certainly," I replied, falsely. Then I murmured something inane, which I prefer to forget for the ninny it makes me; and I think deep down, Jeremiah really must care for me because he chuckled in spite of my stupidity, and he teased me.

I made no attempt to linger after the herbs were collected. So fearful was I of spoiling Jeremiah's nice thoughts of me, that I proffered an excuse of being needed for spinning—though the wheel was in use at that very moment—and left Jeremiah in the road.

"I shall see you tomorrow," he told me, and I smiled and nodded, wordlessly.

I think he wanted to kiss me. I wish I had been confident enough to let him.

Salem, 5 August 1692

Last eve I overheard Mama in conversation with Papa. About me.

"'Tis gotten out of hand," Mama was saying, quietly.

"She's young and impressionable," murmured Papa.

"Those are oft the ones it strikes first, Jacob."

I had risen from bed and gone to the top of the stairs to ask Mama when she would be coming to join me—so fearful was I that Goody Glover would come terrorize me when 'twas only Mercy and I in the chamber—when I heard them. Speaking in hushed tones leads to only one conclusion. No one is intended to overhear. Quietly I sat in the shadow betwixt the wall and the railing, my knees pulled to my chin, my nightdress tucked down under my toes.

Papa said, "She's simply been listening too close to the talk of the trials. Such talk is enough to give anyone visions."

"As vivid as Rachel's? Jacob, you see how she does tremble and go into fits. Even at Meeting—where, if anywhere, the Lord should protect her."

"'Tis a wonder I myself didn't faint in Meeting, Martha. 'Tis hot as Hades in that building!"

"Jacob! Watch your language! And be still your

voice, else the children shall hear."

"About Hades? Or the trials? Rachel hears too much of both, I suspect."

"'Tis what I'm trying to tell you, Jacob. I haven't yet mentioned this to you—for you have been so elated over the mill—but today I found her fashioning a fortune telling device!"

"Aye?" said Papa with concern. "And for what purpose?"

Mama's voice trembled slightly. "I . . . er, don't know, Jacob. She wouldn't say."

Papa paused for a moment. Then he said, "That proves *exactly* what I've been contending, Martha. Something of the same came up in the trial of Goody Black. Rachel is simply using her imagination and putting it to curiosity." His voice lowered a notch. "You, uh, haven't mentioned it to anyone, though, have you?"

"Certainly not! Do you think me witless?! But Mercy, too, saw it; though I don't think she understood. But 'tis not all, Jacob. Goody Bishop came to me with suspicions."

"Goody Bishop has always suspicions."

"Which lead to problems, Jacob. She says Rachel displays disturbing signs, and we should call in Reverend Parris."

"Gossip of goodwives is itself the instrument of the Devil. Have you not said so yourself?"

Mama sounded exasperated. "Jacob, shan't you see? 'Tis no knowing what can happen in circumstances such as this. And how I fear what can happen when that line is passed from being possessed!"

I gulped. I am possessed. It was *awful* hearing it put into words. And 'twas Goody Bishop who reported it. I *knew* she had the smell of danger.

Papa said, "Rachel is just at that *age*. And 'tis an age

which I think should not be witnessing trials or executions. We'll be stopping that now, Martha. For the time, at least."

"Aye, 'tis with my agreement, Jacob. But I think more is called for. I think we should indeed call in Reverend Parris."

"'Tis a poor time to be doing *that*. With the mill getting on its feet."

"But we cannot let it continue any longer. Reverend Parris can perchance rid her of evil demons before they go one step further."

"'Twill be no steps beyond imagination," Papa maintained.

"O Jacob. How can you bear to see her tortured? *You* spend your days at the mill. But I? I see her morn, afternoon, and eve come fleeing through the door with terror in her eyes. Do you not notice the whiteness of her complexion? Do you not notice how distracted she appears? Why, hardly can she concentrate upon a simple chore without leaping up and dancing about to drive away her visions."

"'Tis the energy of the young, Martha."

"Jacob, do be serious. Do you not tire of my sitting with her at night? Do you not miss me in your bed? And what of all the candles you bring? If for nothing else, we need Reverend Parris 'ere we run scarce of candles!"

"I pray the day not to come when we be counting candles."

Mama sighed, a long weary sigh. "Jacob, too weary am I to discuss this much further. Already I expect to start hearing Rachel's cries. If her mind does not go first, 'twill be mine—of that I promise. If you shan't admit possession—only imagination—then Reverend Parris would serve that need as well. We shall ask Reverend Parris to harness that imagination and put it to better reality. What say you to that suggestion?"

Papa considered the matter silently. I could hear the soft puffs of his pipe. "Aye, Martha. To that I be agreeing. Only if 'tis in the harness of imagination."

"Thank you, Jacob. I think I shan't be able to endure another day of this."

"Reverend Parris shall be in town in the morn. When he returns to the village, you shall call. *Without* Goody Bishop."

"Aye, Jacob."

"Mid-aft would be the best. I shall have Daniel with me at the mill. Mercy shall find a friend to visit. 'Tis best your discussions with Rachel have fewest ears."

"Aye, Jacob."

"You shall give him our monthly tithings, so he shan't have cause for unfavorable opinions."

"Aye, Jacob. Now I must go up to Rachel. Shall you follow me with the candles?"

And so ended as much as I heard. Swiftly I disentangled my knees and nightdress and tiptoed back to bed—feeling a wretched burden.

Salem, 5 August 1692 eve

Jeremiah did not come today. I feel hollow and empty. And lonely.

Salem, 6 August 1692

As nervous as a trapped mouse was I waiting for the visit of Reverend Parris. When Mercy was sent away after noonday meal, I wanted to flee out the door after her and disappear into her shadow, so fearful was I of what to expect.

Gloomily I stood at the window and stared out through the small leaded panes of glass. It seemed to take forever for Reverend Parris to arrive. Mama set about making tea, and I heard the bubbling of the kettle in the hearth, but I did not turn, and neither of us spoke.

I found myself wishing I were an orphan, like that child who was abandoned some years back in the village. If I were an orphan, there would be no one upon whom I would bring shame. If I were an orphan, I could indeed flee out the door, and no one would come looking or notice. 'Tis what that abandoned child finally did. After the Disboroughs took him in, he just up and disappeared one day with nary a note nor word. Talk was he went to sea. If I were a boy, I would go to sea.

When Reverend Parris did arrive, 'twas with much pomp and dignity. Reverend Parris has this unsettling way about him of making one feel of lesser station. Sternly he strode up to me, peered down, clasped his hands behind his back, bent over slightly and frowned. "*This* was to be my salvation!" thought I, feeling more miserable than ever.

Taking my place upon the small stool by the hearth, I watched Mama while she took Reverend Parris's hat, served the tea and took her own place in the rocker. Reverend Parris sat in the settle, which he did with much grandiose situating of his long velvet waistcoat.

Both then proceeded to stare at me. My tongue felt like wood. What was I to say? Dumbly, I kept my eyes on the small table between us.

Mama began the conversation by explaining me to Reverend Parris. "Rachel is a quiet, solemn child," explained Mama, "with a very active imagination. The village unrest has piqued that active imagination. You see, Reverend, Rachel does not have many friends; she does not make friends easily. So she has much time by which to let her thoughts wander and run rather . . . well, rampantly."

Mama, I know, was following Papa's orders. Her words were clear and crisp, as if being recited from memory, and vaguely I wondered how often they had been practiced.

Mama continued. "Rachel is extremely close with her thoughts, Reverend. She does not speak much. Yet when she does speak, oft times she is cryptic and abrupt. Oft have I to remind her to soften her tone. I think, perhaps, her lack of softness comes from little practice, for she is very poor at making conversation. 'Tis true, Reverend, that children should speak only when addressed. Yet Rachel oft times does not speak even then."

Uncomfortably I squirmed. 'Tis a peculiar—and unsettling!—experience indeed to sit and hear oneself explained to another. I kept thinking 'twas someone else Mama was describing. I had to pinch myself to remind myself it was *me!* I wanted to say, "Mama, *that* is not me. 'Tis not what I am like at all!" That I have so few friends, I wanted to tell, is a situation of my own choosing. Why, were I to really want, I could have more friends than anyone in the village! I am merely selective, that's all! And as for being abrupt, as Mama described, I am simply straightforward.

All those things I wanted to tell. But I told none of them. Feeling more alone than ever, I fidgetted on my stool.

Mama said, "Rachel also has difficulty completing her thoughts—which is why people oft consider her peculiar."

Peculiar! 'Twas the first I had ever heard of *that!*

Mama said, "And now she feels she has these visions . . ." Her voice trailed off—lamely, I thought. Did I, or did I not, have visions? What was I to admit?

Silence. No one said a word. Awkwardly my eyes peered up from the table to see what the verdict would be. Two faces stared back at me. How I do hate being the subject of staring. I feel as if people can see *inside* me. I feel as if I have nothing left as private. A person needs to have some private things. If everything about a person's character is held up for all to see, 'tis as if one has no clothes.

In the midst of this staring, it occurred to me that perhaps I could squeeze my eyes shut and disappear. If I couldn't see others, they couldn't see me. So I tried it, but it didn't work. When I opened my eyes, both were still there. And Reverend Parris was looking at me *very* oddly. Mama paled—fearing, I suppose, that my squeezing my eyes shut meant I was going into one of my fits.

After what seemed like an eternity, Reverend

Parris finally spoke, with every word punctuated by a pause in its delivery. "Any recent deviations in Rachel's quiet character?" he asked.

Who was to answer? Me? Or Mama? What if I blundered? How I wished Mama had rehearsed me as well as she had rehearsed herself!

Mama said, "Well aye, Reverend, there have been deviations. Sometimes Rachel begins chattering, rather aimlessly."

"To drive away the visions!" I wanted to explain.

Reverend Parris asked, "Any agitation?"

"Oft," replied Mama. "Whenever her imagination conjures up these visions . . ."

"They are *awful* visions!" I exclaimed, suddenly, surprising even myself. I wondered if my blunder had arrived. I didn't care. The visions *are* awful; and if I didn't tell Reverend Parris so, how was he to help?

Reverend Parris then asked, "And what do those visions look like, Rachel?"

Stammering, I told them they were of Goody Glover, all the while anxiously glancing back and forth to Mama for some clue as to how much I was to reveal. Reverend Parris's frown grew deeper. Gravely, he began to rapidly question me while I haltingly tried to answer as best I could; but so frightened was I, my explanations became disjointed, and I began to feel my doctor worse than the disease. Merely I wanted him to pronounce me cured, then depart.

"Does her vision appear to you now?" Reverend Parris eventually asked.

Swiftly I glanced about the great room. I saw nothing. With faint hope, I thought perhaps I was cured. Hesitantly, I shook my head.

"What does she say to you?" Reverend Parris asked.

"N . . . nothing" I stammered. Oddly, I found myself wishing Goody Glover would indeed speak, so I could tell both Mama *and* Reverend Parris what she said.

Reverend Parris prodded, "Any unusual occurrences in the household? Like strange noises? Or pots falling from the hearth? . . . . Or bread not rising?"

"No," interjected Mama, firmly. "My yeast is always faultless."

Uneasily, I shifted. Too well did I remember the day of Goody Glover's hanging, and I wondered how much Mama had noticed.

To me Reverend Parris asked, "Does Goody Glover e'er appear to you in the form of animals? Like birds, or bats, or dogs, or chickens, or—"

"Aye," I said, nervously, ". . . she . . . she has appeared to me in a large orange cat."

"And does she e'er appear as a large, yawning, fiery pit?"

"Nay . . . er . . ."

"When you see her, do your limbs stiffen, then go into spasms?"

"Well, I, er, shake a lot. I . . . I'm just so frightened, you see. But I . . . I don't really stiffen . . ."

"Do you speak in foreign tongues? In some language unknown to others?"

"Nay . . . I, er, not that I remember."

"Nay, she does not," verified Mama.

So swift were his questions, I had the feeling he was trying to trip me.

"Has she struck at you?" the reverend asked. "Fought with you?"

"Nay," I said, quickly trying to remember. "Nay, I . . . I don't think so . . ."

Suddenly Reverend Parris's voice grew quiet and low. "And why, Rachel, do you think Goody Glover wants you?"

My breath could scarce make it past my lips. Never could I tell what little I *do* know—about Mama and

Goodman Glover. And certainly I could make no conjecture. To Reverend Parris, I finally mumbled, "I . . . I don't know."

Reverend Parris then sat back in the settle—from his previous posture of leaning intently toward me—and pondered his conclusion. Nervously I fidgetted with my apron, twisting its corner round and round my finger 'til it crumpled in a tight knot. I dared not look at Mama. He let the silence lie interminably while making his deliberation, until finally he smoothed the front of his linen shirt, and announced:

"'Tis a clear case of possession."

A dropping pin could have been an explosion, so still was the room. Such declaration, Mama did not want to hear. But Mama *believed* it. I *know* she did.

"Not . . . not imagination?" attempted Mama, feebly.

Reverend Parris was certain. "All the signs are present."

Mama's expression was pale and uncertain. Papa was not going to like this verdict.

But Mama, always of poise, quickly recovered herself. Drawing a long breath, she asked, "The cure, Reverend Parris? What say you for recommended action?"

"Aye." Reverend Parris nodded. "The cure. In situations such as this, 'tis usual, of course, to increase Bible reading. Three or four hours a day should give pause to evil demons and provide alertment that the soul is wise to the terrors and tortures of Hell." Too well am I *already* wise to the terrors and tortures of Hell! "Should also be done whene'er the demons appear," continued the reverend. "And in accompaniment, I recommend fasting. Fasting does tear out the demons' sustenance." Glumly, I wondered if that meant no evening meal. "And finally," said Reverend

Parris, "administer Venice treacle. One cup every hour."

That nearly did me in. At the mere thought, my stomach violently heaved. Venice treacle being the most repulsive compound ever imagined, already I could smell the horrid fumes of pounded bodies of snakes mixed with wine and every herb known to a kitchen garden, all boiling in some wretched kettle. Anxiously, I wondered if I could escape it.

"Aye," replied Mama, obediently. "I shall have Jacob search out snakes this very eve."

Then the reverend, after much Scripture reading, left.

I know not at all what to make of his visit. Over and over have I turned his conversation in my mind, yet I feel not at all comforted. When Mercy and Daniel returned, I wanted so much to be able to say I am well—or at least on the road to recovery—but I could not.

In fact, nothing at all was said within the family. Papa returned from the mill, Mama laid out evening meal and everyone acted as if nothing at all extraordinary had occurred—which only increased my discomfort. 'Twas only later, when I had gone to the well to fetch water and had returned, bucket in hand, to find everyone huddled in a corner whispering, that I knew Mama had told. Guiltily, they all immediately straightened. Furious, I slammed the door and returned to the well, whereupon Goody Glover came to me in the form of a small brown bird. Just as Reverend Parris had predicted.

Salem, 7 August 1692

Last eve, so profusely did the blood gush from Goody Glover's snapped neck that it poured into my throat and sent me so choking I could scarce catch my breath.

"Mama! Mama!" screamed Mercy as I lay in my bed, convulsing in terror. "Come quick! Rachel has another of her fits!"

In the rafters a bony head hung upon a square shoulder, neck gaping with a flowing wound, and the saliva that drooled from her lips mixed in with her sticky blood and thinned it to make it run faster. Into my eyes it fell, into my nose and throat, and it matted my hair and covered my face until my whole head was immersed in her blood. I could not close my mouth for its pouring. Choking and gasping, I felt as if I were drowning, and I could think of nothing, not even Mercy's frantic wailings, as I fought to breathe and strained my lungs as they filled with blood.

Frantically I thrashed. My legs flailed and my hands punched wildly, but I could not escape. Her long gnarled fingers reached down and held me fast against my sheets.

"Stop it, Rachel. Stop it," ordered Mama, harshly,

and she slapped me.

But I could not stop. The blood poured ceaselessly, and I felt that my tongue would follow; and all would fill my throat and I would die upon my bed.

Again Mama slapped me, and again; then quickly she grabbed me by the shoulders and shook me. "Stop it, Rachel! Stop it!" she ordered. "Take some of this treacle!"

The treacle became blood, and I gagged and choked until its brownness covered my gown. So miserable was I that I threw myself upon Mama's shoulder and wailed, "Help me, Mama! Help me!"

"Ssshhh, Rachel. Ssshhh," whispered Mama as she rocked me. "I shall help you. I shall try."

But I know she cannot. Goody Glover shall never cease her torture. Until she takes me.

Salem, 7 August 1692, aft

Papa, too, is now troubled. The dam he has built for the mill has caused the English cart road to flood, and Goodman English is in terrible temper over the situation. Today, at the mill, Goodman English vented all his anger, and there was a frightful row. And while Goodman English ranted and raved, Goodman Corwin, for no apparent gain, was vigorously nodding and giving agreement to the tantrum. 'Twas the situation when I found them.

Poor Papa. He tried to explain. "When the rains stop, the river shall recede."

Goodman English would have none of it. "If 'tweren't for the dam," raged Goodman English, "I shouldn't have to depend upon the rains!"

Again Papa tried to reason.

Goodman English interrupted. "How shall I get my milk to town by which to feed my family? We shall all starve! Neither cart nor canoe can get through the mud!"

Goodman Corwin punctuated the ranting with a vehement nod.

Goodman English's snit, I know, was brought on on account of jealousy. He's jealous because we live on

Ipswich Road—which leads directly to town—while the English house sits way back in the village, requiring the family to contend with cart paths which are always marshy, rutted and give one a positive stomach ache for all the jouncing around of innards. And, because of the lack of free land, Goodman English and his family will have to make do with their backwoods farm and its inconveniences—with no hope of improvement.

Goodman Corwin is also jealous, as I have already recorded, because of Papa's inheritance and sudden turn of fortune. Goodman Corwin is not one to be pleased by a turn of fortune, unless 'tis his.

Feeling rather of advantage for a change, I listened to Papa reason.

"Would you have the village deprived of a mill?" Papa asked. "Would you have us all again grinding by hand—else travelling the distance into town? Pray, Simon, would you have your grain not only traversing your cart path, but also spending the better part of a sun going forth then back from town?"

The waterwheel behind me was going "Whoosh, whoosh, whoosh."

Goodman English wanted none of Papa's reasoning. I watched him stalk out, with Goodman Corwin trailing in his shadow, and I made a face at them both—out of loyalty to Papa. Goodman English climbed into his cart, ranting some incoherent threats about taking the matter up with the magistrate. And so fiercely did he whip his oxen, I felt certain those oxen would balk and turn on him.

Sighing, Papa walked over to me. "Be glad you are a woman, Rachel," Papa said. "You shan't have to contend with such burdens. Daniel shall bear them instead."

Secretly, I think the mill no burden at all. I wish I

were to inherit it instead of Daniel.

Later, when Papa arrived home for meal, I learned that Goodman English's cart lost a wheel and crashed on his way home—demolishing the cart, though leaving its shaken, angry driver intact. I am glad about the cart.

Salem, 7 August 1692, eve

Where is Jeremiah when I need him? Every day he calls, yet three have past with nary a visit!

Is it Phebe Jeremiah now takes with him fishing and in slow meanderings through the woods? Is it Phebe to whom Jeremiah now shows off his musket, and with whom he now shares his teasing and laughter?

How I wish I were pretty! 'Tis so horrid being plain. Papa says 'tis what is inside which counts, and vanity shall never bring advantage. But 'tis not at all how the world works. 'Tis not ugly old cows about which people coo and pander, but the soft, silkiness of their calves. Was there ever a homely cur whom people yearned to adopt and nurture? Nay, 'tis the frisky cuteness of a pup.

I do wish my hair were fair and curly, and my nose had not near so many freckles. Boys like pretty girls—of that I'm certain. And are girls no better? Do I not make fun of Joshua Snow for being so ugly? Does Jeremiah ever think the same of me?

My nose is too long. My cheeks are too shallow. How I do yearn for the round, softness of Phebe. O how I hate to admit Phebe is pretty!

Mama says looking glasses are not for admiring but

for adjusting one's cloak, and when she catches me studying my reflection—which I have oft done lately—Mama admonishes me for my preoccupation. Yet how is one to really know oneself if one does not know how one *looks?* Such reasoning sits ill with Mama. "'Tis the inside which one should study," Mama reminds. Yet I cannot help but feel that what is inside is reflected in what is out. I do wish Mama and I weren't always at such cross-purposes.

Perhaps 'tis indeed my inside manner in which Jeremiah tires. Perhaps he is more attracted to the shallow prattle and lightness of Phebe. Perhaps I should try more cooings and panderings, as Phebe does so well. Boys always do seem to like girls who are airy. Why do I torture myself so?

Who am I? What am I to become? Of what substance is my character? Shall I ever be poised and capable like Mama? So many doubts plague me.

How much calmer I shall be when I am free of my possession. Perhaps then Jeremiah will like me again.

Salem, 8 August 1692

I composed a poem today. I shall record it.

> "Like treasures, her thoughts were carefully
> guarded.
> Her feelings were precious jewels,
> To be kept close and shared
> Only with the right, deserving persons.
> And in the end, what was her fortune?
> Loneliness. And a brimming jewel box,
> About which no one knew—or cared."

'Twas in my mind when I awoke this morn. Round and round the words rambled in my head—put there, I suppose, by Mama's description of me afternoon last—and all day they have stayed with me. I feel sad. I think I shall try to change my character.

If only there were someone to whom I could pour out all my troubles, I'm certain I would feel ever so much better.

But to Mama I fear telling too much for fear of causing her further worry. Already Mama looks aged. Yet always her shoulders are erect, and always she holds herself with surety; so, to the outside world anyway, she gives away nothing. But I, who know her so well, see the calmness drain from her expression, and she pauses more often now before she speaks. It wrenches me to think of those times I have made her weep. Mama, who is so stern and constant, brings more fear than my visions when I see her break. Papa is my diversion, my happiness. But Mama is the rock upon which we all rest.

To Papa I can tell even less, so distracted is he with his problems over Goodman English and the dam. And still he refuses to admit anything might be awry with his own flesh and blood. 'Twas exactly as I heard him whispering to Mama. "The Reverend Parris is wrong, Martha. Nothing ails that which has sprung from *my* loins."

Papa likes to pretend nothing is unusual. This is how he acts: He comes home for noonday meal, plops down on the bench at the trestle table, rubs his white sleeve across his perspiring forehead, takes a long swallow from his noggin of beer, glances at me sitting in the great room by the hearth, and asks (matter-of-factly), "How is Rachel doing with her fasting, Martha?" 'Tis as if he's inquiring about some lesson I'm learning!

I like how Papa has a curly lock of hair which always tumbles onto his forehead. Papa is nice looking—have I yet recorded that? 'Tis no wonder Mama took him over Goodman Glover. Papa has a soft face with reddish brown hair, and his shoulders are quite broad. His eyes rather twinkle when he smiles. Papa laughs more than Mama. 'Tis from Mama I get my sharp features and stern appearance. I do wish I looked more like Papa instead.

The other night Papa was playing his jew's harp, and he allowed me to sit at his feet and lean my head on his knee. How I do love Papa's attention—'tis ever so much more comforting than Mama's.

The Venice treacle tastes wretched, but yet has little effect—save for keeping me doubled over with vomit. Goody Glover and her husband spent all last eve in my rafters. Only exhaustion keeps me from recording details.

I should like to record my thoughts on Reverend Parris, of which I recorded only a few in the writing of two days past. His sermons brim with the evils of money and with unfavorable comparisons to successful merchants—so much so that I think the reverend is secretly envious, wishing such prosperity for himself. Oft have I noticed how people who speak so strongly against a thing are concealing some deeper emotion instead. So I think it is with Reverend Parris.

Papa says Reverend Parris squandered a small inheritance on poor investments. 'Tis why he was forced to accept the ministry—for want of any other agreeable station. Yet things have not at all worked as he had planned. It does, I think, quite bother him to have constantly to beg for his monthly salary. And I do think the resentment he harbors spills over into his sermons and teachings. Sometimes I feel his pompousness divides us as much as the issue of the witches—sometimes even adding to that issue. How are we to rid ourselves of our evil demons when our Reverend constantly reminds us of our wicked ways and accuses us of pacts with the Devil?

Please, God, do not think me impious toward one of Your shepherds. Merely am I trying to sort out what I have heard others whisper. Merely am I trying to *understand.*

Now, having recorded all that, I shall record that Reverend Parris returned again today—presumably to check upon my progress. I have the oddest sensation that he almost *delights* in my possession. As if 'tis further evidence of what he calls our "infested village."

Alas, God, I do wish You would redeem those amongst us who are "rotten hearted." So I can be cured.

Salem, 8 August 1692, eve

I saw Jeremiah today. When I was collecting eggs in the henhouse, I espied him leaving the road and entering the woods with his musket. I think he saw me, but I prefer to think he did not. Swiftly I set down my basket and followed.

I caught up with him near to the spot in the path where I had encountered Goodman Glover. Breathless, I called out, "Jeremiah! Wait! 'Tis me!"

When I think back now, for the slightest fraction of an instant, his pause was reluctant. But when he turned, his smile was pleasant. "I've had so many chores . . ." he began, by way of explaining his lack of appearance, and, thus, I knew he felt guilty.

Instantly I forgave him. "So have I!" I echoed with enthusiasm. So pleased was I to be once again within his company that I cared not at all for the days that had passed without him. "Mama has kept me busy morn, aft and eve with carding, spinning, breadmaking and candles! Scarce have I had time to catch my breath!" 'Twas a lie, to be certain. More truly have I been occupied with treacle, prayers and Reverend Parris. But of that I could not tell Jeremiah. "Are you going hunting?" I asked.

"Thought I'd look for some quail," he replied, offhandedly. "I haven't much time, though. My father has much for me to do at the ordinary." He stood facing me, but not really looking at me, and I wondered if he felt awkward for the change that had occurred betwixt us. To put him at ease, I reached for his free hand and squeezed it and smiled. His shyness bolstered my confidence, and I thought, "Even Jeremiah feels foolish at times!" The thought improved my spirits immensely.

"May I accompany you?" I asked.

"Sure," he said; and his musket slipped, so he disengaged his hand from mine to straighten it.

He turned to walk the path slowly, and I walked beside him. Since the path is narrow, and wide enough for only one, Jeremiah politely walked to the side, his steps making crackling sounds in the carpet of dried leaves. I thought how handsome he looked. His head bent toward the ground as he walked, and his musket lay across one of his broad shoulders. His tall, slender frame moved with ease. His dark brown hair was clubbed, and I thought how soft it was.

I said, "It seems so long since I've seen you!"

"I know," he replied, nicely. He related something about the ordinary, but I wasn't really listening. My thoughts were absorbed in merely his presence. Casually I brushed my arm against his, hoping he would take my hand, but he didn't.

"I think about you every day," I told him, and now I could bite my tongue for how eager I sounded.

At last he looked at me, rather sheepishly. Vaguely it occurred to me that perhaps he regretted having kissed me. But swiftly I pushed the thought from my mind and decided he simply felt shy about it, because he's so proper. Impulsively I stood on my toes and kissed his cheek. He blushed the color of a cherry. I waited for him to stop and kiss me back, but he continued walking. How I wanted him to kiss me!

We conversed for a while, but our conversation now seems thin and of little substance. When we paused near some ground scrub where quail might be hidden, I ran my hand along the grip of his musket, pretending to admire it, but secretly hoping he would take advantage of my closeness and touch me. He didn't.

His mind seemed distracted, somehow. Preoccupied. His demeanor was pleasant and polite, yet distant in a way I can't quite put my finger upon. When after a short while he sighed and said, "I guess there won't be any quail today," I found myself vastly disappointed. I wished he hadn't given up so swiftly.

"Shall I see you on the morrow?" I asked when we parted at the road.

"I'll try," he said.

Pray, God, do let him still like me.

Salem, 9 August 1692, morn

Shall Goody Glover never be satisfied 'til I join her in death? Why does she so torment me?

Last eve her blood again spilled into my throat, and so profuse was its flow, the Venice treacle could scarce find its way past. And as the drool dribbled from her distorted lips, her mouth opened into its wide cackle, making the blood flow even faster. So violent were my thrashings, Papa could not at all catch hold of my limbs to tie me down, and Mama had finally to toss upon me a pitcher of water.

Mercy ran wailing to the great room, refusing to return even after my convulsions had subsided. "What if Goody Glover gets me, too?" Mercy wailed.

"Goody Glover shall get no one," Mama maintained, firmly.

Papa said, "I think we should ask Reverend Parris to return."

Mama replied, "He returns every day, Jacob."

Daniel, disgusted, slammed the front door and went to the barn, saying he could scarce catch a wink for his troublesome half-sister.

And I? I exhaustedly helped Mama change my soaked sheets, wondering where all is to end. Pray, God, what plan is for me? Am I forever to be tormented? Or am I to soon indeed choke upon her blood and follow my torturer to her grave?

Salem, 9 August 1692, eve

I hate Phebe! I hate Abigail! I hate Deliverance!

Today I went round to call on Ann Sibley, and with her were the three people I now most hate: Abigail, Phebe, and Deliverance. All were tossing horseshoes beside Ann's barn. "No one," thought I, suddenly miserable, "had thought to invite *my* inclusion." Too soon did I know the reason, because at my appearance, all motion instantly stilled. For a moment I wondered if I had grown horns, so strangely did all stare at me. Remembering my resolve for a change of character, and all too clearly hearing Mama's description of me as friendless, I smiled. So seldom do I smile, I expected everyone to excitedly greet me. No more in error have I ever been.

All stared at me in nervousness. It made *me* nervous just watching them. Phebe actually took two steps backward. Abigail tossed another horseshoe. For a moment I thought everyone was going to pretend I didn't exist! Hopefully—expectantly!—I looked at Deliverance. Surely Deliverance would bid me a greeting. Deliverance was my best friend. Deliverance always wants to be *liked!*

Obviously Deliverance did not care about being

liked today. Deliverance half smiled awkwardly, and when Phebe said something about leaving, Deliverance almost tripped over Phebe's heels to follow. Abigail was in close pursuit. Phebe could not, of course, resist acting catty. Still not addressing me, she excused herself to Ann by saying *very precisely,* "My mother has given me strict instructions as to certain persons I'm to avoid."

Stunned, for a moment I hadn't a clue as to her meaning. Deliverance didn't even glance at me. Then I realized. 'Tis because of my possession. How swiftly its news has spread.

As if Phebe's claws hadn't yet made their mark, she then tossed her head in that irritating manner and said, meanly, "O Ann, do tell Jeremiah if he comes round that I shall be at home. He was expecting me here today."

I felt mortally wounded. If Phebe's claws had reached into my chest and ripped out my heart, I could not have felt worse. So Jeremiah has indeed replaced me with Phebe! Has he kissed her, too, I wonder?

Wretched, I glanced at Ann, mortified at what she must think. Had she told the others about Jeremiah and me? What a fool they must think me to be!

My insides writhed as I watched the trio walk across the fields, whispering, giggling, their heads bent as close as thieves. No need had I to wonder of what they were whispering. 'Twas of me!

Miserable, I wanted to put my face in my hands and run home weeping. But so desperately alone did I suddenly feel, that I needed a friend, any friend, no matter how reluctant that person was for my company. I again looked at Ann. She had a strange expression on her face, rather like when one has eaten something foul and wishes to be able to spit it out. But Ann is too sweet to be unkind.

Bluntly I asked, "Do you want me to leave?"

Ann began picking up the horseshoes, presumably to give herself time to think, but finally she answered, softly, "Of course not."

She didn't mean it. But I didn't care. Nervously I began helping her collect the horseshoes, hoping she wouldn't change her mind, and eventually she asked in her sweet voice, "Mama asked me to pick wild-flowers for the table. Would you like to help?"

At that point I would have picked ragweed, so desperate was I for company. We went to the meadow and meandered slowly over its small green hills, picking daisies and buttercups and Indian paintbrush, and so relieved was I that I had not been completely ostracized, I didn't care whether Ann talked to me or not. Which, for a while, it looked as if she would *not.*

I was relieved, however, that Ann was too kind to mention Jeremiah. Were she to have referred to him in any manner, even to express sympathy, I am certain I would have wept.

Yet Ann's curiosity about other things did not go unspoken. As she reached down to pluck some paintbrush, she softly asked, "What's it like, Rachel? Being possessed?"

So startled was I, I did not answer for a moment. 'Tis the first time anyone has ever mentioned my condition so naturally, just as naturally as if she had inquired: "What's it like, Rachel? Living on Ipswich Road?"

Pondering the question a moment, I wondered if I really wanted to answer. Normally, 'tis exactly the sort of personal probing I would avoid, replying with some cryptic statement which would close off any further curiosity. But, remembering my resolve to change my character and to be more open, I heaved a long sigh and said, honestly, "Ann, 'tis the most dreadful thing you can ever imagine."

Slowly, and in vivid detail, I then began describing much of what has happened to me, feeling a sense of release in finally having someone to whom I could spill out all my troubles. I probably should not have told so much, but Ann listened with such interest, and with such sympathy, I could not stop myself. Sometimes I even made my visions sound worse than they are, just because I needed the sympathy. Alas, my pride, I fear, went the same way as my reserve, and I felt not a whit of shame or reluctance in what I told.

At the end, Ann—dear, sweet, gentle Ann—put her arms round me in a hug and told me how glad she was to be able to understand.

"Dearest Rachel, I am so glad you have confided in me." Her voice was sad, and I truly think she felt some of my pain. "Please do feel you can always count on me should you ever need help . . . or just to listen should you need to talk."

I think she meant it. Oddly, I suddenly had a deep desire that some of her peace and gentleness could be a part of me, that if it were, it would soothe me; and I impulsively removed a pin from my hair and pled, "O Ann! Do let's be blood sisters! You are the only one who cares about me! Truly you are! Do let's seal our bond!"

Ann looked startled, but she was kind. Stammering, she put me off with: "Er . . . umm . . . your, uh, pin shan't, uh, be sharp enough. Perhaps we . . . uh . . . should do it another time."

She probably would have done it had I pressed; but I didn't press. I think I know why she refused. She, just like the others, thinks me contagious.

Feeling awkward, I instantly regretted my impulsiveness and was about to tell Ann that I hadn't really meant it and was merely jesting; but I hadn't the chance, because suddenly a bumblebee swirled out of a clump of daisies that Ann had reached to pick, and its black and yellow fur landed on her hand. I still feel badly for Ann. I know it hurt. Tears welled in her eyes, and she whimpered as she ran to the house for her mother.

On the way home, a chicken flew into my path and opened its mouth into a loud cackle—Goody Glover's cackle. Its feathery body kept flying at my legs and pecking at my ankles, and it chased me all the way home, 'til I was nearly driven to distraction and finally collapsed on the great room floor, wailing. It seems I never escape her! And now she has taken all my friends! Even Jeremiah!

Salem, 10 August 1692

How lonely I am for Jeremiah. Does he not think of me at all? I turned thrice and ten today, and he did not even remember.

Mama and Mercy presented me with a pewter spoon for my bridal chest; Papa and Daniel bestowed me a cup and saucer. I wonder if I shall wed to ever use them.

Salem, 11 August 1692

I could bear it no longer. Being the direct person I am, I had to hear Jeremiah himself explain why he has replaced me.

I went to the ordinary, which was the only place I knew to find him. The dust from the road made small, dry puffs as I walked, clinging to the hem of my skirt and streaking it gray, which quite ill-humored me, for I did so want to look my best for this occasion.

I had hoped to find Jeremiah outside; but I did not, and so I took a deep breath and marched up the three small steps and proceeded to enter—which, as a girl, and as a villager, is quite unheard of, ordinaries being licensed only for men and for travellers, and considered wasteful idleness for villagers, who should be putting time to better use.

Tentative at first, I pushed open the large, heavy door a small crack. Six or seven men sat at trestle tables, cooling themselves with tall draughts of beer. I recognized no one, of course; but at the far end of the room, the taproom door stood slightly ajar, and behind it I could see Jeremiah doing something with a stack of kegs. My heart began to pound nervously.

Pushing the door a bit farther, I stepped inside.

Some of the men set down their wooden noggins and watched me. Quite naughty did I feel, standing in an ordinary. Swiftly my eyes took it all in, from the warm coals in the enormous hearth to the rows of shelves with empty noggins reaching almost up to the low ceiling, to the neat samplers hung on the plaster walls—every detail of which I tried to remember so I could relate it to Deliverance, or even Abigail, if ever again they decided to speak to me. Then Jeremiah stepped from the taproom and stopped dead in his tracks.

His jaw dropped open in amazement. I giggled awkwardly. Quicker than I could blink, he was beside me and hustling me outside, giving me quite the lecture for my erring ways and speaking softly 'til we reached outside so as not to cause a commotion amongst the travellers.

As soon as we were in the sunlight, I abruptly interrupted and defended myself. "Had you come to call—as you used to," I said, "I shan't be forced to such erring!" What courage I displayed!

I had meant it half in teasing and half in challenge, but my abruptness gave him pause from his lecturing, and I could almost see him gulp. Suddenly he looked guilty. I was glad. I wanted him to feel guilty for ignoring me.

Hands on my hips, I defiantly repeated, "Why *have* you ignored me?"

Still Jeremiah did not give a direct answer. Looking vastly uncomfortable, he mumbled something I could make neither head nor tail of, then finally he repeated what he had said two days past—how his father had been keeping him quite busy at the ordinary. Stammering, he said, "'Tis . . . er . . . been a time of, uh, so many travellers that I guess . . . well . . . the days have all drifted into one."

Trying to decide whether his answer was genuine, I

stared him straight in the eye to try to determine if he meant it. I couldn't decide. So with even more directness, I then asked, "Have you replaced my company with that of Phebe?"

Jeremiah snapped, "I told you my father has kept me busy."

I decided I did not believe him. Whether he had indeed replaced me with Phebe, I still did not know; but I *did* know, and I knew *he* knew, that he had been avoiding me. Bluntly, I said what I knew to be filling his thoughts.

"So. I suppose you've heard about my possession."

"Well, er, yes," he stammered. "I have, uh, er, heard of it."

His discomfit increased to the point of pain. And while his long legs shuffled around in the dirt, I could see him visibly wince. Deliverance once said Jeremiah's arms and legs look like they are growing too fast for his body. At that moment, his gangliness seemed to grow immeasurably.

Vexed at not having the conversation going at all as I intended, I started to morosely sit down on the steps; but no sooner had my knees half-way bent than Jeremiah swiftly caught hold of my elbow and led me round to the back, toward the chopping stump, which I thought to be because he felt it not seemly for a girl to be sitting on the steps of an ordinary. Brushing off the wood shavings on the stump, Jeremiah prepared me a place, but perversely I now decided I wanted to stand.

"Well?" I demanded. "'Tis my possession, isn't it? That is why you've been ignoring me."

"Nay, nay. 'Tis not true at all," he denied. "We're still friends. I promise we are."

Startled, I asked, "Why would we *not* be?"

Again Jeremiah was awkward, moving round on the stump, and I could tell this conversation was something he vastly wished to avoid. His feet kept self-consciously burying themselves in a pile of shavings, until finally he asked, "Do . . . do you have these . . . er . . . fits often? I mean, could you just be standing somewhere and . . . uh . . . fall into a fit?"

Somewhere deep inside me a light dawned. Furiously I spat out, "So that's why you hustled me outside, then so swiftly round to the back! You fear I shall scare away your father's customers! Well, if you worry whether I shall fall into a fit on the steps of your father's ordinary—I shan't! My visions have to drive me to distraction before I give in, and I promise I shall leave well before that!"

By Jeremiah's scarlet face, I knew I had read his thoughts precisely. And so burning was a lump in my throat, I could scarcely swallow.

"'Tis not what I thought at all," Jeremiah swiftly lied. "Truly 'twas not! I was . . . er . . . just curious, that's all."

Contemptuously I shot back, "What a fraud you are, Jeremiah. You're just like Deliverance and all the rest. You're afraid of me, aren't you? You're afraid I'm contagious!"

The chill in my voice could have frozen tea. But inside, that lump scorched a hole through my throat, and I wanted to sob.

Dejected, Jeremiah said, "I've missed you, Rachel. Truly I have. Don't leave. Let's talk—like we used to. About, er, other things."

"Things which are not important to *me?*" I hissed.

"Rachel, pray . . ."

"Don't 'pray' me, Jeremiah Moore! You're no better friend than any of the others! And you, of all people! You're the one person I thought I could count on! The one person I thought would understand me!"

I suppose Jeremiah felt miserable. His face was pale,

and his eyes were sad and repentant. I didn't care. I rushed on, my words withering and sharp.

"So, I see your friendship runs no deeper than a shallow puddle! You're even worse than the others, who at least *admit* their intentions!"

"Rachel, that's not fair—"

"Not fair! Not fair, Jeremiah Moore! And whom are you to speak of fairness? You, who deserts a person just when they need you the most! Well, I shan't vex you with my presence any longer! You shall have no more fears of my having fits on your father's steps!"

Hurt to the quick, I turned on my heel, blinking back the tears, but swiftly Jeremiah caught my hand and pulled me back.

"Rachel, listen. Pray, listen! You're right in some ways. I . . . I am not a very good friend. But . . . but you know how it is when people are accused of . . . er . . . possession." I could tell it pained him to speak the word. "Everything around them gets . . . well, er, confused. And everyone starts talking about . . . well, about how maybe something worse might happen. . . ."

"Like being witched!" I spat.

"Well, er . . ."

"You needn't worry about that either, Jeremiah Moore. If I do become a witch, you shall be the last person upon whom I cast a spell! You shan't be worth it!"

I knew my words were dangerous, but I was too angry to care.

"Rachel!" gasped Jeremiah. "Do be—"

"Careful?" I snapped. "O wouldn't you and all the others just love to see me hang from a noose!"

"Rachel, that's not true! I—"

"Or would you rather see me driven insane from the terror of my visions? With not one friend in the world to turn to! Aye, 'tis indeed what everyone wants, isn't it?"

"Rachel—"

"Well, upon my life, you shall have neither! I shall . . . I shall kill myself first!"

With that I did turn on my heel, and raced away, blinking back tears of hurt and frustration.

'Tis strange, how I have always felt about Jeremiah. All my thirteen years he has been my playmate and my protector; always around him I have felt soft and kind, a softness and kindness which has extended beyond him to all else and all other persons in the world. So much more pleasant, and pretty, has the world always appeared when Jeremiah was there. And when he has not been there, my feelings have been just the opposite; instead of large and bright, the world has seemed small and unfriendly and frightening, and inside I am closed, sharp, wary.

Now I wonder whether all these years I have made a mistake, whether the person I thought to be so steady, so caring, was merely a figment of my imagination, another vision which has deceived me, a vision having no more substance than the soft, ill-formed shape of a clam, a vision having no more strength of character than a rope, which, when its ends are loosed of its bounds and it has lost its constrictions, falls limp and useless and serves no purpose.

I had hoped Jeremiah would follow me. When I arrived home, I sat in the shadow behind the barn, and I watched the narrow, dusty road for hours. But he did not come.

Salem, 12 August 1692

Today was *awful.* Even do I fear to write it.

'Twas started when I was on an errand for Mama and took the shortcut through the woods. Always this past fortnight I have been so cautious, for fear of encountering Goodman Glover, so I have taken the road. But today, so low in spirits was I about all that has happened, I wanted to think. The solace of the woods is best for thoughts.

Upon returning from my errand, having forgotten my fears and feeling secure, I took the longer path through the forest, near to where the river widens.

Male laughter floated intriguingly through the trees. Instinctively I knew some of the village boys were swimming, and being of curiosity, I stealthily tiptoed off the path and peered round a nice fat maple.

Deodat Easty was there (Ann's desired intended), as was Peter Cook (whom Deliverance's heart beats for), as well as homely Joshua Snow and others. In all there were about seven, all hooting, hollering, splashing and having a merry time of it. Engaged in rough horseplay, as only boys can do, they had fashioned a diving position from an old log floating in the middle of the river. But most fascinating of all was they were stark naked!

Flushing, I quickly dodged my head back round the tree. Yet curiosity again plagued me. Gingerly I peered out again.

How funny they were! Their hands and faces were brown as berries, while the rest of their bodies was white as baby's skin! Deodat Easty climbed on the log, looking like some sprawling, leggy frog, then turned, stood and, with a yelp, leapt into the air, arms and legs wildly flailing, his small white dingle bobbing like a fish, until he landed with an enormous splash into the water. I smiled.

"If sweet, shy Ann could see Deodat *now,"* I thought. "Ann would positively faint with embarrassment!"

Smiling, again, I continued to stare, my eyes taking in their naked bodies and always travelling toward their bobbing dingles. Always, for some perverse reason, I have been fascinated by boys' dingles. Once I saw Daniel, 'twixt the curtains, climbing from the bathing tub, and I thought of it for days. His dingle is larger than Deodat's. Probably because Daniel is older.

I decided no one would know if I took another peek.

Ugly Joshua Snow—who can't tell one end of a mallet from the other—clambered up on the log, fell off, tried again, fell off again and finally made it. I giggled softly. Can Joshua do nothing right? His dingle poked out like a short skinny sausage. How I wished I could tell Abigail! 'Twould serve her right for her recent attitude!

Suddenly leaves crackled behind me.

'Twas Goodman Glover!

Stunned, I stood petrified like wood. Goodman Glover had seen me spying!

His thin lips opened into a grin, and his teeth were all

yellow and misshapen. "So, 'tis watching the boys you like, is it?" he said.

Horrified, my hands flew to my burning face. What if the boys heard him speak? What if everyone came bounding from the water and found me spying?

Goodman Glover's grin became a low chuckle. "So the pretty one likes the boys, does she?" he repeated.

His small hand reached toward me, pulling me against him, and frantically I tried to wriggle free. I could not believe the strength of his grasp. Before I knew what happened, his other hand had covered my mouth, and he shoved me to the ground. Terrified, I wanted to scream, but I couldn't. Someone might hear! While male laughter floated through the trees, my mind spun, trying to grasp what was happening. Terrified, I fought. Those thin evil lips and those gaping yellow teeth closed over my mouth, and the smell of liquor made me want to wretch. Hands were all over me. Something large and hard pressed against my leg. 'Twas a dingle! Pray, God, how could such a small weasely man have a dingle as large as that!

Through liquored breath, I could hear soft, low laughter. "Your Mama once joined her body with mine. She liked it. Joined me often, she did."

Aghast, I felt my stomach heave. What was he saying? What had Mama done? Surely 'tis a lie!

I heard his low, evil laughter again. "Now 'twill be *your* body I'll join! And you'll like it, too! Just like your Mama did!"

Kicking and biting, I felt his quick, small hands tear at my buttons, then suddenly I felt one hand on my flesh! On my small breast! Struggling, with all the energy within me, I wanted to cry out but could not, for fear of the sound. His small weight lay atop me heavy as a boulder, and no matter which way I fought, I could not wrench myself free.

The world swam in horror, and his sharp teeth upon my lips bit in pain. So firmly were they fastened upon my mouth, my choking sobs strangled in my throat. I could not breathe. Frantically I struggled, and within my struggle, I heard a rip, then felt a grasping hand within my underclothing. Something hard and stiff moved upon my leg. It pressed against my privates, and though my legs were pinned, I kicked and scratched and pommelled.

Through labored grunts, I heard a curse, then suddenly a deep pain shot through me. My privates and my insides felt as if they should split apart, and suddenly I froze, so great was my pain, and so terrified was I of greater pain which came with every movement. His sickening body went into a spasm. His foul breath made short, swift "oofs," and his small hand pressed my chest flat to the ground while his spasms came with such speed and such pain that no longer did I fear sound; but my screams stuck in my throat and made only silent sobs.

Suddenly I felt one enormous spasm, then heard a high, whining wail—like an animal caught in a trap. His weasely body stilled, weighted atop me. It was only then the real horror enveloped me. He was inside me! Goodman Glover, with his disgusting, large dingle, was inside of me!

Every fiber within me renewed my fight. Kicking, biting and heaving, I fought with all my might. His body began yet another spasm, but somehow I threw him off and tore myself free. Frantically I stumbled to my feet. A bright trickle of red blood leapt out upon my torn clothing. I nearly wretched. His weasely body lay at my feet, doubled over in curses from where my foot had kicked, but I did not stop to watch. A sob rose to my throat, and I turned to flee.

Behind me, he growled, "Tell your Mama of this,

and the whole village shall know of her past!"

Swiftly I ran, stumbling, weeping. A large hairy boar leapt out at me, snarling, and then I *did* scream, as loud as my lungs would allow me. In his beady eyes I saw the eyes of Goody Glover. He charged, chasing me, his cusps fierce and ugly, and in even further terror, I scrambled up a tree, then hid myself in its limbs, sobbing. For hours I sobbed, until my throat was raw and I could not breathe.

When finally I reached home, I tore off my dress and shift and threw them, wadded, into a corner of the chest; then collapsed upon my bed. No one must ever know what has happened. I have been defiled by Goodman Glover! Mama could have been his wife! And 'tis a horrid, horrid tale which lies behind those facts!

Salem, 13 August 1692

I feel physically ill and shamed to write. All came back to me in last eve's nightmare, and I do not think my mind can continue.

Betwixt Goody Glover's cackling laughter sounded the soft, low chuckle of her husband. He tugged at my dress. His hands were on my flesh. His large, hard dingle pressed against my leg. His thin lips and liquored breath covered my mouth and swallowed my lips. I wanted to cry out! Scream! Flee! But I could do nothing. My body was made stone from some wicked spell his evil wife had cast upon me.

Dingles—big dingles, little dingles, fat dingles, soft dingles, all sizes and shapes of dingles—whirled round in my brain, until suddenly Goodman Glover stood before me naked, as if he had stepped from the throng of raucous, bathing boys.

His thin lips curled in a smile. The tip of his small pink tongue moved round the top of his yellowed, gaping teeth. His wandering eye darted this way and that. A tail curled from his buttocks. His dingle was enormous, the size of a tree. Sobbing, I tried to step back. I wanted to vomit. His hand reached for mine to draw it toward his dingle.

A low voice said, "Your Mama joined her body with mine. I might have been your father."

'Twas the voice of the Devil! From nowhere a pitchfork leapt into his hand, and with its tines, he stroked my breast.

Sobbing, I screamed, "Be gone! Be gone, you vile, vile man!"

Blood trickled down to my stomach, oozing from the marks of the sharp tines. 'Twas warm and stinging. I screamed. Amazingly, my body became unloosed, and I fought. Fought with all my strength.

"I hate you! I hate you!" I screamed. "You shan't take me! You shan't!"

From a mist appeared Jeremiah. He, too, was naked, and his hand was held out to me. When he spoke, 'twas as if his voice drifted from a distance. "Do not fear, Rachel," Jeremiah said. "'Tis merely a dream. Waking shall set you free."

"Nay!" I cried. "'Tis no dream! 'Tis real! Can you not see? My visions are real! They have come to get me!"

Jeremiah smiled, a kindly smile. Fiercely I grabbed at Goodman Glover and shoved him forward.

"Look, Jeremiah! 'Tis real! Can you not see the tail?"

Again Jeremiah smiled, touching me, then shaking his head, his vapor disappeared.

Goodman Glover laughed evilly. He moved toward me, closer, closer. Frantic, I kicked and sobbed. His pitchfork aimed at my cheek, its tines sharp and jagged. In terror I covered my face; but the force, when it hit, nearly made me swallow my tongue, and I cried out in pain.

But the pain was not that of the pitchfork. Nor of his vile dingle. 'Twas of Mama slapping me. And I was tied to the bed.

Salem, 13 August 1692, early eve

I fear to leave the house, so frightened am I of encountering Goodman Glover. All day I have spent at my spinning.

I cannot look at Mama, for knowledge of her horrid past. And for what she has caused me to suffer. She tried to come converse with me, sitting beside me at my wheel, but I mumbled something unintelligible and short, until finally she sighed, stood wearily and returned to her bread baking. To Mercy, I heard her say, "'Twas a poor night for Rachel. 'Tis best we leave her to her thoughts." She left two cups of Venice treacle on the table beside me.

I marvel that Mama—pious, sedate, poised Mama—could contain such a vile secret, could so naturally continue with her chores, could so often have been held up as a perfect example of goodwifery! And all this time beneath that calm exterior has lain something too detestable to even imagine. Does she not know what it would do to Papa were he to learn the truth? Does she not know Papa would be destroyed?

Upon pain of death, I swear Papa *never* shall learn of it. Even have I to kill Goodman Glover—or Mama herself!

So sorry do I feel for Papa, for what he does not know, that my heart nearly tears in two and aches in my breast. At midday meal I watched as he and Mama conversed, even laughing over something, and I wanted to weep for what a fraud Mama is. My throat stung from unspent tears for how Mama has deceived him. At evening meal, when Papa was so upset over the English suit and Mama comforted him, I hated Mama for how sincere she sounded, for how she touched Papa's hand as once she had touched Goodman Glover's.

And what of me? Am I no better than Mama? Has my body not also joined with Goodman Glover's?

Aye, I *am* better than Mama. I must persuade myself so, to keep my senses. My joining was not of my own choosing, and I do not have a husband from which I practice concealment. By these two sins, Mama has created my doom, which I must bear wordlessly. How I hate her for where she has led me. I cannot think where all will finish.

The peace of confiding is not allowed me. My tongue, always so wooden, must become more wooden still. 'Tis only you, dearest journal, who may hear my thoughts and my confession and therein provide me sanity.

Salem, 13 August 1692, late eve

So many troubles weigh upon Papa's shoulders. Troubles which are oblivious to Mama's past. Goodman English has filed suit, as he threatened, and demands that Papa dismantle the dam, which would destroy the mill.

After evening meal, I walked with Papa back to the mill, not speaking, wanting our mutual presence to console us both. We sat on the steps in the dusk, and the whoosh of the waterwheel felt oddly reassuring. Something permanent still remained.

In front of us, the road lay silent. So different our road is at dusk than during the day. In the day that winding, dusty thread teems with activity: nicely dressed gentlemen ride past on their way from Boston; travellers stop at the ordinary; rickety carts, harnesses jingling, go clattering past, piled high with timber, vegetables, beef, pork and all sorts of farming yields headed for the coast, thence to other ports and other towns and other places, all so unknown to me.

Occasionally, as I did tonight, I sit on the steps and think about those other places. I try to imagine that vast, mysterious world which lies beyond our mill. And so close are we to the sea, some days I can even smell the pungency of salt cutting through the air.

The setting sun eased behind the trees and cast the world in a dim, sad light, matching the mood of Papa and me. Soon it would be dark, and the hills would be shapeless, black forms; the empty road would be hidden, trailing off into some vast nowhere around the bend. Sighing, Papa placed his arm round my shoulders and laid my head against his chest.

"The Lord constantly tests us," Papa said. "Every hour, every day, He tests us. Always observing, always watching to see if we keep constancy in our faith. 'Tis why He now sends the devil to our midst. Testing us in yet another manner."

Glumly, I nodded. Fervently I wished the Lord would send the Devil away, at least from me.

Lost in thought was Papa, trying to sort out the reason for his troubles, and he continued with: "So much strife between village and town. So many jealousies between our poor, beleaguered husbandmen of the village and the more prosperous merchants of town. Were those jealousies to cease, God would surely remove His thorns. Because Satan would find no fertile valley for temptation. Do you not think, Rachel, that contented hearts leave no room for evil?"

Papa was referring to the jealousies of Goodman English and Corwin. I wondered if such men would ever be content; yet it pleases me when Papa addresses me as an adult, so I did not argue. Nestling further into his chest, I told Papa I thought this to be a horrid summer; I did not tell him why.

"Aye." Papa nodded. "One can only hope the riddance of these witches shall clear us of our strife. Perhaps then neighbor shall again be in concert with neighbor. Perhaps then we shall once more enjoy our sense of community. 'Tis the root of the problem, Rachel—our lack of community. Selfishness—selfishness and covetousness are what have brought Satan amongst us. Does not the Good Book say 'Love thy neighbor as thine self'? How have the Book's words gone so unattended?"

I said what I have been thinking for some time now. I said I thought the riddance of witches seems to be curing nothing. That the village is more unsettled than ever. That for every witch we rid, thrice more appear.

My words were disturbing to Papa. He said, "We have to depend upon Reverend Parris to bring us back into the fold."

"Mostly what Reverend Parris cares about," I observed, "is his salary." My bitterness for all things that have happened showed in my tone.

"With cause," Papa countered. "That salary is now overdue for many a fortnight. And that, too, brings grumblings of begrudgement from half our neighbors. Truly the Reverend Parris is an instrument of our Lord. Else long ago, he would have deserted us."

I told Papa I thought Reverend Parris to be the source of much grumblings and begrudgement himself. I reminded him of how Reverend Parris had spent months negotiating very favorable terms before even accepting our community of lost lambs.

Again Papa was perturbed by my bluntness. "Rachel, you must not be so vocal in your criticism. 'Twill bring you difficulty and ill will."

"But 'tis the truth," I maintained.

"Aye." Papa nodded. "But truth is not always best spoken."

"Aye," I thought, bitterly, "like the truth about Mama and Goodman Glover. And about me."

With weariness, Papa said, "I have always tried to do my best by you children and your mother. If God be willing and show me the way, I shall endure this new test He has presented me. But you must help me, Rachel."

"Aye, Papa."

"You must try to be obedient and pious, and you, too, must fight the test the Lord has given. You must try not to imagine things which aren't really there. Such imaginings do so sorely trouble your Mama. I love your Mama dearly. As do I love you children. And the conflict which divides the village weighs a hundred times heavier on my heart when it spills into our home. Can you do that for me, Rachel? Can you help us find that contentment we have lost?"

How my heart cried out for the tenderness with which he spoke Mama's name! With such affection does Papa hold someone who has so monstrously deceived him! I could not look into his eyes for what evilness I knew!

"What hurts your Mama," Papa said, "hurts me, too. You do know that, don't you, Rachel? Your Mama's happiness is mine, as well. Will you try, Rachel? Pray, promise me you shall."

Finally, after a long while, I murmured, "Aye, Papa. I . . . I shall try." But inside I knew it would kill me.

Salem, 14 August 1692

I have *tried* to keep my word to Papa. All day I have tried. But I have disappointed him.

To Mama, I have been polite and have attempted not to show at all how much I hate her. I helped her with the soap making and thought I was quite civil. I helped her gather up all the lye and put it into the large black kettle, and I even helped her collect wood in the field behind the house to build the fire beneath it. Even did I take the paddle from her and stir for a while, the foul smells of the thickening lye nearly choking off my breath. My tone, when I spoke, was cool, however, and I could not resist slyly asking:

"Mama, how well do you know Goodman Glover?"

Mama stammered. Calm, self-assured Mama stammered! "Why . . . why do you ask?"

I hated her more than ever. "No reason," I replied, letting my voice trail off vaguely. "I just wondered."

Mama did not answer. I despised her. At midday meal, Papa gave me a stern frown for my disposition, but I didn't care.

Salem, 15 August 1692

Again I have disappointed Papa. For at long last, after continual inquiry by both Mama and Reverend Parris, Goody Glover has finally spoken.

I had gone to fetch some butter from the churn in the icehouse when it happened. 'Tis an errand I do so dread to do, because the icehouse is always so creepy. Sides of beef, venison and mutton hang from the rafters, and always I am afraid the spindly, blood-red legs shall brush against me and touch me. Daniel says 'tis absurd, my reaction. 'Tis only meat which finds its way into our stomachs, Daniel says. Of course, 'tis so. Yet I do positively detest looking at animals without their skin.

Being in a hurry to be in and be gone, I left the door open a crack, swiftly edging my way round the blocks of ice, which Papa cut from the river last winter. The sawdust floor was damp and soggy from the ice being half melted. Sides of meat hung over me like eerie critters, smelling strongly of pickled brine, and I crouched low so as not to touch them. The stream of light from the cracked door led me toward the back and the butter. Almost had I reached it when I saw her. Goody Glover. Her face rose up in a mist from the top of the churn.

Startled, I stumbled backward into a side of beef and let out a yelp. Leaping in the other direction, I fell into another side, then dove for the floor. I was trapped! The small, dank room began echoing with cackling laughter, and faces leapt from a side of mutton, grinned, then drifted up to the ceiling, disappeared and suddenly shot out of another. Her blood dripped down onto the critters and made them redder. Frantic, my heart nearly pounded out of my shift. Edging toward the door, my back plastered to the wall, I screamed in terror. Laughter deafened my hearing; my hands flew up to muffle my ears. Constantly I cried out, "Be gone! Be gone! You evil witch!"

Finally my lungs could scream no longer. I had to pause to catch my breath. Sobbing, I asked, "What do you want? Why do you so torment me?"

The voice was gravelly and jarring, strained, as though its wind was cut short from the pull of a noose. Stunned, I was not certain at first if I had really heard it.

"I want you to sign my book," she said.

"Wh . . . what?" I stammered.

"I want you to sign my book," she repeated.

Book? What book? The Book of the Devil?

"Wh . . . what book?" I pressed.

"Satan's book," she said. "He wants your soul beside me."

One long, bony hand held out a piece of parchment. The other held a pen. Further did I plaster myself to the wall, agape and staring.

Finally I knew what she wanted. To sign away my soul to the Devil! Somehow I had always known it. 'Twas why Goody Black was convicted. For the same contention.

"No!" I screamed. I found my lungs again. "No! I shan't sign your evil book! Not even . . . not even if you slit my throat! Be gone, you evil witch! Be gone from me forever!"

Shrill laughter trailed after me, even after I flung open the icehouse door and fled.

Sobbing, I ran past Mama and on to Papa and threw my arms round his waist and poured out my story.

"She shan't have it!" I wailed to Papa, in determination. "She shan't have my soul, even . . . even if she slits my throat!"

Papa said nothing. He merely looked down at me in confusion. Behind me, in a calm voice, Mama replied, "She shan't slit your throat, Rachel. Of that I promise you."

"But what about my soul?" I cried, as I frantically looked up into Papa's eyes. "Can you keep that from Goody Glover, as well?"

Papa just shook his head, sadly.

Salem, 16 August 1692, morn

"Slit your throat! Slit your throat! Slit your throat, Rachel!"

On and on the raucous voice cackled, all through the night and into the dawn. From the rafters her evil face glared down at me. Her cloying fingers reached out, grasping for me, and blood gushed from her neck in torrents, soaking my linens. Again and again, tossing her head back in laughter, she chanted, "Slit your throat! Slit your throat! Slit your throat, Rachel!"

Goodman Glover appeared, too, in the same disgusting manner; and Jeremiah, and Mama. This time 'twas not I caught beneath Goodman Glover's disgusting spasms, but Mama, and a smile played upon her lips. A deceitful smile, that made me want to wretch and strangle.

Goody Glover snarled. The blood that spewed from her neck oozed into my mouth making my screams frantic with chokes, until I was not certain whether 'twas her blood I tasted or my own.

And all the while I choked, her yawning mouth

curled in laughter. Her shrill, mesmerizing litany—"Slit your throat! Slit your throat, Rachel! Do it now!"—nearly drove me to madness.

Again I was tied to the bed, but this time when Mama tried to comfort me, I spat at her. And Papa slapped me.

Salem, 16 August 1692, aft

More sadness there was today.

Goody Hale was convicted. Tomorrow she is to be hanged. Bethshaa Abbey is said to be no improved. I wonder what solutions these hangings bring.

Tomorrow also holds the trial of young Goody Lawson. Are Goody Lawson and Goody Hale fortunate, I wonder, to have their trials be so swift? Is hanging better than languishing in that dirty little prison, which happens to so many who have been arrested? Goodman Lawson would not think so. Goodman Lawson would wish his new wife were indeed allowed to languish. 'Tis said he stands at the hut's window, holding his wife's hand through the bars, his eyes red from weeping, fervently pleading his wife's innocence and begging anyone who passes to listen. 'Tis said, if not cautious, he will join his wife.

Daniel continues to strut round the house and makes no secret of his pride at winning the unattainable Prudence. How it does nettle me to see such pleasure when all round *me* caves in like gloom! Afternoon last, when Daniel returned from midday meal with the Cory's, his face was flushed, his chest swollen, and so superior and conceited was he while describing the beauty of the Cory home, I burst into tears. My depression was more than I could bear!

Deeply upset is Papa over the English matter. Goodman English now goes from neighbor to neighbor to rally support, while Papa mournfully tries to carry on. The countersuit is to cost £21. We do not have it. I heard Papa whispering to Mama that it shall have to be borrowed.

Ann came round today, improving my disposition slightly; but after she departed, Goody Bishop arrived to spin with Mama, and my mood sunk to gloomier depths than ever. Not two moments had passed when Goody Bishop asked how my Scripture readings were progressing. I knew at once why she had come—not to spin but to supervise my cure.

Morosely I sat on the lean-to floor across from them, carding, numbly listening to the whirr of their wheels.

Goody Bishop asked, "Do you take your Venice treacle regularly?"

"Mmm," I mumbled.

"And your fasting? How does *that* progress?"

"As much as I can endure," I sullenly replied. "I must have *some* food to survive."

A tall, prepossessing woman is Goody Bishop, having large bones and rather sharp features. Always I have envisioned her standing sternly at the gates of heaven, meticulously checking through some thick ledger to determine whether each quivering, waiting soul should be allowed to pass. I wonder if Goody Bishop is indeed as perfect and as Godly as she pretends. I wonder what she would say if she were to learn about Mama.

Her stern voice suggested, "Perhaps you should try more hours with the Scriptures."

It did not surprise me that Mama immediately bid me to take up Goody Bishop's suggestion, even though

Mama had just previously lectured me upon my neglect of the wool. Mama always weakens under Goody Bishop's will. So, fetching the Bible, I obediently returned to my position on the floor to read under their watchful gaze, my mind not concentrating, my innards wriggling under Goody Bishop's constant stare. I saw her frown. I marvelled she could spin so instinctively while being so watchful of my reactions. Her eyes narrowed. I knew what she was thinking.

Peevishly I said, "Aye, I do pay attention to my reading."

Startled, Goody Bishop exclaimed, "Why, Rachel Ward! How you do read my thoughts!"

"Hmmph," I thought. "You are as obvious as cream that has curdled!"

Mama's brows knit at my temperament, and I was then forced to endure Goody Bishop's suggestions of other supposed cures for my condition, all of which were addressed to Mama. Carrying charms was recommended with great emphasis, as was standing upon my head thrice daily to drive out the evil spirits. All, maintained Goody Bishop, have worked for others. Then, lowering her voice, Goody Bishop ominously said to Mama, "Of course there was the case of the little Tompkins girl. Nothing worked. She simply turned out to be a witch."

I pretended not to hear.

Salem, 17 August 1692, morn

Another eve Goody Glover has terrorized me.

"Slit your throat! Slit your throat, Rachel! Slit your throat with a knife from the kitchen!"

So mesmerizing were her orders, and so frantic was I from madness, that I nearly rose from my bed and carried out her bidding. Pray, God, provide me with sanity. And strength.

Salem, 17 August 1692, aft

Tragically, the Disborough house has burned to the ground.

How swiftly things do happen. Only this morn Papa went to see Goodman Disborough about borrowing the £21 for his countersuit. Goodman Disborough refused him, though, and I heard Papa and Mama whispering about it later.

Apparently Papa promised Goodman Disborough to pay the money back by winter, after the fall harvest brings more business to the mill, but Goodman Disborough replied: "Winter's honoring depends upon the verdict of the court. From whence comes the honoring if the mill is shut down?"

Papa was angry. Harsh words were exchanged. 'Twas not highly honorable of Goodman Disborough, I think, after only last year when Papa was so helpful with the Disborough plowing because Goodman Disborough had hurt himself in a tree felling accident. Papa reminded him of that.

At any rate, not hours later, a spark from a brush fire Goodman Disborough had lit—burning scrub and tree limbs from a field just cleared—strangely caught the grass afire and headed straight for the house. 'Tis mysterious indeed, what with the sogginess of the ground from all the rains we've had.

So now the Disborough's home lies in ashes. Only the stone chimney remains. And a stricken Disborough family has taken up residence with the Englishes. They all probably sit round the great room and talk about how much they dislike Papa. And the rest of the village prattles about how peculiar the incident is.

"'Tis the Devil's work, again in our midst!" declares Reverend Parris.

He called again today, asking if I had yet had a fit where my limbs stiffen and my eyes roll round in their sockets and I babble as if in a trance. Surprisingly, not two hours after he departed, I had one. 'Tis peculiar how he always seems to know just what's to happen. I suppose he has seen so many cases like mine, he just knows the pattern.

I'm glad I did not go to the hanging of Goody Hale. 'Tis said to have been most morbid. Goody Hale vowed to cast a spell over the entire village, making all our crops wither and our stock sterile, and the audience was frightened to the tips of their shoes. Reverend Parris read from the Scriptures for two hours after she died, to counteract her threat.

I would so like to see Jeremiah. All day I found myself standing at the window and gazing down the road, waiting. Deep down I know 'tis senseless.

Salem, 18 August 1692

Mama bade me accompany her today to lecture. I did not want to go, not only for the deep disregard in which I now hold Mama, but because I feared Goodman Glover might be there. Usually we do not attend lecture, the Sabbath already requiring a day absent from chores; but Goody Bishop suggested that my condition requires as much exposure as possible to pious matters, and Mama, to be sure, obeyed the suggestion.

"We must not provide Goody Bishop reason to prattle," Mama said.

I said, "Goody Bishop *always* prattles. She's a nosy old busybody who finds nothing much at her own hearth, so attends to everyone else's."

Mama shushed me with sternness and said if I did not watch my tone, I would find myself spending my days in the lean-to. I wonder if Mama has guessed that I hate her.

So off I was marched to the Meetinghouse for the second time this week. Goodman Glover, to my vast relief, was not there. But I did not escape him for long. On the return home as Mama and I walked with Ann and her mother, whom should we encounter on the road, but *him.* And he tried to engage us *all* in conversation!

Desperate, I edged in between Ann and her mother, trying to conceal myself behind Goody Sibley's short, round figure. That evil, weasely man tipped his hat. "Good aft, ladies," he greeted, and he said it in a soft, low voice that was O so falsely charming. I wanted to wretch! I dared not look at him, so keenly could I feel everything he had done to defile me. I could not help flushing with shame, either, that I had not been able to stop it.

"Good aft, Goodman Glover," replied Mama and Goody Sibley in return.

"Lovely day, is it not?" he said, real friendly.

I wanted to kick Goody Sibley. She, with her ever cheery nature and high chattery voice, stood as if she were ready for a day's conversing and made not a motion to budge. She was enjoying the company! While her nasal chatter rattled on and on with that despicable man, I kept my eyes to the ground, but every so often I glanced up and caught his one good eye darting in my direction. How dirty and unclean I felt! As if he were once more pinned on top of me!

Then Mama entered the conversation. Goodman Glover said, "You look handsome today, Goody Ward."

"Thank you," replied Mama, in a polite tone.

"Your husband does well by his mill, I assume."

"Aye," replied Mama. "Very well, thank you."

I wanted to scream for the sarcasm which lay behind his question and for the casualness of Mama's reply. Goodman Glover knows as well as anybody about Papa's troubles—the whole village knows—and both he and Mama pretended nothing at all was wrong! Is this some secret code betwixt them?

Goodman Glover said, "I hear the son does well,

also. Courting the Cory girl, is he not?"

"Aye," replied Mama. "'Tis a good match. They complement each other well."

"With a marriage planned next spring?"

"Aye. Daniel nears eighteen then."

"A good age to be wed. Were *you* not eighteen when wed?"

Mama's voice grew soft, and her cheeks betrayed a light flush. "Aye, Goodman Glover. Just eighteen I was."

I felt ill down to the pit of my stomach. Mama and Goodman Glover were remembering the time before she was promised to Papa—when she and Goodman Glover were suitors—and I wanted to bury my face in my hands for knowledge of what that meant. Mama had joined her body with *his!* Mama had for some unGodly reason shared everything with this small disgusting man! I saw his thin lips curl into a smile, and I had all I could do not to pick up a clod of dirt and throw it at both of them. I marvelled that Mama could remain so calm and poised—as if nothing at all had happened. What a fraud she is! Only a slight rise in her color betrayed her.

"'Tis exceptionally warm today," remarked Mama—I suppose to explain her flush.

"O 'tis! 'Tis!" chattered Goody Sibley. "What heaven would lie in a glass of cider. Do you not think so, Goody Ward? Do, do stop at our house and have one. Goodman Glover, I do wonder that your waistcoat does not make you faint. The cloth is so heavy. And you without a wife to make you another. You poor, poor man. Perhaps were you to chop some wood in exchange, I could put my needle to task . . ."

On and on she chattered, like some squeally mouse, until I thought my nerves would snap. Ann, sweet, shy Ann, stood obediently by, never once showing impatience, except when once she softly whispered to me about a butterfly which flitted onto her arm. But as I softly whispered a reply, I caught Goodman Glover watching me, so I abruptly halted our exchange, not wanting to do a thing to call attention to myself.

Finally, after what seemed an eternity, adieus were bid, and I hated Mama doubly over for how calm she sounded. How had she the nerve to speak so naturally to this man after what they had done!

As "gooddays" were exchanged, I swiftly tried to edge my way round the other side of Goody Sibley, so as not to come within an inch of that evil man; but somehow, in a way that I am not entirely certain, he brushed into me, and I heard a soft chuckle which sent my flesh crawling. My eyes were to the ground, but in that instant, something was pressed into my hand. By that evil man! 'Twas a piece of paper!

Frantic, I knew not what to do. I could not call attention to it, for I knew not what it said. And neither could I drop it on the road, for fear of who would find it. All the way home I had to carry it, all the way past Ann Sibley's house when Mama declined Goody Sibley's offer of cider for how weary she felt, all the way with just Mama and I walking alone, saying nothing and walking in silence, I despising her more than ever. All that way I carried it, it burning a hole in my hand, wondering what that despicable man *now* has done. Finally, as I left Mama at the hen house and I went in to collect the eggs, I quickly unrumpled it and read.

Scrawled on that crumpled piece of paper, by some demented hand, was the warning:

"Be good to me, pretty girl. Else the entire village shall learn your Mama's past. More to come from me soon."

Pray, God, what am I to do?!!!

Salem, 19 August 1692

All day I have not moved a muscle from the house. What did he mean "More to come from me soon"? Is he to leave another note? Are instructions to follow? Dear God, I feel ill from panic!

Pray, God, let this demented man leave me alone. Is it not enough his evil wife tortures me? Is it not enough I live daily with threats of slitting my throat if I do not sign my soul to the Devil? Why, God, do You let Satan do this to me? Have I been such a straying lamb that You do not wish me back into Your fold? I try, God, I *do* try, to be Your obedient servant. So often do I read Your Scriptures that my eyes burn and my head constantly aches. Tell me any chapter and verse, and I can recite it in slumber! Nay, not in slumber! For that is when she torments me, wanting my throat! Constantly do I fear already it is slit. Is that what You intend, God? That some night those long, bony hands shall reach down with a gleaming knife, and blood shall soak my pillow? So tormented am I, dear God, I fear some night

I shall do it *myself!* Pray, God, don't desert me! You are all I have left! There is no one else to whom I can turn!

Can You hear me, God? If You can, pray redeem me! Do not let this wicked woman and her demented husband wrench me into their grasp!

Salem, 20 August 1692

"Slit your throat! Slit your throat! Slit your throat, Rachel!" she tells me over and over.

Salem, 20 August 1692, aft

I fear even going to the barn without someone beside me. When Mama bid me put out salt licks, I feigned a fit so as not to have to walk round the pasture. Daniel did them instead. In the kitchen garden, I made Mercy go with me, so fearful was I Goodman Glover would sneak up behind me. Mercy whimpered to Mama, "Mama, please don't make me go with Rachel." In two fortnights she has not been alone with me. Sweeping the front yard, constantly do my eyes dart this way and that, ready to bolt should they catch sight of some small weasely shadow creeping up to snatch me.

Everyone thinks 'tis only my visions which plague me. Mercy, white and trembling when we picked squash in the kitchen garden, pleadingly asked, "Can't . . . can't you do something about them? Your visions?" O that I could! O that I could make that fiendish woman depart, taking with her, her vile and disgusting husband!

Papa angrily took me aside after morning meal and admonished, "Rachel, you promised you would put that woman from your mind! You gave me your word!" O were it so easily accomplished as promised! How I do weep for how I have disappointed Papa. But how much more disappointed would he be to learn the truer reason for my daily torment!

So blatant is that torment that even Ann—dear, sweet, timid Ann—asked as we sat with our spinning, "Rachel? Does your possession grow worse? Do forgive me for prying. But I cannot help but notice how deeply it ails you."

"Aye! Aye!" I wanted to scream. "My possession does indeed worsen! But worse still is what it brings in its shadow!"

Reality and visions oft mix into one, and my head throbs for not being able to determine which is which. Is the husband the vision and the wife the fact? Pray, what happens to my mind? Is it lost?

Mama and Papa forced me to the hanging of Goody Lawson, thinking visual reminder of the riddance of a witch would pluck out my imagination, leaving me free. But so fearful was I of the encountering of Goodman Glover that I huddled with my back up against Papa's as he drove the cart; and on Witch's Hill, while we waited, so close did I stand near Papa's side, he had constantly to shake me off.

The hanging did nothing for my imagination—save to increase its vividness. 'Til the very end, Goody Lawson wept and wailed and maintained her innocence, and it seemed to take forever for her to die. Her body dangled and twitched while strange gurgles came from her throat, until finally her poor distraught husband tore from the crowd and threw himself beneath her feet, sobbing. His mind is gone. Goody Bishop whispered to Mama that he shall have to be watched.

Pray, God, don't let *my* mind go as well!

Salem, 21 August 1692

Papa has borrowed the £21 from Goodman Bishop.

I wonder if it stung Mama's pride for the money to have come from the husband of her best friend. Always they have been on equal footing, Mama and Goody Bishop, with Mama last year rising one step higher after Papa's inheritance. And now Mama not only moves a step below, but is beholden to someone who, in the subtlest of manner, will constantly remind her of her inferior position.

So self-righteous is Goody Bishop, so certain of herself, that she will not admit for a moment that she might have been too hasty in her reporting of Goody Short, who purportedly caused a pot to fall from the hearth as she passed the Pearson home. That the hook on the iron was later found to be at fault makes little difference. Goody Short was already arrested. And Goody Bishop, when asked whether she wished to recant her charges, staunchly maintained, "'Tis my duty to report unnatural occurrences which infect our village." I wonder that Goody Bishop can be so confident of her *own* perfection and purity.

Being wash day today, Mama bid me help her at the stream, and fearfully my eyes darted this way and that, keeping watch amongst the trees, trembling for who might appear. I did not think he would harass me with Mama near, but I was taking no chances. At the merest shadow of a shuffling, stoop-shouldered form, I was ready to bolt.

Perspiration running down our backs, Mama and I knelt at the water's edge, dipping and scrubbing the clothing, the harsh soap stinging my hands, the sun as hot as fire, until I, too, wanted to be in the cool water along with the wash. Mama bid me remove my dress and refresh myself, but at first I declined, fearing *he* would appear; yet finally the baking sun held me back no longer, and I stripped down to my shift and wriggled round in the water. How cool it felt. The rocks along the bank lay strewn with clothing stretched neatly and drying.

Suddenly, from out on the road, such a din erupted that Mama and I both stood in startled paralysis. Horses whinnied, a cart crashed, and the quiet gurgle of the stream was shattered by screams, wails and the high pitched yelps of children. In a flash, Mama dropped her laundry, I rose from the stream, and we dashed toward the frantic cries for help.

Instantly my eyes took it all in. Bridget White, tall and enormous, was surrounded by six of her brood of tattered, wailing children while trying to remove an overturned wagon from the body of another, impeded in her attempt by the rearing, frightened horses, still harnessed to the wagon and stumbling and careening to their knees trying to tear themselves free. Without a moment's hesitation, Mama rushed to the horses. And I? Dripping wet, clad only in my shift, I instinctively raced to the wagon and lifted. In seconds the child was free.

A frantic Goody White gathered up her dirty screaming child, then halted and looked at me in amazement. I suppose I appeared like something beyond description. Did she thank me? Did she fall at my feet and cover them with kisses? Nay, not for a minute!

Goody White—she who was once a widow and bought an indentured servant, who let that servant share her bed, then wed him only to one day find him disappeared while she was left saddled with debt, making her forever after bitter and sullen—merely squeezed her child tightly and spat to me, "You have broken his leg!"

Dumbfounded, I knew not what to reply. Finally, I breathed "But . . . but I saved him from death!"

"Hah!" snapped Goody White. "'Tis what you'd like to believe! Nearly did I have him free, when you *mangled* him!"

Her wailing, dirty brood tugged at her skirts, while the boy in her arms screamed in pain for how tightly his leg was being gripped in his mother's firm hold, shoving it toward me for inspection.

Mama had by this time calmed the horses and set them free. Efficiently she ordered, "Let us go to the house, Goody White. We'll see to the child's repair. Rachel, collect your clothes at the stream, then return to us, for we shall need assistance."

"But, Mama . . . !" pled I, in my defense.

"'Tis no time to talk, Rachel. Do as I say. Goody White, we may have to call on the physician. I shall send Daniel."

Disgusted, I returned to the stream, leaving Mama with the ranting Goody White and her wailing, scruffy brood, all headed toward the house, with Mama all the while attempting to bring order and control to the chaotic assembly while leading the skittish horses. I was sorry I had even considered rescue. I should have let the child be squashed. Such thanks do I get when I *do* try to be kind.

In the end, the physician came, the child's leg was set, the sullen, bitter mother and dirty tattered children were invited to stay for midday meal and no one ever once turned to me with a whit of gratitude.

Later, Mama said, "I know you tried to do a nice thing, Rachel. But as Goody White does not see it so, we shall let it be. 'Tis best to leave a thing unmentioned than to have it raise quarrels."

So, dear God, my better side shall go ignored. But *You* see it, don't You?

Salem, 22 August 1692

A most fearsome storm swelled over our little village. In midmorning, the skies turned suddenly from a calm, clear blue to midnight black, and the wind arose with such ferocity that trees were felled, malt houses collapsed and livestock were tossed into fences. Rain poured down in torrents. The river swelled, and the road became a quagmire so deep even a horse could be lost. Fields became raging lakes. Lightning crashed, thunder boomed and the tea cups rattled in the cupboard. We all feared for our lives, so tumultuous were the elements.

Then, just as swiftly as it arose, it left. Skies were again a blinding blue, and the sun beat down warm and hot like fire. Goodman Sheafe said he used to see such storms at sea. He said from nowhere they appear, tossing a ship like 'twas at the mercy of monsters amidst the snarling waves; but just when the last mast is to shatter, the storm suddenly moves on, and once again the sea sings calm and steady. I do not think I would like the sea.

Reverend Parris says the storm is another sign of the Devil's intervention. "Satan once again rears his ugly head!" bellowed Reverend Parris as he surveyed the destruction. "He shall not let us rest in peace! We must continue to drive out all his sinners! Nothing but witches cause these unnatural events!"

Cows were lost, sheep battered senseless, fences destroyed and Goodman English's roof was gone. I was pleased about the roof. Now both the Disboroughs and the Englishes are without shelter. Though by eve, 'twas almost replaced. And both families again take lodgings together.

I wonder if 'twas Goody Hale and her spell that made it all happen?

Salem, 23 August 1692

Today I talked to Goody Glover. In the barn I was when she came at me with threats to slit my throat. Papa's gleaming scythe stood near, and so frightened was I that Goody Glover would pick it up and use it, that I very nearly signed her book!

"Leave me be! " I cried, sobbing. "Can you not see how miserable you make me? And call off your demented husband, as well! Both of you drive not only *me* to misery, but my whole family!"

Betwixt her cackling laughter, I heard her say in that strained, shrill voice cut short by a noose, "'Tis as I intend!" Then the laughter grew louder.

That was when I got the idea to bargain. "I shan't sign your book!" I cried. "I shall never sign! But if you and your husband leave me alone, I shan't tell anyone you were second choice! No one shall ever know your husband never loved you!"

For a moment, I thought it might work. The barn was silent, and I could hear only my own heavy breathing. Perhaps Goody Glover was considering my bargain. But just as my breath started coming more evenly, the barn again rang with cackling laughter.

"Do you not hear me?" I shrieked, angrily. "Do you

care nothing for your pride? If you do not bid your husband to leave me be, the whole village shall learn you were never wanted!"

Mercy, standing at the door, glanced round in confusion. Her small voice said "Is . . . is someone with you?"

Wearily, I told her nay; 'twas only me. Trying to bargain with Goody Glover.

Mercy's eyes grew as large as moons. "You're . . . you're making *pacts* with her?" she breathed.

"I was trying to bid her riddance." I replied.

Naturally Mercy told Mama. And Mama was appalled. So I told Mercy I wished *she* would go to the Devil for being such a tattletale.

At that, Mama gasped, drew a terrified Mercy into her arms, bade me apologize and commanded, "There shall be no more talk like *that,* Rachel Ward! And no more pacts with the Devil, either!"

To end the day on a fitting note, Goody Lawson's husband—the one who lost his mind—is accused of being a witch. Goody Bishop reported him.

Salem, 24 August 1692, dawn

I am exhausted and frightened. Goody Glover's litany started last eve 'ere I scarce blew out the lamp.

"Slit your throat, Rachel! Slit your throat! Take a knife from the kitchen!"

Angrily I put my hands over my ears to drown out the voices. I didn't scream, for screaming would only bring Mama.

On and on her orders droned 'til my head felt as if it would split into a thousand pieces. "Where were you today?" I whispered. "Where were you when I made you a bargain? Did you not hear what I promised?"

Her cackle nearly rendered me deaf. "Slit your throat, Rachel! Slit your throat! Take a knife from the kitchen!"

"Be gone!" I whispered. "I shan't listen to you another moment!"

Mercy called out from her bed. "Rachel? Is that you? Did you say something?"

"Nay! Nay!" I replied, cryptically. "Now, hush! And go to sleep!"

"Slit your throat, Rachel. Slit your throat. Take a knife from the kitchen."

Her cackle calmed to a short cajole.

"Slit your throat, Rachel. 'Tis the only way. Your only escape."

"Why do you torture me so?" I whispered. "What have I done? Why do you hate me?"

"Your body has joined with my husband's," she said, and I shuddered. So she had seen even that! What else had she seen?

"Why did you not stop him?" I softly pled. "You must know how I detest him! I did not want to join!"

Her voice erupted into a jarring cackle. "Why did *you* not stop him?" she said, and I wanted to weep for the answer to the very same question. "You wanted it, didn't you? Just like your Mama!"

"Nay! Nay!" I cried. "I hated it! Every moment I hated it! And I hate you, too!"

Mercy said, "Rachel? Are . . . are you having one of your fits?"

"Go to sleep!" I snapped. "Leave me alone!"

Goody Glover threw back her head in laughter.

"If you go away," I whispered, "I shan't tell anyone about your husband and Mama. I promise I shan't. You don't want people to know, do you?"

"You shan't tell even if I stay," she said. "You shan't tell because *you* don't want anyone to know."

Miserable, I knew she was right. Harder I pressed my hands against my ears to muffle her cackle. "When did it happen?" I asked. "With your husband and Mama?"

"A long time ago," she said.

"Shall you tell me about it?" I softly pled. "Shall you tell me so I can understand?"

Again she threw back her head, shrilly, and would tell me nothing. Then she whispered, "A secret. A secret. A secret you must learn. Slit your throat, Rachel. Slit your throat with a kitchen knife. Come with me, and I shall tell you everything."

"Stop! Stop!" I cried as her bony fingers reached out

for me.

Mercy called out, nervously, "Rachel? Shall I call Mama? What's going on?"

"Nothing!" I snapped. "Nothing's going on! Now go to sleep!"

Goody Glover said, "There's no way out, Rachel. You have joined your body with my husband. You are unclean."

I choked back a sob.

"No one shall want you, Rachel. Not even Jeremiah. Have you told him, Rachel? Have you told Jeremiah of your joining?"

"Nay," I whispered. "I can't tell him. I . . . I can't!"

"How did it feel, Rachel? How did it feel when my husband lay atop you? Did you like it? Is that why you didn't flee?"

"I hated it," I sobbed. "I tried to flee. Truly I did. I . . . I just couldn't, though."

"Why, Rachel? Why?" she pressed. "Why couldn't you flee? Because you teased him, didn't you?"

"Nay! Nay!" I whispered frantically. "I didn't tease him! I didn't want it to happen! I couldn't flee because . . . because I just couldn't! He . . . he was too heavy!"

Her laughter tortured me to the very depths of despair. "My husband is a slight man," she said. "And yet you could not move him?"

"But I'm only a girl!" I wailed. "I'm not very strong!"

"Strong enough for water buckets, are you not?" she said. "Strong enough to lead the stock and manage the cow."

"I . . . I know," I said, sickened.

"But not strong enough to move my husband," she said. "No one shall ever believe that, Rachel. Not your Papa nor your Mama, nor even Jeremiah. You are spoiled, Rachel. You shall never wed. No one shall have you."

"I know," I sobbed.

"Slit your throat, Rachel. Slit your throat. 'Tis the only way. Put your family from their misery. Have you not caused them sufficient grief? Slit your throat, Rachel. Slit your throat. Rise and get a kitchen knife."

All she had said was true. I have caused the family grief. Continuous grief, and with no end. No one wants me. Even now Jeremiah avoids me. I shall never wed. I shall always be a burden.

Slowly, methodically, I rose from my bed, trance-like, moving quietly toward the door.

Mercy called out, "Where are you going, Rachel?"

"Hush," I ordered. "Go to sleep."

The stairs creaked beneath my feet. All was dark below, lit only by a thread of moon seeping through the open windows. I did not need a lamp; I knew where I was going. Numbly, I seemed to float to the cupboard, and I opened the drawer. The wooden handle felt cold on my fingers, and the smooth steel of its long blade caught the glint of moonlight and shimmered silver-blue. Slowly I ran my finger along its edge. It was sharp. Papa had sharpened it evening last. Dazedly I stared at it. For how long, I do not know. I remember feeling the cool breeze of night as it gently caught my gown. I am not certain what I intended. Mixed with the soft breeze was a whisper. "Slit your throat, Rachel. Slit your throat. Slit it with the knife."

I do not think I would have obeyed. But I am not certain. Like a leaden weight, I felt powerless to move or think. The glint of steel mesmerized me and carried me away into the caressing voices.

"Slit your throat, Rachel. Slit your throat. Slit it with the knife."

Then I heard Mama behind me.

"Rachel! Pray, God, what are you doing with that

knife? Give that to me! Give it to me this instant!"

Her voice was sharp and frantic. Still powerless to move, I stood frozen while she grabbed my hand and threw the knife across the floor. It made a sudden clatter. Angrily she grabbed me by the shoulders and began shaking me.

"Give me your ear, Rachel! Give me your ear! This nonsense must halt immediately! Do you hear? You must halt this at once!"

I said nothing. Like a rag doll, I stood limply within her grasp, my head bobbing backward and forward as her hands shook my shoulders.

"Rachel, what ails you?" she demanded. "Why are your eyes so glazed? What did you intend with that knife? Speak to me, Rachel! Tell me what you intended!"

"I . . . I don't know," I murmured, and I am certain I spoke the truth. Even still I do not know my intention, and not knowing fears me. Would I have done as Goody Glover ordered? Or would I have turned the knife on Goody Glover instead?

Mama ordered, "Up to bed with you! I shall be up in a moment! Then we shall speak this thing through!"

As I climbed the stairs, Mama remained in the kitchen, and I knew she was searching out all the knives. I knew she would hide them. I thought, "She doesn't need to hide them," and I started to tell her so, but I didn't. Because I wasn't certain.

Salem, 24 August 1692, eve

I dreaded today's sun to rise. Mama was furious because I would not speak to her last eve of my intentions. She sat on the edge of my bed for what seemed an eternity, attempting to draw everything out of me; but I told her nothing. Nothing was I able to tell. Too much pain would be caused.

I dreaded also that, miserable and exhausted, I must face a house-raising. Even Mama, I know, did not want to attend. At morning meal her face was strained and heavy, and only through her strong force of will was she able to match Papa's eagerness.

We had to attend because of Papa's mill. The mill fares poorly, and two factions have developed in the village: those who side with Papa, and those who side with Goodman English. Papa, of course, bears the brunt. People stay away in droves for not wanting to get involved.

For this reason, Papa was determined the whole family would be in attendance for the raising of a new home for the Disboroughs. Papa wanted to show the village that we bear the Disboroughs no grudge, even though Goodman Disborough refused Papa the loan of £21 and moved his family in with the Englishes.

Papa's intention is to persuade as many people as possible over to his side, thence have them bringing back their grain to the mill. "'Tis good business," I heard Papa explain to Mama. "If we wish neighbors to bring us their grain to grind, we must in turn show we wish to help others. By raising a house."

How I dreaded going. Everyone I did not want to see would be present. But no choice had I. After sun-up, Daniel went to fetch Prudence, since the Cory family as a rule is above such common activities as house-raisings, and I resigned myself to piling into the wagon with the rest of the family, all the while fervently vowing to stick close to Papa for protection against Goodman Glover.

Only once had I seen the Disborough farm since the disaster. That time it had been a desolate and lonely place, its acres of charred grasses looking like a black dried-up lake bed, and its lone chimney rising from a forlorn cellar hole which was filled with rubble and ashes. How different it looked today. Neighbors from every corner of the village swarmed round the blackened field, the men intent upon the raising of a house, the women quilting or setting out tables of food, the laughing squeals of children drifting all the way down the road, well past the bend; and while the grass remained charred, the scene was much improved because the rubble and ashes had been cleared, and the solitary chimney did not look half so forlorn with the heavy oak framework which was being lifted around it to provide it with a shelter. Soon, after today's framing and fall's finishing, a new house would stand; and after winter's snows and spring's growth, the field would return to its soft, fertile green, and only a memory would remain of this summer's tragedy.

Papa tethered the horses, then went to help with the house. I turned to follow, but before I could climb from the wagon, he was gone. Clearly men's work had no room for a child.

It seemed everyone had some purpose to attend but me. After Mercy and I helped Mama carry the food we brought, Mercy trotted off to giggle with her friends. Daniel, with Prudence on his arm, also disappeared into the throng, with Daniel playing quite the sophisticated suitor. That left only Mama. And I followed her like a lost puppy clinging to heels.

From across the field, I watched Papa talking with a group of men who were inspecting the framing, and I saw him make a special effort to approach Goodman Disborough. Even did Papa lay an arm around Goodman Disborough's shoulders. I ached for how Papa was swallowing his pride and being so pleasant; and I thought of all those times Papa had helped the Disboroughs, yet the one time Papa asked for assistance in return, Goodman Disborough had refused. Goodman Disborough smiled as if he remembered nothing. Then Goodman English walked up. I held my breath. Even from the distance, I could see Papa's jaw tense. Yet still Papa was pleasant; their conversation was brief, but while Goodman English looked surly and seething, Papa remained calm. Later Papa told me he said to Goodman English, "'Twill be settled in the courts. Today let us leave our differences behind us." How *could* Papa be so civil!

Daniel moved confidently and easily amongst his friends as well as the adults, and it surprised me how friendly and well-liked he seemed. He even took charge of attaching the lifting ropes and lining up the framing. I began to wonder if there is a better side to Daniel after all. Prudence smiled over at him, a soft, flushing, adoring smile, and when I saw Daniel return that smile, my heart did a sharp twist. Once I had seen Jeremiah return *my* smile like that; once I had expected the day would come when Jeremiah, turning of age, would be officially asking to call on *me*, just as Daniel had done for Prudence.

Nervously I espied Goodman Glover. His stooped, weasely form was planted at the barrels of beer, already into the spirits. Cringing, I edged closer toward Mama. He did not see me. Noggin of beer in hand, he took off toward the framing, his walk hinting at a drunken swagger, rather like a sailor attempting to maintain his balance on some rolling deck.

All this activity I noticed. But truly my eyes were fastened like buttons to buttonholes to the far end of the field, to that vexing spot where Ann, Deliverance, Phebe and Abigail stood surrounded by a cluster of boys, the entire group teasing, laughing, flirting and having what was clearly a marvelous time of it. Jeremiah was with them. He was demonstrating how to make a whistle from reeds; I knew it to be so, because he had shown me the exact same trick years ago when we had been sitting by the river with our bare feet wriggling in the water among the stones. But whom was Jeremiah most intent upon impressing with his current demonstration? None other than Phebe. My heart tore into shreds.

Miserable, I listened to Mama and her group of goodwives chatter on and on about the selection of food. I felt like a pariah. No one talked to me; no one took note of my presence; and, save for Goody Bishop, who pointedly inquired as to how my Scripture readings were progressing, thereby making me wither with the attention given to my possession, not one word was addressed in my direction. Dumbly, I stood like a weed, and being about as popular.

"Rachel," whispered Mama. "Go play with your friends."

"Friends?" thought I, gloomily. "I have none, save

for Ann, and she stands in the midst of that laughing throng. No one even knows I'm alive! No one even waved a greeting!"

"Rachel," hissed Mama, again. "Do go see to your friends. Else people shall think something is wrong!"

"Wrong?" I wanted to say. "The whole world is wrong! I am friendless! Forgotten!"

Mama left me no choice. I was as unwanted with her as I was with the others. Hesitantly I moved from Mama's side, slowly making my way past the quilters and spinners, trying to melt into the activity so as not to provoke the attention of Goodman Glover. I tried to prolong every moment before I reached Jeremiah, Phebe and the others, and when I did reach them, I glumly held back, remaining a few paces off from the group, running my foot round in the grass, pretending to look for clovers. I hoped Ann would notice me and say something nice.

But Ann was too absorbed in something being said by Deodat Easty; she was blushing furiously. Abigail giggled stupidly, in some secret with ugly Joshua Snow, and villainously I wondered what Abigail would say if she knew about Joshua's silly looking dingle. Deliverance made some clever remark to Peter Cook, making him laugh uproariously, and Phebe tossed her curls and openly flirted with Jeremiah, who seemed to be enjoying the attention immensely. Phebe was the only one who I was certain saw me. But she pretended she didn't. Too delighted was she in captivating Jeremiah.

Amongst that long, agonizingly self-conscious search for clover, I eventually heard Ann's soft voice, kind and pleasant, and my hopes soared. "Rachel! How pleased I am to see you! Do come join us!"

Everything was going to be all right! By Ann's acceptance, the others would follow, and no longer would I be some misbegotten pariah! Relieved, I edged forward. But as I did so, all conversation stopped with faces turning tense and ill at ease. Smiles drooped. I glanced at Jeremiah. He paled in discomfort. Clearing his throat, Jeremiah started to bid me a greeting, but no sooner had he distracted his attention from Phebe (who probably inwardly raged, and who was sufficiently confident of her ability to gain everyone's approval of her forthcoming cleverness), than Phebe dropped to the ground and began writhing. "Don't let her take me!" Phebe screamed. "I'm to sign her book! Don't let her make me! Is that a bird I see on your shoulder? Nay, bird, don't attack me! Help! Help! He flies to attack!"

Aghast, I stared down at her in horror. Then the worst happened. Everyone began to laugh! Phebe mocked me for all to see, and everyone applauded!

Something inside me snapped. With venom, I cried, "Phebe Edwards, you're a gurley-gutted Devil and I hate you!"

"Taa, taa, taa," chanted Phebe, airily as she rose and dusted herself off. "She thinks I care that she despises!"

The laughter grew more awkward, and I turned to flee, gulping back tears of mortification. In a flash, Ann caught my arm—dear, sweet, quiet Ann—and turned round on the group with a ferociousness that left me stunned and startled.

"You ought be ashamed of yourselves!" snapped Ann, her eyes lit like fire. "Some friends *you* are when another is in need! I cringe to admit I know any one of you!"

I know Ann was trying to help, and I was truly grateful for her kindness, yet only did I want her to let me loose so I could flee! Where did Ann find such strength? Where has that strength been all these years?

Ann ordered, "Rachel, if you turn round, these

people shall present their apology. Which is sorely needed, indeed."

Stammering, I murmured, "That's all right, Ann, I—"

"I don't blame you, Rachel," interrupted Ann with renewed vigor. "I should want no apology from their kind, either. Come, let us help with the food. I'm certain I see a nicer sort by the table."

With that, Ann led me away, no one bothering to call out or to follow—being too embarrassed, I supposed—with Ann saying softly, but firmly, "Pay no attention, Rachel. They don't mean what they do. They know nothing of how you feel. They only do such things in shortsightedness and sport. Later they shall come to you, one by one, and apologize. You shall see."

But no one did. Not even Jeremiah.

The only one who did seek me out was Goodman Glover. When I went to water the horses. Fortunately, he was too drunk to make his threats coherent.

"Pretty girl," he said, his words thick and slurred. "Be nice to me."

Before I could tear from his grasp, he loosed his breeches and *exposed* himself to me!

"Like my organ?" he said, with a drunken grin. "You remember it, don't you? You liked it, didn't you? Want to touch it, pretty girl?"

I stared, sickened, at the small floppy dingle which stood out white and shriveled against the dark cloth of his breeches. Too vividly did I recall what had so recently transpired. Had that small floppy thing really grown to such enormity? How could I not have stopped his vile mutilation of me?

He fumbled for my hand, trying to draw it toward that thing of which he was so horridly proud, and I felt ill for all the memories that leapt out at me. Angrily I wrenched myself free. Stunned, I watched him fall to people shall present their apology. Which is sorely needed, indeed."

Stammering, I murmured, "That's all right, Ann, I—"

"I don't blame you, Rachel," interrupted Ann with renewed vigor. "I should want no apology from their kind, either. Come, let us help with the food. I'm certain I see a nicer sort by the table."

With that, Ann led me away, no one bothering to call out or to follow—being too embarrassed, I supposed—with Ann saying softly, but firmly, "Pay no attention, Rachel. They don't mean what they do. They know nothing of how you feel. They only do such things in shortsightedness and sport. Later they shall come to you, one by one, and apologize. You shall see."

But no one did. Not even Jeremiah.

The only one who did seek me out was Goodman Glover. When I went to water the horses. Fortunately, he was too drunk to make his threats coherent.

"Pretty girl," he said, his words thick and slurred. "Be nice to me."

Before I could tear from his grasp, he loosed his breeches and *exposed* himself to me!

"Like my organ?" he said, with a drunken grin. "You remember it, don't you? You liked it, didn't you? Want to touch it, pretty girl?"

I stared, sickened, at the small floppy dingle which stood out white and shriveled against the dark cloth of his breeches. Too vividly did I recall what had so recently transpired. Had that small floppy thing really grown to such enormity? How could I not have stopped his vile mutilation of me?

He fumbled for my hand, trying to draw it toward that thing of which he was so horridly proud, and I felt ill for all the memories that leapt out at me. Angrily I wrenched myself free. Stunned, I watched him fall to would I be some misbegotten pariah! Relieved, I edged forward. But as I did so, all conversation stopped with faces turning tense and ill at ease. Smiles drooped. I glanced at Jeremiah. He paled in discomfort. Clearing his throat, Jeremiah started to bid me a greeting, but no sooner had he distracted his attention from Phebe (who probably inwardly raged, and who was sufficiently confident of her ability to gain everyone's approval of her forthcoming cleverness), than Phebe dropped to the ground and began writhing. "Don't let her take me!" Phebe screamed. "I'm to sign her book! Don't let her make me! Is that a bird I see on your shoulder? Nay, bird, don't attack me! Help! Help! He flies to attack!"

Aghast, I stared down at her in horror. Then the worst happened. Everyone began to laugh! Phebe mocked me for all to see, and everyone applauded!

Something inside me snapped. With venom, I cried, "Phebe Edwards, you're a gurley-gutted Devil and I hate you!"

"Taa, taa, taa," chanted Phebe, airily as she rose and dusted herself off. "She thinks I care that she despises!"

The laughter grew more awkward, and I turned to flee, gulping back tears of mortification. In a flash, Ann caught my arm—dear, sweet, quiet Ann—and turned round on the group with a ferociousness that left me stunned and startled.

"You ought be ashamed of yourselves!" snapped Ann, her eyes lit like fire. "Some friends *you* are when another is in need! I cringe to admit I know any one of you!"

I know Ann was trying to help, and I was truly grateful for her kindness, yet only did I want her to let me loose so I could flee! Where did Ann find such strength? Where has that strength been all these years?

Ann ordered, "Rachel, if you turn round, these

Salem, 25 August 1692

Imagine my excitement when Jeremiah came to call. 'Twas in midmorning, when I was glumly at my spinning, not wanting to leave the walls of the house, that Mama came into the lean-to and clearly announced, "Jeremiah waits by the fence. He says he would like to speak with you."

My heart nearly leapt from my shift! Mama, too, was pleased. I could tell because she was smiling, which she so seldom does. Nervously, I straightened my apron and went outside to greet him. We went round to the barn and sat with our backs to it, to afford ourselves some privacy.

Jeremiah was somber. He knew he had done something wrong, and I think he regretted that he had shown a chink in his upright armor and now had to admit to a fault. Awkwardly, he said, "I'm . . . I'm sorry, Rachel, for how I acted yesterday. 'Twas coarse of me."

I wanted to believe him, certainly. But I was suspicious. Testily, I asked, "Do you really mean it, Jeremiah? Or are you saying that because Ann made you?"

the ground, his drunken, weasely form too intoxicated to rise, his glazed eyes unable to focus. Even his laughter was slurred. Then swiftly I returned to the house-raising.

And so, God, not a soul in the world cares what happens to me. Except Ann, of course.

"Ann made me do nothing."

"Except feel ashamed. Which you should have done on your own." I could not resist rubbing it in. Sometimes I hate myself for how vindictive I can be.

Soberly Jeremiah nodded. "'Tis true," he replied. "I should have known. But will you forgive me, just the same? I really didn't mean to hurt you. 'Tis just that I . . . well, I didn't think."

Absently, I picked at a blade of grass and chewed on it while I sorted out my feelings. All last eve I had lain awake with those feelings, deciding just what I would say if the chance presented itself, which, truthfully, I had given up all hope of ever occurring; so now I tried to put those thoughts all together, in some coherent fashion, so I could explain them to Jeremiah in a way that he could understand how he had hurt me.

"I do not forgive easily," I said. "My temper is not like yours, which is quick to flare and swift to abate. My temper seethes before I show it, and it lasts longer."

"I know that," Jeremiah said.

"I think 'tis because I don't care about many people. There's only a few I pick out to be my friends—like you. You see, what most people do neither riles nor elates me; it merely interests me. But those people I do care about—those few I have picked out—I care about deeply, and everything they do matters. So when they hurt me, they hurt me to the quick."

"Like I have?" asked Jeremiah, softly.

"Aye, like you have. Because I trusted you. Trust means a very lot to me, Jeremiah, because I give it so rarely. Those I do give it to, I expect to be worthy of it. I expect them to live up to my trust."

"'Tis a weighty burden, Rachel. We all cannot be perfect."

"But *honorable* you can be. We may disagree,

Jeremiah—and often we do, because we are different people—but there should be honor in that disagreement."

Jeremiah, too, began plucking at grass blades, feeling, I suppose, the churl for how he has acted. "I've let you down, haven't I?" he asked.

"Aye. You have. But you know that. Even before Ann had to point it out, you knew it. But what hurt worst of all, Jeremiah, was not just your ignoring me, but how you so obviously showed that someone else was more important. I'm talking about Phebe, in case you haven't guessed. How do you think I felt yesterday when you were flirting with *her* while letting *me* stand there like some lump of earth? And when everyone knows you're supposed to be my very best friend."

"Forget about Phebe."

"How can I forget her when 'twas *her* you were giving all your attention?"

"I was only talking to her because . . . well, because she can be amusing sometimes. She isn't such a bad sort, really."

"O?" I said, feeling the anger rise in my throat. "And I suppose ridiculing me—*mortifying* me—in front of all those people isn't a bad sort!"

"'Twas only done in teasing."

"That's not true at all, Jeremiah! And you know it!"

"Rachel, I came to apologize. Not to start an argument."

"What kind of apology is *that?* Defending someone who has made me feel smaller than a pence?"

"You weren't exactly at your best, either. Calling her a gurley-gutted Devil!"

"Which I'd call her again a million times over! And wipe that smile off your face, Jeremiah Moore! Phebe deserved every word of that description!"

"O, I guess she does sometimes. She can be a little

empty headed and silly—"

"A *little!*"

"'Tis really just her way of being friendly. I feel sorry for her sometimes. And if you'd seen her later after she smashed her hand—"

"Phebe smashed her hand?" I was delighted!

"Mmm. 'Twas not long after you left. She was watching the house being raised, when one of the ropes suddenly slipped round, knocking her off her balance, and as she fell to the ground, her hand got caught 'twixt the cross beams."

I could not have been more pleased. "I hope she was in enormous pain."

"Rachel! That's a terrible thing to say! She nearly fainted from agony, and 'twas all I could do to help her mother take her to the physician, the tears all the while running down her cheeks; but never once did she scream or wail. What an oak she was! But did you not see us leave? We practically walked right over you while you were talking to Goodman Glover."

Goodman Glover! Horrified, I breathed, "You . . . you didn't see anything, did you?" What if Jeremiah were to find out the total tale of my anguish!

"He was drunk, if that's what you mean. But then he is always drunk. A queer man, isn't he? They say his wife was a terrible rail. Henpecked her husband to death. 'Twas no wonder she was discovered a witch. The poor man was probably pleased as punch to see her hang from the noose." Remembering, Jeremiah suddenly stopped dead, then stammered, "O . . . er . . . I forgot. She's the one who now, uh, causes your . . . your possession."

Silently I turned over this new piece of information about Goodman Glover. So Goody Glover was a rail who made her husband's life miserable. I wanted to tell Jeremiah that Goodman Glover is not a "poor man" at all. He is vile and disgusting.

Aloud, I said, "Jeremiah, why do you so hate to say that word—'possession'? Why can't you sit and talk about it with me?"

"We've been through that before."

"Not so I can understand. 'Tis not as if I've been accused of being a witch, and—"

"Rachel, I don't want to talk about it."

"That's the trouble, Jeremiah. You don't want to talk about anything that's *important*. But sometime we have to. Sometime—"

"Nay, we shan't. We shan't have to talk about it at all."

"But I want to. I'm tired of you stradling a fence. Are you on my side, or not?"

"Don't force me to make a choice, Rachel."

"A choice? All I'm talking about is whether you're with me or against me. You're my *friend*. Or have you suddenly forgotten that again?"

"You're asking whether I support your possession, or I don't."

"Well, *do* you?"

"Don't do this to me, Rachel."

"Do *what?*"

"Make me tell you that possession has ugly implications, and I want no part of it."

"Jeremiah! Is that how you *really* feel about me?"

"Not about *you*. About your possession."

"But . . . but that's part of me right now. There's nothing I can do about it. I do try, but—"

"Then talk of it with someone else." Abruptly standing, he said, "I have to go now, Rachel. I've thought of something I must do."

"But, Jeremiah! I thought you came to apologize!"

"I have apologized. But you're too selfish to think of any problems but your own. You won't even consider my side."

"Because you won't tell me!"

"You just haven't listened."

Watching his back, I scrambled to my feet and spat out: "I suppose that 'something you have to do' is Phebe!"

Evenly, he said, "It is. I promised I'd call to see about her hand."

"I hope her hand rots with the Devil!" I cried.

"You'd best be more careful with your words," he said, with a coolness that sent chills up my spine. "Considering your present situation of being possessed. And what it can lead to next."

Angrily, I took the wad of grass in my hand and threw it at him.

Salem, 26 August 1692

For the second morn in a row, I have felt so ill I could scarce keep down morning meal. I know 'tis because of worry for all that has happened.

When I rise, I feel light-headed and dizzy, and the smells from Mama's cooking hearth come drifting up the stairs to set my stomach so churning that I am fearful of descending to the kitchen. This morn I sat wearily playing with my food at the trestle table while Papa bid me eat.

"Growing girls need sustenance," he reminded. "Else they shall wither to a thistle."

Obediently I forced down a piece of corncake. But so violently did it begin tossing about, that finally I had to race to my chamber pot to dispel it.

Mama loses patience for the suffering of my morning chores. She knows 'tis merely the aftermath of the prior eve's nightmares and cacklings, for by noon I am able to swallow; but the knowledge makes her no happier.

Salem, 26 August 1692, eve

As there seems to be no one else with whom I can discuss my possession, I decided to go talk to Eunice Flint, who is just my age and who a fortnight ago was discovered also possessed, by Goody Warren, who has since been arrested. I asked Mama if I could take the horse, Eunice living way back in the village. I told Mama of my intention, saying that if I did not converse with someone where I might find understanding, I might possibly go mad. I was surprised at how readily Mama agreed. I think at this point, Mama, too, would try anything to have me cured.

The Flint house is a crude one, being nothing more than a cabin, and surrounded by land that is scrubby, marshy and rutted. How glad I am that we live on the better side of the village, where the earth is more inviting. As I approached, I saw Goodman Flint out harvesting his corn, a young son trailing after him and dropping ears into a sack fastened to the back of a mule. 'Twas a peaceful, idyllic scene, one that I soon found deceiving. For when I reached the cabin door, the clatter of noise emerging from within made me think some calamity had occurred. At least eight small children, or as near as I could count, all under the age of six, filled every corner of the tiny room, their high pitched voices and frenetic activity making such a commotion I wondered how a body could think. Triplets lay in an enormous cradle, screaming to be fed. Twins toddled round banging on benches with wooden spoons. Toddlers I judged to be three and four squealed over the possession of a cornhusk doll. A five-year-old attempted to help prepare midday meal, constantly dropping utensils every which way and manner. And over all this clatter presided a young, serene Goody Flint and a clearly capable eleven-year-old Eunice. I marvelled at their patience!

Yet for all the chaos and the smallness and simplicity of the cabin, all was clean, neat and scrubbed. Clothes were decidedly threadbare; but they were mended, and not an ounce of dirt marred the children's happy, active faces.

Not really knowing the Flints, having only seen them in Meeting, I attempted to introduce myself through all the din, and as near as I could make out, they recognized me, being familiar with our family through Papa's mill. Goodman Flint had apparently been hired by Papa in the mill's construction, as a part of the labor. Though 'twas Eunice I came to see, 'twas clear another pair of hands would be useful, and I set about helping to feed the triplets, glancing tentatively over at Eunice from time to time, thinking she looked as normal as I, wondering if her possession was as wretched as mine. Just as I had about decided that Eunice appeared much too capable to suffer the torments which plague me, an astounding thing happened. Eunice, feeding one of the twins, dropped the earthen bowl with a crash, and she herself clattered to the floor.

All chaos came to an immediate halt. Eyes were on Eunice. Writhing, she screamed, "Nay, Goody

Warren! I shan't assist in your spells! Be gone with you! Be rid! A cat! A cat! A cat creeps upon the mantle! 'Tis you! Nay! Nay! Your claws reach for my eyes! You shan't have them! I shan't join you with the Devil! A bird! A bird! Now a bird you are! Your talons reach for me! Be rid! Be rid! Gone with you, you witch!"

Writhing, Eunice's soft brown eyes turned to glass, her tongue lolled from the side of her mouth, and her limbs alternately froze in paralysis, then frantically fought.

"She chokes me! She chokes me!" cried Eunice, hysterically.

It was unnerving. Suddenly I realized the effect of my own fits upon observers. Is Mama as distressed as Goody Flint when she watches me thrash and quake? Is Mercy as terrified as this roomful of gaping toddlers? Even the mewling of the triplets was stilled.

When all was finally over, Eunice, limp and exhausted, threw both hands over her face and softly moaned, "Where am I?" Goody Flint, relieved, swiftly went to her side and, cradling Eunice's head, helped her drink some cider. So guilty did I feel, knowing the pain I have inflicted upon others, I could scarcely watch.

Later, as we sat on the hitching post out front, I asked Eunice if she, too, felt guilty about the distress she causes.

"O aye," she sighed. "It does so trouble me, for Mother does so depend upon me. She is not my real mother, you know. My real mother died when I was a child, then Papa married this mother, and O what a brood they have!"

"Indeed," I chuckled.

"And I am so dearly necessary to help with it all. Almost never do I find time for myself."

"You seem quite capable," I remarked, thinking Eunice had probably not had a day to herself in five years. Particularly with a mother but ten years older than herself.

"I do try to be," Eunice said, valiantly.

We then exchanged occurrences of our possessions, our exchange making me feel ever so much better knowing someone else experiences the same torments as I, and oft when I described something about Goody Glover, Eunice would exclaim, "Aye! Aye! Goody Warren does that, too!"

Feeling sorry for both of us, I sighed heavily, and asked, "Why do you think we have been singled out? Why is it *us* who have been possessed, and not someone else?"

"Perhaps," suggested Eunice, tentatively, ". . . perhaps 'tis because we are special."

"Special?" I said with a blink. "You . . . you make it sound as if 'tis *admirable.*"

Eunice smiled, a soft little smile, and two pink spots colored her cheeks. Quietly she said, "Perhaps it is. Perhaps God has chosen us to be tested. To see if we are able to withstand the Devil's challenge. And if we do, think how much stronger we shall be. Why, we could be heroines in our struggle!"

Never had such a possibility even remotely occurred to me. I turned it over in my mind, thinking I rather liked it, and was still deep in consideration when Goody Flint called out to Eunice for help with the twins, who had dampened their gowns and needed changing. And hardly had I started to think one small part of me might be, just *might* be, heroic, than Eunice, returning to the house, fell into another fit over a butterfly which flitted in the door before her. The butterfly was Goody Warren. "She's giving me warning!" cried Eunice, writhing. Again all other motion stopped. And again, when 'twas over, a consoling mother pressed a cup of cider to a step-daughter's lips, who smiled weakly in gratitude. I was beginning to have suspicions I did not like. Too evident was it that Eunice's fits brought attention to a step-daughter who was overworked, saddled with responsibility and neglected of notice. I tried not to think of the implications for Goody Warren.

Cheerfully Eunice called from the hearth as I left. "Do come back, Rachel. We shall talk again. For you, our latchstring is always out."

"Aye. Aye, I shall," I said absently.

But I knew I wouldn't.

Salem, 27 August 1692

This morn Mama bade me dispense with the Venice treacle, for suspicion that it is the culprit in making my stomach toss. I did not protest. I hate the Venice treacle. But I know the culprit is truthfully Goody Glover, and so does Mama.

Salem, 27 August 1692, eve

Papa's countersuit is constantly delayed. Not only do the witch trials bog down the courts, but other suits as well. Goodman Sibley (Ann's father) now sues Goodman Watts (Abigail's father) for slander, saying Goodman Watts called him a "Devil's issue" and his chattery wife "a turtle-headed fool," and all over some posthole digger which Goodman Sibley borrowed and neglected to return. Ann and Abigail are not speaking. It seems the whole village is rife with accusations and counter-accusations for one thing or another. As for Papa, in a way I am glad for the postponement, for the mill still stands. But Papa says he wishes 'twould be decided, for he feels a heavy weight dragging down his shoulders. Too well do I know his meaning.

Daniel arrived home in mid-aft in a rage. It seems Goodman Cory thinks it best that Daniel and Prudence cease their courtship for a time until Prudence grows older. I am certain his decision is due to the uncertainty of Papa's mill and our financial situation. But Daniel thinks otherwise.

"'Tis *you!*" he cried out at me as he came storming through the door and bore down on me at the hearth, where I was making stew. "'Tis *you* and your possession that have brought my ruin!"

"M . . . me?" I said, in amazement.

"Aye, *you!*" he practically screamed, jabbing his

finger into my chest. "The whole village talks about you and your strangeness! Any day they expect you to slit your own throat! You are mad! That's what they say! And 'tis only a matter of time 'til they find evidence that you are a *witch!*"

Startled, I nearly dropped my spoon. Is *that* what everyone thinks of me?

"You have ruined my life!" Daniel cried. Now he shook me by my shoulders. "The one girl I have ever loved—*will* ever love—is torn from me because of a possessed sister! Do the Corys want such strangeness in their family? Do they want a son-in-law the brother of a soon-to-be witch?"

I trembled to the tips of my toes for what he said. I think I would have burst into tears right then and there if Mama had not stepped from the kitchen and torn him from me.

"That is enough!" Mama ordered, sternly. "I'll have no son of mine torment his sister."

"You!" Daniel raged, wheeling. "You are *not* my mother! My mother was gentle and saintly! Not some stern, pretendingly pious, penniless beggar as you! Had Papa not taken you, you would never have been wed!"

Aghast, my eyes almost bulged. Never have I realized how much Daniel hates Mama. Two scarlet circles burned on Mama's cheeks.

Calmly she said, "I am your mother, now. And I shall have no talk of . . ."

Daniel would not be calmed. Taking an earthen bowl, he threw it against a wall, smashing it into a thousand pieces. Mama and I both jumped.

"You shall *never* be my mother!" Daniel raged. "You care only for pious appearances! If Goody Bishop says jump, you leap! If your saintly Reverend Parris says tithe a pence, you tithe ten! Aye, so quick you are to spend my father's money! Because you never had a nail to call your own! Had Papa not taken pity on you and taken you without dowry—aye, and sheltered your sickly parents, too, and got you all out of debtor's prison, all out of his own pocket!—we'd never have to worry about a mill! We would never have had it! We'd have had money for that property in town like Papa wanted! You think I don't know about that, don't you? You think I don't know how you ground down Papa's ear and talked him into the mill when 'twas really the land he wanted! But nay, you spent all his savings, and when his inheritance came along, you spent that, too! Well, you can't buy your way into heaven, no matter how hard you try! And you shall never be anything but what you really are—some base backwoods ruffian who played on Papa's sympathy! And if 'tweren't for that sympathy, you'd be some miserable spinster grovelling at our feet!"

I took a deep breath. Warily I glanced from Mama to Daniel, wondering what would happen next. Nothing. They stared each other down.

With one last attack, Daniel turned on me and cried, "And *you!* You have ruined my life forever! The whole town just waits for you to be arrested! Ask your mother if that is not true! 'Tis fitting indeed that a mother who clawed her way to means should have it crumble about her for giving birth to a *witch!*"

With that, he turned and stormed from the house. Mama and I stared after him in silence. Then slowly Mama walked over and began picking up the pieces of the shattered bowl.

Trembling, I asked in a small voice, "Is . . . is it true? About . . . about what the town says of me?"

Mama's voice was soft and shaky. "Aye, Rachel. 'Tis true."

"And . . . and the part about Papa paying off your debts? And . . . and getting you out of prison?"

"Aye, Rachel. That's true, too."

I did not ask anything else. I was too shaken.

Salem, 28 August 1692

The house is like a graveyard for how few words are spoken. Mama moves about the kitchen, depressed and silent, and I have not asked her further about the tale which Daniel hinted at afternoon last, for I do not think she would tell me.

Papa worries constantly about the mill, coming home late for meals and leaving early, his forehead creased, his gloomy thoughts kept to himself. I think my own gloomy thoughts, which are mostly what I now know the village says of me. Mercy, poor soul, tiptoes round the house like a frightened mouse, warily glancing from face to face, wondering why her beloved Mama speaks to her in such cryptic tones.

And Daniel? Daniel has fallen ill. He complains of severe pains in his stomach and is able to keep nothing down except broth or tea, which Mama brings to him in silence, and neither speaks. No one seems to know quite what is wrong with him. I think 'tis the aftermath of his fury. So riled was he, I wonder his stomach did not turn inside out, which I think perhaps it has. So he lies abed in his chamber, shutters drawn, his eyes staring up at the ceiling.

Mercy thinks Daniel's ailing is related to mine, that

my daily upset is contagious. Tiptoeing to his room, she suggested as much, trying, I think to be helpful. Her suggestion set Daniel off into another rage, which ended with a pillow being tossed at Mercy's face and Mercy wailing down the stairs to Mama. Little does Mercy realize how odious Daniel considers contracting anything from me.

And adding to my general gloom is the fact that I have received another message from Goodman Glover. 'Twas left in the door of the hen house, and I found it when I went to collect the eggs. My first thought was "What if someone else had discovered it instead?"

Its scrawly hand read: "Meet me on the morrow by the river. By the stand of birch. After midday meal. Else I shall tell the whole village."

I did not need to wonder what he would tell. What am I to do?

Salem, 29 August 1692

I did not sleep at all last night for worry of what today would bring, and for the horrifying sarcasm of Goody Glover's cackling laughter. If I did *not* go, Mama's story would be out, and our already gloomy family would undoubtedly fall into the depths of Hell; never again could it return as before. But if I *did* go, I felt as ill as Daniel for thinking about the consequences—which are too vile to describe. All night and half into the morn, I vacillated about my actions, sometimes thinking one evil the more monstrous, sometimes thinking the other. Both made my nausea worsen, causing my head to pound so painfully I could scarcely think.

At mid-morn I was briefly distracted from my anguish by the appearance upon our doorstep of Bridget White and her sniffling, tattered brood of seven. The courts had seized the White land and property to pay off long overdue debts: so they were not only roofless, but completely bereft of future provision, and for some reason I have yet to understand, Bridget White felt *our* family should provide *hers* with shelter. Nay, she very nearly demanded it!

"We'll be needing food and a place to stay," said

Goody White, her tone bitter and scowling. 'Twas as if she blamed *us* for her misfortune! "And the boy with the mangled leg needs a soft mattress for his pain."

The boy, dirty and picking his nose, stood leaning upon two pathetically fashioned crutches, which were no more than some gnarled old tree limbs. Another child sat perched upon one of Goody White's ample hips, and the rest either climbed all over the hitching post, or sat morosely in the dusty yard, the dirt hardly making their unkempt appearance any the worse.

Mama was speechless. I watched her, wondering what was to happen. Finally she said, "Come in, Goody White. You may cool yourself with a glass of beer. Then I must go speak with my husband."

I, of course, was left to provide the beer. Mercy went with Mama to the mill, and I could scarcely wait for Papa's decision. He must have approved, because Mama returned, cool and efficient, and said, "You may stay with us, Goody White. Your children shall sleep upon quilts in the lean-to, and you shall have Mercy's bed. Mercy shall sleep in the trundle near Jacob and I."

Leave it to Mercy, I thought, sourly, to get the favoritism. While I am stuck with Bridget White!

Goody White acted as if 'twere *she* granting the favor—and an enormous favor, indeed! "I hope the bed's big enough," she said. I doubted that! "And the boy with the leg must have *two* quilts." I noticed Goody White did not offer to trade the bed with her son, herself taking the floor.

"Aye," said Mama, evenly. "And now, I was preparing noonday meal, and you may assist."

"Have to settle the children first," said Goody White.

"Certainly," replied Mama. "And then you shall assist. Everyone in this household pulls his weight."

And that, I thought, while staring at Goody White's enormous figure, is a lot of weight, indeed! I hoped she didn't eat as much as she appeared. She did. And her children ate as if they hadn't seen food in a fortnight. Noonday meal was a horror. Dirty children whined and cried and stuffed food into their mouths as if no more were forthcoming for a week, grabbing dishes and platters from beneath our very noses, and leaving gravy spills on every inch of table and braided rug. No matter how much order Mama tried to bring, no matter how much firmness she applied, things remained as they were. Tumultuous. Papa left early for the mill.

Goody White glanced over at me, her eyes hard and narrowed in her horsey face. "Hear your eldest daughter's possessed," she said.

I stiffened. Before I could answer, Mama replied, "Rachel is having some difficulties at present. 'Twill improve."

"'Tisn't contagious, is it?" demanded Goody White. "Don't want some spell cast on my children. Or me kept awake nights."

"You needn't fear," Mama said. "Nothing is contagious."

"'Tisn't a witch, is she?" asked Goody White, suspiciously.

"Nay," answered Mama, evenly. "Rachel is merely possessed."

"And about keeping me awake nights?" she then demanded.

I said, "With *you* there, I'm certain no visions shall *dare* haunt me." And I meant it!

"Those visions the ones that made you mangle my son's leg?" she accused.

Mama replied, with shortness, "Rachel was trying to help."

"Some help," sniffed Goody White, caustically. "Poor child can't hardly walk—maybe never will. And that son you have lying upstairs. He sick? What ails him?"

"Something he has eaten," replied Mama, becoming colder by the moment. "He shall be up and around on the morrow."

"Don't want my children getting sick," Goody White reminded.

I can see we are in for a bad time of it. Such a cantankerous woman I have never imagined. Even Mama was on edge. After the table was cleared, and the dishes cleaned, I whispered to Mama in the corner of the kitchen, "*Why* did you let her stay?"

Mama said, "Her pride is wounded that she must beg. We must be understanding." Her voice was toneless.

"Why *us?*" I pled. "Why can't someone *else* be understanding?"

"I don't think anyone else has ever been kind to her."

Perhaps that is so. But I don't believe that is the real reason Mama took her in. There is some other reason which Mama isn't telling.

The afternoon progressed from bad to worse, with me being put in charge of harnessing that unruly brood, washing them, putting them to chores in the barn and contending with Goody White's commands, such as new crutches for the boy with the mangled leg. How we are going to survive under the same roof, I do not know. And I fear to contemplate.

So in the end, with all the commotion, and with every moment filled, I did not go to Goodman Glover. I can only shudder for what he will do with his threats.

Salem, 30 August 1692

All day I feared to look at Papa. When he arrived home for meals, I stared at him intently, fearing against fear to see some awful knowledge etched within his glance. Was his brow more deeply creased? Did his jowls sag lower than afternoon last? Were his clear blue eyes dark and cloudy, wracked by pain? Oft did I consider going to the river, making apologies for being a day late, pleading for reprieve; but I convinced myself no one would be there to hear my plea, and even if he were there, the plea would not be heeded. Fate was irreparably cast. But deep down I know I did not go because I did not want to. Dear God, is that so wrong of me? Is it wrong to allow Papa to be so pained, as surely he soon will be? How long before Goodman Glover tells? How long before Papa learns? Dear God, would that You could reach down with Your all-powerful hand and guide me.

That Papa does not yet know, I am certain; for if he did, 'twould have come out this eve, in the argument betwixt him and Mama. 'Twas an argument following a day of tumult, for I knew the Whites could never live under our roof with peace.

Goody White does not do a lick of work, thus being

not only surly but lazy, and anything she *does* attempt, she makes a frightful mess of, thinking, I suppose, that she will not be called upon to do another. At pain was she to complain all the day long about her weariness and loss of sleep due to her disturbance by my visions, which I did try so hard to control. Yet so often did Goody White's house-rattling snores jolt me from slumber, and so startled was I upon each waking by the loudness and strangeness of those wheezing sounds, that I kept thinking it was Goody Glover; and before I could will her away, she instantly swirled up in front of me, with all her cackling laughter. And blood. I think that is what aggravated Bridget White the most. How I kept washing my hands.

The noisy, ill-mannered brood is no better. Even Daniel, in all his moroseness and self-imposed silence, complains. Daniel's illness gets no better, and he says bitterly that if those ragtag ruffians do not refrain from bolting into his darkened chamber, he will roar up from his weakened sickbed and pound them into the floorboards. For once, I wish Daniel well with his venom.

So seldom have I ever heard Papa and Mama argue, that I was startled when even *this* horrendous situation brought them to such lowered depths. Mama, particularly, attempts harmony at all costs. Yet Mama's voice was raised like the shrillest shrew, and poor Papa, with all his troubles—and more to come of which he does not yet know!—was forced to drive his own voice sharper; so that in the end, I could not at all recognize these two people who had for all my thirteen years kept such stability under our roof. They were in the malt house when I heard them, Papa having ordered Mama there after evening meal. I heard that whispered order and tiptoed out soon after, leaving Mercy to contend with the unruly Whites and knowing not of whence we had all disappeared.

"She has to go," said Papa, firmly. His voice was scarcely muffled at all through the stone walls.

"She can't," said Mama, with conviction.

"Let someone else take her in," commanded Papa.

"No one else *will!*"

"Then let her rot in the woods! My conscience shall be bothered not a whit!"

"Rotting in the woods is *not* what I fear, Jacob!"

"You *live* by your fears!"

"And do you not also? Is not everything you do ruled by fear of losing the mill? Then make *this* one of those fears, as well!"

Curiously, I wondered what Bridget White had to do with Papa's troubles with the mill, or Mama's fears, whatever those fears are, but I had scarce time to think about those perplexities, because Papa said:

"Nay, I'll *not* make it one of my fears! I'll not have my home wrenched limb from limb!"

"And would you live with the consequences?"

"Consequences be damned! You must—"

"Jacob! I'll not listen to your curses!"

"Curses I'll say if I wish! If you want to rid the fear, then rid the problem!"

"You sound like your son!"

"So today he's *mine!* Afternoon past, you damned him for disclaiming to be yours!"

"He made clear his desires! So it shall be! Why do you not reprimand him for how he addresses me!"

"Love is earned, not ordered!"

"Earned only when 'tis given encouragement!"

"Encouragement! Encouragement it should be when now he lies ill and cursed?"

"Jacob! God still your tongue! May your voice be rent forever should you put such a thought into his head!"

"'Twill occur to him soon! I'll stake my life!"

"Nay, if 'tis not given seed! And when you talk of earning, you'd best look beneath your own hat for that! Else you stand to lose love you once cherished!"

"If you wish to speak further of *that* situation—"

"I do *not!* I wish you only to be the husband and father I wed!"

"So you now regret *that* as well?"

"I regret nothing! Save for your lack of feeling!"

"My feelings are stretched to their limits! Tomorrow that woman and her odious family *go!*"

"They stay!"

"They go!"

"They stay, I say!"

"By tomorrow they are rid!"

"And Rachel and I go with them!"

"Damn you, Martha!"

I heard the heavy stomp of Papa's boots, the slam of a door, and by the light of the stars, I saw Papa's tall angry figure stalk off into the fields, his arms swirling round like windmills. Mama remained in the malt house, weeping weary and heartbroken tears, and for all I despised her, I could not help but feel pity. She sounded like a lost child, deposited in some ditch. 'Twas perplexing indeed, hers and Papa's altercation. Why would Mama leave with Goody White, and take *me* in the process?

Salem, 31 August 1692

I have stumbled upon a piece of information so grotesque I can only write it. To not a soul can I breathe a word, for 'twould bring destruction to someone I still hold so very dear were it to become common knowledge, as I fear it soon shall be, and I must figure out how to stop it from becoming so. Nay, even do I fear writing it for the risk that this journal may someday be discovered, may someday even be presented by me to prove my innocence. But write I must, for I cannot hold such monstrosity inside, needing somehow to sort it all out, of which recording shall assist me. And so I shall record.

Two travellers paused for refreshment today at the ordinary of Jeremiah's father. 'Tis not an unusual occurrence for travellers to pause, yet the circumstances surrounding these two particular travellers were indeed unusual, and I cannot help but think the wicked hand of the Devil has made it happen.

With the travellers were their two servants, an old Indian woman and a colored coachman, and 'tis around the Indian woman the tale unfolds. I became aware of the first part of the tale when Ann came to spin with me, bringing me the news that the Indian woman once was servant to Jeremiah's mother, Jane, when Jane was a child. Such rejoicing took place at the ordinary over the unexpected reunion that the whole village soon knew of it, Jane and the old Indian slave having thought they had lost each other forever. From the pieces of gossip which Ann and I fitted together, I learned that Jane's father had been a sea captain, he and Jane's mother residing in Boston. The Indian slave had belonged to the family, and to the slave Jane had been greatly attached, the slave in return being equally attached to Jane. Sadly, though, when twelve, Jane's father was lost at sea; sadder still, Jane's mother soon after died of heartbreak, having been deeply in love with her husband and disconsolate without him.

Homeless, and having no brothers or sisters, a gentle and timid Jane had no choice but to hire herself out, thus being taken in by an ill-humored family who abused her and required no less labor than sunup to sundown, and still more labor until late eve when finally Jane could rest her weary head upon her straw mattress. Her clothes were threadbare and scant, for her new family had no use for Jane but to cook, clean and tend to their family of numerous demanding children.

In this sorry state did Jane reside for four years, until she was sixteen, at which point her new "father" passed through our village on his way north, stopping at the ordinary for ale, and causing a great sensation for his ill-treatment of his adopted daughter. Jeremiah's father promptly took pity upon the girl. The young, dark-haired Jane gazed up at him with wide, appealing eyes, and Jeremiah's father, Oliver, having just buried his second wife, promptly fell in love, Jane so strongly reminding Oliver of his first wife. Aye, Oliver told Jane, she was equally as gentle and quiet as that first wife, and being so similar in appearance to that beloved, she brought him great joy, for he dearly adored his first wed and had not been truly happy since he had lost her. A bond instantly formed between Jane and Oliver, as if they had been destined for each other.

Negotiations were advanced, with Oliver offering a "dowry" of a grand ink-black mare and £10 in exchange for Jane, and Jane in turn bringing no dowry but herself. All were greatly pleased, even the ill-humored adoptive father. The next day, Oliver and Jane were wed. And Jeremiah eventually was to be their son.

So ends the lovely part of the tale. Parts of it I had once heard from Jeremiah himself and still think it touching and romantic. The grotesqueness, I was to learn later.

So pleased were Jane and the servant woman over their unexpected reunion, that Jeremiah's father carried out two barrels of ale to the edge of the road and proceeded to offer free refreshment to all who passed. I accompanied Papa to witness the reunion, myself being more interested in the possibility of seeing Jeremiah. Jeremiah, however, was busy assisting his father as host, both animatedly handing out noggins this way and that, which resulted in the busy Ipswich becoming quite jammed at the ordinary hitching post, because it seemed no horse or driver wished to refuse the opportunity for free refreshment, or the chance to listen to such an enchanting tale. 'Twas fate, they all decided. Fate with another of her surprising twists.

Aye, fate had indeed been surprising—much more than anyone suspects!—and now I shall move on to that other part of the story.

Being overlooked in the excitement, and never having been proficient in seeking out conversation, I wandered round to the back of the ordinary and headed down to the river. There I heard, and saw, the old Indian woman in agitated conversation with the colored coachman. Such agitation was highly curious to me, since not moments before I had seen the old woman and dark-haired Jane walking arm in arm, in joy, the two whispering and laughing like children. In fact, never had I seen Jeremiah's mother look quite so radiant and lovely. I remember thinking that she was a beautiful woman indeed, and 'twas no wonder Jeremiah's father had fallen instantly in love, plus paid a worldly sum for her hand.

The old Indian woman, begin short and squat and having a broad, square wrinkled face with much gray streaking her coarse hair, pulled her woolen shawl round her shoulders and clutched it tightly to her, the clutching being solely from agitation, for the day was bright and warm.

"Me poor little Jane," the woman was wailing, softly, to the colored coachman. "Whatever are I to do? O the wickedness that has been did to her!"

The coachman looked as perplexed as I, his two white eyes narrowed in his black face like half moons in a midnight sky. And so nervous was the old Indian, I found myself nervous and agitated simply watching.

Standing silent and obscured by a thicket of birch, I did not move, and they did not hear me. I hoped dearly the coachman would ask the old Indian to explain her agitation, for if he had not, I, out of great curiosity, most certainly would have stepped forward and asked myself. What wickedness could have been done to such a lovely dark-haired woman who moments before had been flushed with radiance? Soon I was to know.

The old Indian wailed, "You swear as a Christian ruled by our Christian God never to repeat a word of the tale I will tell?"

Eagerly the black coachman nodded, his white teeth gleaming, he being just as curious as I. The old Indian woman, to insure his loyalty, softly chanted some Indian words and made unusual signs which I did not understand, then proceeded, in her illiterate grammar, to relate the tale which is so grotesque.

"Me little Jane," she said, "not be the Captain's daughter, like she think. Her real father give her to his sister's watch when she not be yet a year. And all because he so aggrieved over the dying of his wife and not able to tend to such a tiny babe. The watch were to be temporary, he riding her all the way to Hadley hisself. The sister take her and say she keep the babe as her own, 'til the father find a new wife. But the sister not do that. She sell the babe to Captain Bradley and his wife. I be with them, when they be up in Hadley settling the inheritance of an old aunt. The Captain and his wife be wonderful people. Best masters ever owned me. But they be sad without child. No child come year after year. So when the sister approach them with a babe for sale, they take it and pay £30 gold. All the dead aunt just willed. Then they go back to Boston. And the sister write the father that the babe had took sick and died. And Captain Bradley and his wife be joyful and think their Indian servant be without ears. She never tell. Which I don't. For I love that babe and help make her grow to girl. How pretty she be. Grow prettier all the time. I tend her like my own. And she mind as sweet as a lamb.

"But the Captain and his wife must feel bad for what they do. One day Captain Bradley returns from sea with a gold locket for his little girl. And inside that locket be etched 'REM,' and the words 'from birth.' The child don't know what REM means. The Captain tell her it be initials for a long and enchanted life, that the initials be for some foreign words he learn in some island. The child delighted. But I know the truth. I know what the letters mean. They mean Jane's birth name. And I know the Captain someday want Jane to figure it out so she know who her real father be. But she never did. Because she gave the locket to me, to keep our spirits always as one, when we be torn apart after the Captain died. And this be the locket. I wear it round my neck ever since. See? See if it don't say inside what I tell."

Wrinkled hands trembling, the old Indian woman removed the locket from her thick neck, opened the catch and held it out for the gaping colored coachman to see. The old woman continued, her voice shaky and disturbed.

"You know what REM mean? It mean Rebekah Elizabeth Moore. Not Jane Bradley, like Jane think. And that man in there she so love? That man who adore her so, and with her produce a son? That man be the same man who all those years ago ride a tiny daughter up to Hadley to be safe in the care of his sister. That man be Jane's father!"

Is it clear, now, the monstrosity of the situation? Jane has married her father! Jeremiah is the son of his father and sister!

Scarcely can I believe it myself, and would not had I not heard it with my own two ears. Now I know why Jeremiah is an only child, why all other children have died even before birth, and I find it only a miracle that Jeremiah survived.

So "unnatural" is all that has transpired that I can only guess at its effect were the village to learn of it. Every evil that has ever befallen us surely would be attributed to this one unnatural event, and even I am not certain it should not be, not certain whether it does not indeed bear the mark of that diabolic Prince of Darkness who may have long ago sent us his wicked stroke which caused us all our witches. If not true, surely it would be interpreted so.

Silently I stood in the thicket of birch, trying to absorb this enormity, and so close to me did the agitated old Indian and the grave colored coachman finally pass that I marvel they did not see me. I can only attribute their blindness to their agitation and state of worry. They and their masters soon departed the ordinary, before the barrels were emptied, but afterward the situation grew graver still.

As I, stunned and numb, moved silently through the imbibing throng in front of the ordinary, that throng intent upon watching a serene and happy Jane Moore wave goodby to her long lost servant while the coach disappeared to a small cloud of dust in the distance, I spotted a drunken Goodman Corwin reaching down and picking up a small shiny object fallen in the dusty road. 'Twas a locket, delicate and gold. Like two bright stars Goodman Corwin's eyes lit. He, who has for years struggled to feed a family of ten on land which makes crops wither and wilt, had finally found his fortune! I could read those thoughts as if they were my own. Swiftly Goodman Corwin looked round, then dropped his discovery in his pocket. And his normally downtrodden expression miraculously transformed itself into delight, a dozen years falling from his defeated slump as he pranced off down the road, whistling.

O how I wanted to run after him and snatch from him that damning piece of evidence!

'Tis only a matter of time, I know, before Goodman Corwin loses caution, forgetting any fear that if his prize is made known, its rightful owner will return to reclaim its possession. Goodman Corwin, 'tis certain, will proudly display that prize. Conceit will guide him. And when he does, Jane will recognize it, Jeremiah's father will guess the truth, and the results will be too disastrous to imagine. I must figure out how to prevent it. I must save Jeremiah. I cannot let such suffering befall him, for dearly do I still care for him, even if he does not return that caring.

Salem, 1 September 1692

All day I have wracked my brain for a plan, yet no solution will come to me. My sleep was so fitful last eve, and so terrorized by all sorts of horrid visions, that Goody White, after seizing me by the shoulders and roughly shaking me until my neck nearly snapped, announced that if I were to continue to shriek and wail so as to send the walls shuddering, she would toss me into the barn. Mama went with me. The two of us walked like apparitions ourselves, our long white nightdresses like white mist in the dark dead of night, moving in silence the short distance between house and barn. We climbed into the loft, making our beds in the hay, listening to the screechings and burrowings of rats, as I tried to will away the horror of my visions.

Mama's voice was strong and stern. "Tell me, Rachel, what you see. Why do your visions continue to worsen?"

I could not tell her. My head was too full of all the vile things I know yet cannot breathe. Dear God, why have you given me so many burdens? Am I destined to be heroic, as Eunice Flint portends? I do not feel so at all.

Papa said this aft that Goodman Corwin came into

the mill with a swagger. Papa said Goodman Corwin jauntily hinted at purchasing a bull and leasing it out, and adding a lean-to to his shabby cabin. Papa wondered how Goodman Corwin has found the means. Papa talked of Goodman Corwin's astonishing lightness of character. Goodman Corwin is not yet telling. I must figure out how to stop him.

I did not remark upon Papa's recountings, which he said to no one in particular, he and Mama still not speaking nor meeting each other's eyes, and the chaos produced by the unruly Whites distracted the curiosity of anyone else, were anyone else to have reason for curiosity. Which they don't. Not yet. But if bragging has reached Papa, other ears are certain to follow.

Salem, 2 September 1692

I shall record today's events exactly as they happened.

At morning meal, so weak and wretched did I feel, that Bridget White moved her entire brood to the other end of the table for fear my illness was terminal. Truthfully, I had begun to wonder so myself. Tiresome indeed it is to always rise with nausea, and I had wondered if I should ask Mama if 'twas part of becoming a woman. Many ploys has Mama attempted to settle my stomach, but the only one which meets with any success is the sprinkling of salt upon a dried piece of jerky. The two taste like pungent hide, but my stomach accepts them.

This morn, as Mama and I sat at one end of the table, I caught her watching me, pensively. Uncomfortable, I said I felt well enough to do the milking and immediately rose to escape both her scrutiny and the clatter of children. However, not moments had I settled myself upon the stool, when Mama appeared in the barn beside me.

"Leave the cow," ordered Mama, tonelessly. "I wish to speak with you."

"I shall be only a minute," I said, stalling. I did not

know of what she intended to converse, but I had an eerie premonition that I did not want to hear it.

"I wish to speak with you," she repeated.

"Cornflower needs milking," I said.

"Cornflower can wait," she replied.

"But, Mama," I reasoned obstinately, "she's ready and—"

"I am ready, too," Mama interrupted.

The strain of all these past weeks was evident in her voice, for it rose and verged on anger, which is unlike Mama with her poised control. I decided I had best be obedient. Collecting the milking bucket with its shallow puddle of milk, I patted Cornflower's neck, then sat down beside Mama on the rickety bench we use to hold odds and ends, such as curry combs and horse blankets. Mama moved the combs and blankets.

Her voice was calm when she spoke, but her gaze was piercing. "I'm going to talk to you about being a woman," she said.

I could feel myself flush. I did not want to talk to Mama about something so intimate because I so despised her.

"'Tis been over two fortnights since you've bled," she said. "Have you not bled since, Rachel?"

My flush went deeper. I thought of other bleeding, but it didn't count. 'Twas a different bleeding.

"Rachel?" Mama repeated. "*Have* you bled?"

I didn't look at her. "Nay . . . uh . . . er . . . nay," I said, and I hated how timid I sounded.

"I see," Mama said. She seemed to turn my answer over in her mind for a long while; and when she turned her gaze back upon me, it was veiled and controlled, and I could not read what she was thinking. "I'm going to ask you something, Rachel," she said. "And I want you to tell me the truth."

I froze. "O God," I thought. "What if she asks me

something about Goodman Glover!" So vividly was that grotesque situation on my mind, and so fervently was I trying to conceal it, that naturally it was the first thing that popped into my thoughts.

"You and Jeremiah are very good friends," Mama said, which startled me, for it was so removed from what I expected. "He has not called on you recently. Is there a reason?"

How I hated her for that observation! Miserable as I was for Jeremiah's avoidance, I like to pretend that no one else notices. Nothing could have alienated me more than for Mama to have stated her observation so baldly.

"Is there a reason?" she repeated.

Seething, I said, "I . . . I don't know. Perhaps he tires of me."

Such pain was contained in that admission. Yet I could think of no story to contrive, no other excuse to advance. Denial of Jeremiah's avoidance had already been withdrawn from me.

Mama asked, "Is there a reason he tires of you?"

Cryptically I said, "I guess he just doesn't like me. I . . . I think he likes Phebe instead."

Steeling myself, so the pain would not be so jagged, I stared at the wall. Mama paused for a moment before she continued.

"Is there nothing you did, Rachel, to cause him to dislike you?" How well I knew the answer to that question!

"Aye," I said, finally. "I . . . I am possessed. He's . . . he's afraid that I'm also a witch."

"I see," said Mama tonelessly. Her deep breath was audible before she proceeded. "Rachel, sometimes when a boy and a girl have known each other for a long time, they . . . they become familiar with each other. Have you and Jeremiah . . . become familiar with each other?"

Confused, I said, "I . . . I don't know what you're talking about. If you mean . . . how well do I know him . . . I think I know him pretty well. Well enough anyway to know he would not wish to be the subject of this conversation. He likes Phebe now, Mama! How clearly do I have to tell you!" If she forced me to admit his replacement one more time, I knew I would burst into tears.

"Has he ever kissed you?" she pursued.

"That's none of your concern!" I quickly snapped, which, of course, gave Mama her answer.

"Has he ever done more than kiss you?" she asked.

Angrily I said, "Do you want me to tell you he's held my hand! That he's touched my arm! Tugged on my hair! Do you want me to tell you every little thing he's ever done!"

"I want you to tell me if he's shared your womanhood with you," she said. "If he has lain with you as man and wife."

Shocked, I wheeled round to face her. So far from my mind was the question she advanced, that I could scarce believe she had asked it. Immediately I cried, "Nay, Mama! Nay! We have done nothing! I swear on my life!"

The sweetness and innocence of Jeremiah's kisses instantly vanished like a puff of smoke in the presence of Mama's accusations, and I hated her for that spoiling, hated her for thinking that Jeremiah had used me, then discarded me. My one pleasant memory was swiftly erased like wind on dust!

Now I realize why she asked. Because her next statement was "Rachel, I fear you are with child."

So swift was this accusation on top of the other that I could do nothing but gape. A knot formed in my stomach. I felt violently ill.

Mama continued. "You are past your time of bleeding," she said. "Your morning nausea is that of a woman who holds another life inside."

She paused for a moment, allowing her words to absorb meaning, and during that pause, my eyes burned with tears for a realization Mama did not understand. Never have I felt lonelier, or more lost.

Mama said, almost pleadingly, "Now, Rachel. Is there something you would like to tell me about Jeremiah?"

Blinking back the tears, I said miserably, "There is nothing to tell, Mama. Nothing. Jeremiah and I have done nothing."

"I see," Mama said. Suddenly her head dropped into her hands, and she was visibly and surprisingly shaken. Quickly she leapt to her feet and began pacing, back and forth across the barn floor, her feet leaving swift, small remnants of footsteps, her fingers wringing themselves one into the other, and so distressed was she, that I was certain she knew the whole story. But she did not know.

Agitated, Mama sat back down on the bench and grasped my shoulders. "Your visions, Rachel . . ." she said, and her voice broke into a short wail. "Your visions . . . have they . . . have they threatened you with . . . with anything like this?"

"Like . . . like what, Mama?" I said, frowning, not able to grasp her reasoning.

"Like having a child!" she said frantically, and her fingers clutched like nails into my shoulders.

Dumbly I stared. "Like having a child?" I repeated.

"Rachel!" she cried out, and her fingers pained me so greatly that I could think of nothing but their hurt. "Have your visions given you a child! Are you carrying the child of the Devil?"

Aghast, I could scarce find my voice. My own

mother accused me of bearing the child of Satan! Pray, God, how could all have come to *this!*

Instinctively, I told the truth. For far less ghastly was the truth than the accusation.

"Nay, Mama!" I said, fiercely. "'Tis not of the Devil! 'Tis of Goodman Glover! 'Tis Goodman Glover's child, I bear!"

Oddly, I expected to see relief. But there was no relief. Mama's frantic face turned ashen, and for a moment I feared she would faint.

"Goodman Glover . . . ?" she repeated, and her voice seemed to come from a great distance.

"He defiled me!" I said. And because I hate her so much, I added, "Just like he defiled *you!* Only you *wanted* to be defiled! *I* was *forced!*"

Bracing myself, I waited to see how she would react to this piece of information. Fully did I expect her to slap me. But more than anything, I yearned to hear a denial. I hoped above all hope that none of what I thought was true, that this terrible nightmare would suddenly vanish, and we could all go on with our lives just as always. Yet my last thread of hope was not to be. No denial was spoken.

Mama's voice was small and quiet. And heavy. "What else did he say?" she asked.

"Nothing," I said, bitterly. "Only that you used to lay with him. And that you liked it!"

Still I yearned for a denial, and my bitterness grew as it was withheld.

"Who else knows of this?" she asked, desperately.

"No one," I said. "I would not want to mortify Papa."

"And of you?" she pressed. "Who else knows of you and . . . and him?"

I sneered. "Do you fear to speak his name?" I asked. "Once you must have spoken it often. Nay, I have told no one of myself, either. Nor do I intend to."

"You mustn't," she said rapidly. "No one must know. No one. Not until I think of an explanation. For . . . for the child."

Mama left then, swiftly, her face creased with worry, and I remained on the bench for a while, thinking, feeling not at all like a mother with child. Then I went back to the milking, for I knew not what else to do. And all day I have simply gone through the motions of living.

Salem, 3 September 1692, morn

Last eve Goody Glover's terrorizing was more jolting than ever. She reeked with fury.

"You bear my husband's child!" she cried, and her cackle was devoid of its usual sarcasm. It was seething and stormy.

Her enormous bony head was distorted with rage, pulling the skin taut across her angular cheekbones and making her jaw jut out with horrifying protrusion. Blood poured from her throat onto her gnarled hands, and with those hands, she clasped my neck to choke me.

"I don't want it! I don't want it!" I cried out over and over. "Stop it! Stop it! I can't breathe! You're cutting off my breath!"

Her hands pommelled my stomach, to snuff out its life, and in desperation I cried out, "Stop! Stop! 'Tis yours! I'll give it to you when 'tis born! I promise I shall!"

Bridget White called out, frantically, "What's going on here? Are you having one of your fits?"

Goody Glover roared, "'Twill be no birth! I'll kill it first! I'll kill you both!"

"You shan't!" I screamed. "God shall protect me!

Stop it! Stop it! I can't breathe!"

Bridget White cried, "Martha! Martha, come git your possessed daughter!"

Goody Glover stormed, "Take the knife, Rachel! Slit your throat!"

"I can't!" I screamed. "Mama has hidden the knives!"

Mama said sternly, "Rachel, sit up! Sit up, this moment!"

"I can't!" I screamed. "I can't! She's choking me!"

Bridget White cried, "Let her be choked!"

Goody Glover roared, "You bear my husband's child! 'Twill be your doom!"

"Be gone! Be gone!" I screamed. "I can't breathe!"

Mama said, angrily, "Come with me, Rachel! Come with me this moment! Come to the great room!"

"I can't, Mama!" I screamed. "She'll follow me! She's choking me!"

Bridget White cried, "Let her be choked! Put an end to it all!"

Goody Glover roared, "You bear my husband's child! 'Twill be your doom!"

Mama grabbed me by the arm and pulled. "She shan't follow you Rachel! She shan't! Rise this instant!"

Bridget White cried, "Praise God! Praise God! 'Tis lunacy! The Devil has come to take us all!"

Mama snapped, "Hush, Bridget!" and slammed the door behind us.

Goody Glover did not stay behind in the sleeping chamber. As I sat upon the settle, her face suddenly rose out of the embers and thundered, "Slit your throat, Rachel! Slit your throat! Else I'll reach inside your stomach! I'll pull out the babe!"

"Nay! Nay!" I screamed, more terrified than ever. Frantically I raced to the hearth and began tossing out logs of red hot embers, desperately attempting to make her disappear. With a sizzle the logs fell to the carpet, scorching my hands but not burning, for so swiftly did I toss, my palms held their fire for only an instant.

Horrified, Mama grabbed a blanket from inside the settle and began furiously beating, all the while trying to push me aside. "Stop it, Rachel! Stop it!" she cried.

Goody Glover stormed, "Slit your throat, Rachel! Slit your throat, else I'll wrench out the babe!"

"Be gone!" I screamed. "Be gone you evil demon! I hate you! I hate you, you ugly witch!"

From upstairs, Bridget White yelled, "What goes on down there? Is that smoke I smell!"

"Hush!" Mama cried. "Back to bed with you, Bridget!"

Papa's heavy foot clamored down the stairs, his strong arms suddenly coming up behind me and clasping me in a vice-like grip. "Good God!" he swore. "What goes on with you, girl? Are you to drive us all to madness! Calm yourself this instant!"

At Papa's voice, Goody Glover vanished. Spent, I turned into Papa's chest and sobbed. "O Papa," I wailed. "She causes me to do such fearsome deeds! What am I to do? How am I to rid her? I'm so terrified of her!"

Papa's answer was simple and deceived no one but himself. "Will her away," he ordered. "Use the same imagination that brings her."

I did not argue. To my deathbed, Papa shall refuse to recognize that my torments are beyond my control; that he has not yet tamed me by means of a throttle, I can only attribute to his gentle disposition.

"I'll try, Papa," I whimpered. But I knew it was no use.

Salem, 3 September 1692, aft

Late morn I found another note wadded into the hen house door. Its scrawly hand read:

"One more chance. Then I tell the world. This aft. By the river."

Sickened, I crumpled it into a ball. This monstrous man is the father of my child. How odious the thought does cut. Even still, all seems so unreal to me. Perhaps the enormity will later find realization. Right now I cannot think of it. I do not feel like a mother.

Wearily I sat on the fence rail and pondered what to do about the ultimatum. Briefly I considered showing the note to Mama and asking her advice, hoping she might provide a solution that would spare me a dreaded confrontation. But presently I abandoned the thought. Knowing nothing of Mama's past with this man, or of how she truly regards him, puts me at a disadvantage in weighing her advice. What is more, I fear a solution by Mama might entangle all of us further. The only way was for me to handle it myself.

I left while Mama was supervising the Whites with the haying. With Daniel still abed and unable to resume his chores, the haying has now fallen to Mama, and one would think all the White hands should provide more than sufficient labor. Alas, 'tis not so. When I left, the Whites were making unthinkable disorder as a result of their clearly disinterested efforts, and Bridget White was complaining how her back ached from bending. Mama cryptically replied that Bridget White has the largest back under our roof, and it must bend to earn that roof.

The river was quiet and cool. I sat down amongst the reeds, put my feet in the water and watched a snake wriggle past. I wondered how long it would take Goodman Glover to appear. I hoped he wouldn't appear, but he did.

His small stooped form crept up behind me, yet I heard him, and I turned round, saying nothing, wondering what he would do and what I would do in return. His eyes were pink and squinty. He smiled, and his thin lips opened to reveal his yellowed, gaping teeth. I think he waited for me to scream, and when I didn't, it confused him. Standing with his hands on his small hips, he stared down at me, his smile wavering, and finally he sat down beside me. Liquor reeked from his breath. His shoes were getting wet, but he seemed not to notice.

"You're a pretty thing," he said.

"Thank you," I replied, curtly. Oddly, I felt a strength and a coolness rise up in me, and it surprised me.

Tentatively, not knowing what to make of my demeanor, Goodman Glover put his arm round me. I pretended not to feel it. I kept my gaze upon the river.

"Would you like to kiss me?" he asked.

"Not particularly," I replied.

He did so anyway. I tried not to gag. I sat like a rock and pretended not to feel his small, wriggly tongue move round in my mouth. It felt like that snake that had slithered past.

"Did you like that?" he asked, grinning.

"Nay," I said.

He laid one hand on my breast. Then he squeezed, and I felt repulsed. I heard his soft chuckle.

"Your Mama's a harlot," he said.

"I don't believe you," I replied. I don't know whether I did or did not, but I was beginning to ask myself why I was placing such store in the word of this weasely man who is always drunk, shuffling and disgusting. It didn't make much sense, I decided.

"'Tis true," he said. "Your Mama used to be real free with her favors."

"I still don't believe you," I said.

I think that made him angry. He said, "Ask lots of men round here. They'll tell you. They'll tell you what your Mama was like before she married your Papa."

I thought I had found a hole in his story. Curtly I pointed out, "So you were not the only one? You were not so special?"

That threw him. Sputtering, he maintained, "O aye, I was! Your Mama used to do it with me all the time! Right here on this very bank! Aye, right in this very spot I used to lie atop her! And she loved it!"

"What about the other men?" I coolly asked.

"They weren't special!" he sputtered. "Your Mama *liked* it with me. Not with the others. She told me so. All the time!"

"I don't believe you," I said. "Mama would never like someone like you."

"Aye, she did," he maintained. "And you like it, too. And you'll get to like it better. Just like your Mama did!"

Repulsed, I tried not to shudder. "What do you want from me?" I asked.

His soft, low chuckle sent shivers up my spine. "I want you to join your body with mine," he said. "Just like your Mama did. And you'll like it! O aye, you will! Every day you'll come back pleading for more."

"And if I don't?" I replied coldly.

"I'll tell the whole village about your Mama. I'll tell them how she used to lay with me—and with every other man in the village, too. And see how you like *that!* See how your Papa likes it, too!"

I said, "I don't believe you. I don't believe a word you tell me. And I don't think anyone else will, either."

Now he was really annoyed. "O?" he snapped. "Well, see if you believe *this!*"

With that, he grabbed hold of my hand and shoved it toward his breeches, toward where his legs come together, and his small dingle jutted out hard and straight beneath the cloth, like Goodman English's bull. Both fascinated and repulsed, I let my hand lie there a moment while Goodman Glover, his pink eyes gleaming, laughed his soft low chuckle.

I thought, "This is what gave me a child."

"Feels good, don't it?" he said. He pushed my hand along his dingle, and as he did so, a strange look appeared on his face. Suddenly I squeezed, as tightly as I could, as if his dingle were a vicious bug and I was trying to kill it, and he let out a pained howl.

Rising, I spat out, "You're disgusting! And I don't believe a word you've ever told me! You can tell anyone in the village whatever you wish to tell, but I don't think they'll believe you, either!"

With that, I stalked away, leaving him moaning in the reeds and clutching onto his dingle. Where I summoned up such courage, I do not know. Perhaps because so much horrid has already happened, I can imagine nothing being any worse. And if I can save no one else, at least I can save myself.

Salem, 4 September 1692, morn

Goodman Lawson was hanged today. At dawn he went silently to the gallows, ready to join his hanged wife. I do not think his lost mind realized what was happening, or of what he was accused, for his eyes were vacant, and he walked to the noose in the slowness and dumbness of a trance. Goody Bishop smiled in satisfaction. She said, "One more witch is rid."

Salem, 4 September 1692, aft

I have a premonition. 'Twas a dream I had last eve. A house was built of straw. A vast wind arose, swirled round and blew the house into a thousand pieces, casting its walls across the open fields, into the forest and onto the gurgling river, until the house was strewn into oblivion, with not a trace remaining, and no one could ever remember where it stood. And no one cared. I think that is what is to happen to all of us. To Jeremiah. To Mama and Papa. To the village. The terror of witches shall destroy us. Already that vast wind is rising, and there are murmurs that the straw house is hung together by naught but a thread. The prison bulges with the accused, the arrests still mount, the hangings continue, yet nothing has brought solutions, nor provided prosperity, nor instilled contentment where disharmony prevails. Slowly that realization is being whispered. It is being carried by the breezes preceeding the wind. But fanatic believers keep those whispers fearful, and the judges still threaten God's wrath to any who dare disagree. They will be proved wrong, though. With the wind that takes us all.

I have not, and shall not, tell this premonition to a soul. Only witches have premonitions. But this one, I think was provided to me by God. To give me strength.

Salem, 5 September 1692, morn

This morn, as I sat morosely idling with my food, unable to eat, Papa snapped at me.

"Shall you never stop making an amusement of meal, and eat!" he said. "Is this your mulish way of avoiding your morning chores?"

Tears sprang to my eyes. 'Twas the first time Papa has ever spoken to me so harshly.

Mama said, "Leave her be, Jacob."

Angrily, Papa replied, "This foolishness has gotten out of hand. If you shan't eat, Rachel, then leave the table. I'll not have my own meal spoiled by your glumness and idling."

Mercy whined, "Rachel never eats, Papa. Goody Glover won't let her."

Mama said, "Hush, Mercy!"

Papa slammed his fist on the table, making our trenchers so rattle that all of us jumped in fright. "Goody Glover, be damned! I'll not have that name mentioned again in this house! 'Tis the end of this nonsense! Now eat, Rachel!"

"I'll try, Papa," I whimpered.

Mama said, sharply, "Jacob! I'll not have curses at this table!"

Bridget White, clutching as many of her mewling

brood as possible within her hefty arms, cried out, "Curses! Strangled throats! Screams in the night! Praise be to God, what else infects this household! Another day and my children and I shall be forced to seek other shelter!"

Papa roared, "My blessing to do so today, Goody White! You and your insufferable brood have caused nothing but chaos!"

Meekly, I said, "I'll try to eat, Papa," trying to appease him.

Mama said, "Goody White, you are welcome to our shelter. Jacob, I'll not have you speak to our guests in this manner."

"And I'll not have chaos, free-loaders and children who don't appreciate their food!" Papa yelled.

With that, he shoved back his chair, plopped his felt hat upon his head and stomped out the door.

Mama called out, "Jacob! You haven't finished your meal!"

Papa roared, "My appetite holds nothing for clamor!"

The door slammed with a jolt, making my stomach do flips. If I possessed little appetite before, I now had even less.

I know Papa's short temper is a result of his problems with the mill, and I try to tell myself that 'tis those troubles, and not me, which cause him to be so out of sorts. Yet deep down, I cannot help but think I am truly the cause of it all. I do wonder, in light of all that has happened, if life might not be better for all if I simply disappeared. 'Tis this thought I am considering, dearest journal, as I sit here and record.

After Papa left this morn, all eyes were fastened upon me, in silence, and if nothing else caused me guilt, their silent staring did so, causing me to wither. Promptly I did the only thing I could think of. I picked up my wooden spoon, ladled it into my suppawn and took a large swallow. I nearly gagged. Quickly I grabbed a handful of shortbread to keep it down. Then, clasping hand over mouth, I raced up the stairs to relinquish all into the chamberpot.

Mama sat on the edge of my bed and wiped my face with a damp cloth. Softly, so that Bridget White would not hear, she asked, "Have you bled yet, Rachel?"

How dearly I wish I could have replied, "Aye, Mama. I have!" But I couldn't. My crestfallen face told her her answer, and Mama in turn looked even more wretched than I.

"I have an errand," said Mama, after awhile. "Can you manage the Whites?"

I knew her errand. But its intention, she kept silent from me.

Fearful, I ventured, "Mama . . . you . . . you won't make me wed him, will you?"

My voice held a heartfelt plea, for truthfully, dearest journal, this expectation has plagued me dreadfully; and I know should it ever come to pass, 'twould cause me to run away without slightest regret or hesitation. Mercifully, I do not think this option even occurred to Mama. Her eyes widened in horror at my mention, which surprised me, for I would have thought her to have at least given it consideration.

"Nay! Nay!" said Mama, vehemently. "That shall never be, Rachel! *Promise me!* That shall never be!"

"Aye, I promise, Mama," I said, much relieved. "I should wish . . . I should wish to die before such happened!"

For a long while Mama was absent. Taking her shawl from the peg beside the door, she silently swung it round to her shoulders, then purposefully set off down the road, her head high and proud, her jaw set with tension. Despite myself, I felt admiration. I watched her through the window, her long dark skirts kicking up dust, her back straight, and no matter what deceit she might conceal, I could not help but wish that I myself could move with such sureness and certainty. What a child I am. How much learning remains for me. And yet soon I shall be a mother.

Anxious though I was for her return, I tried to remove it from my thoughts. With determination, I occupied myself with the Whites, tried to will away my nausea and attempted to accomplish something of my chores. Yet all the while I felt a rising hope that Mama, with her proud head and resolute disposition, would somehow provide a solution.

Thus, it was with vast disappointment that I saw her return. A small speck on the road she was when I glimpsed her. Only then did I realize how eagerly I had awaited, and swiftly I set down the bread dough, wiped my floured hands upon my apron and rushed out to meet her. As I neared, and her speck grew larger, her arched back was no longer rigid, and her proud head faced to the ground. Without speaking, I knew nothing was solved.

Slowly she approached me, and when she drew close, she did not look at me. I was crushed. She had provided my last hope, and now she had failed me.

Wearily she laid her arm around my shoulders and walked beside me. Her face was ashen, and her red eyes told me she had been weeping. Her voice, when finally she spoke, was bitter and full of despair.

"He is a despicable man," she said, and still her gaze was directed at her feet. "You must avoid him in every way." Ever so quietly, she added, "I . . . I did not tell him about the child."

That is all she has related. When we reached the house, she set her shawl upon its peg, then silently completed the bread. I yearn to know what occurred, but I shall not ask, for I know she will not tell.

And so, dearest journal, 'tis only for me to reach a decision.

Salem, 5 September 1692, aft

A sultry, late summer aft, it is.

Daniel lies upstairs languishing, his body growing thin and weak. He worsens, I think, by the knowledge that Prudence Cory is officially being courted by someone else; I was the one who brought him this news afternoon last. I thought perhaps the information would provide him reason to rise from his bed by giving him the strength of anger to fight for his beloved. How different Daniel is than I always thought. Resigned to his fate, he merely turned his head dully, when I related the news, then tonelessly bid me leave his chamber. Only in his eyes did I see that old fire of hate.

Goody White announced at noonday meal that I am the most peculiar child she has ever encountered—an observation brought on by my wooden tongue and my reclusive demeanor, which today is heavy with thought and decision. I replied caustically that I have no wish to be a cantankerous complainer such as she. Mama then intervened, with some of the few words she has spoken since she returned from Goodman Glover, and told me I must practice charity toward Goodwife White. Heatedly I told Mama Goodwife White deserved what she doled. Still I do not understand why Mama defends her.

Papa's mood at noonday meal was curt and cryptic. His suit is to be heard in a fortnight, and I know he is sick with worry for the countless hours required in preparing his defense. Yet of the details, he speaks nothing to neither Mama nor I. Oft he climbs the stairs and sits with Daniel, and of what they converse, or whether Daniel talks, I do not know.

Oddly, not hours after Mama's return, I found another note left in the henhouse door. I marvel at its boldness.

It said: "This is a warning! I mean what I say! Meet me again by the river!"

Disgusted, I shredded it into a thousand pieces, then tossed it into the hearth and watched its edges flicker then curl into flame. I spat upon its ashes.

Yet I am thankful for its appearance. It helped me to make my decision.

Salem, 6 September 1692

All is set now. I have collected a small parcel of my most treasured possessions and hidden it in a corner of the chest in preparation for my departure. I shall go north, in a direction as far from this curse of witches and all its biting accusations as I can travel. I shall go alone. I shall leave even Goody Glover behind, and I shall tell no one of either my intention, or, when I arrive, of my destination. And I shall go two days hence.

How simple it all seems. I wonder that I did not think of it before. How I hate myself now for so allowing a shrewish woman and her vile, repulsive husband to repeatedly terrorize me. Once I would have wept to have lost Mama and Papa and all that I knew and loved; now I see my loss as my salvation.

Where I shall finally arrive, I do not know. Nor am I certain as to how I shall eat or sleep, or how I shall care for a child. God must be my guide. He must provide me strength and vision and wisdom to survive.

Yet before I go, there is one more thing I must accomplish. I have not forgotten Jeremiah.

His cruelty toward me at Meeting today cut like a sharp scythe. As I passed by him, he neither acknowledged nor spoke to me, glancing past me as if I were made of air, and I flushed with mortification as he called out to Phebe, who danced toward him, then giggled flirtatiously as he inspected her hand. How tenderly did he touch its bandage. And though he pretended not to notice me, I knew he did, and I knew that his avoidance was as much a spoken word as if he had said, "I don't wish to be your friend." What would he say, I wonder, if he knew of my intentions to save him?

So broken was my heart at his treatment of me, that momentarily I abandoned all those good intentions and bitterly considered marching to the top of the Meetinghouse steps and blurting out the whole grotesque story. But I did not. I watched his parents climb into their wagon, I saw his father's arm linger just a moment longer than necessary as it circled his wife's waist and I heard Goodman Corwin brag to the Englishes about his intent to purchase a bull. With all that I saw and heard, I could do nothing so cruel as to destroy Jeremiah's family.

Aye, I shall save him. I shall do so on the morrow, for finally I have devised a plan. And then the morrow following, I shall gather up my small parcel and depart.

Perhaps, God, You shall more carefully watch over me for my charity toward others.

Salem, 7 September 1692

Today, on the scheduled barn raising for the Disboroughs, I set my plan into action.

The occasion for the barn raising was the completion of the exterior of the Disborough home, which leaves only the stock to require suitable shelter before winter howls with its ice and chill. Most of the village, I knew, would be attending. Goodman Corwin would be there, I was certain, for he would not be able to resist another opportunity to hint at his sudden change in means, but I did not think he would bring the locket. I reasoned so, because I thought he would fear losing it in all the exertion of labor.

When it came time for the family to depart, I stayed behind. 'Twas my plan. Feigning an increase in my illness, I stood in the doorway and watched Mama, Papa, Mercy and the entire White brood clambor into the wagon, thinking how 'twas perhaps the last time I would see them all as such. On the morrow I would be gone.

I watched until they disappeared from view and I could hear the creaking cart no longer, then quietly I closed the door behind me, taking care Daniel would not detect the latch, and hurried through fields and forest toward the farm of the Corwin family.

The distance was great from our house to the Corwins', and I rapidly tired as I ran; but I had dared not take the mule for fear someone would see me, and neither did I chance using any roads, which would have been smoother, for the roads would be well trafficked today. As I ran, I began to worry about the time that was required and I feared I should not make it back home by evening, and I wracked my brain as to how I was going to explain my absence. I decided I would think about it later.

The sun was quite high in the sky when I reached the mean and scrubby farm. My chest heaved with breathlessness, and as fast as I could still muster, I crossed their rutted fields with their sharp little hills and entered the cabin.

I was glad for its smallness. It gave me fewer places to search. But I was disgusted at its filth and saw the remains of morning meal still upon the table. Two mice scurried across the earthen floor, which had not been swept in days. Goody Corwin was as poor a goodwife as her husband was a husbandman.

I began in the most obvious places. The wooden till on the rough hewn mantle. Beneath the lid of the settle. In the blanket chests, which smelled musty and unclean. The sugar bowl, which was empty. Beneath the limp straw mattresses. In chamber pots. Behind the hanging samplers. Along the ladder rails, leading to the sleeping loft. Beneath the faded rugs. In the wood box. In the water pitcher. In bread bowls, baking tins, and wooden trenchers. Even in the ashes of the hearth. Not a drawer nor a container remained unsearched, and I was nearly in tears for my frustration. So untidy was the house, with so much clutter strewn this way and that, it could have been beneath my very nose, and I would not have seen it. So I began re-searching all the

places I had already looked, willing my eyes to be keen and alert. Still there was nothing. Disappointed, I sat in a corner, put my head in my hands and nearly wailed. This was my only chance. If I did not find it now, I never would, for I could scarce walk up to Goodman Corwin and boldly snatch it from his pocket!

As I sat there, I noticed the cupboard beside me had recently been moved. Its legs had made a small scrape in the smooth earthen floor. Curious, I reached over and carefully edged the leg across the scrape. Then my heart beat with joy! Beneath the leg, the gray earth had recently been disturbed. Swiftly I began to dig with my nails, and in only moments a shiny gold circle appeared. Hastily I opened it. "REM, from birth." Elated, I dropped it into my shift and shivered at its coolness as it slid past my small bosoms and onto my stomach. Carefully I moved the cupboard leg back into place. Taking one last look around to make certain I had left no trace of my search, and satisfied that Goodman Corwin could not report missing what was not rightly his, I opened the door to race toward home.

Then I stopped dead in my tracks. There, in front of me, dismounting from a horse, was Goodman Corwin and his youngest son! My first thought was "You're not supposed to be here!" Later, I was to learn he had returned for a mallet. At the time, however, I surely did not ask the reason for his presence.

I don't know who was more surprised at the confrontation—he or I. For we both stood stock still in amazement. Instantly my feet became unglued, and I did the only thing that came to mind. I ran.

It took a moment for him to grasp the situation, and I had covered quite a distance before I could hear him racing after me. Weary from the pace I had kept in reaching the farm, I could not run as fast as I normally can; still, my young speed was swifter than his elder, heavier one, and I had very nearly made it across some overgrown pasture, when I tripped upon a half hidden rotted bucket, which enabled him to close in on me. As I scrambled to my feet, I felt his hands on my shoulders, and he whirled me round to face him.

His round face was flushed and perspiring, and his voice came in heavy pants. Still, he managed to make his words quite loud and angry.

"What were you doing, girl?" he bellowed. "What were you doing in my house?"

"I . . . er . . ." My mind reeled, trying to think of an explanation. The locket felt like ice against my stomach, and I was glad I hadn't lost it.

He shook me. "Tell me, girl!" he demanded. "Tell me what you were doing in my house!"

Blankly I stared up at him. I could think of nothing. Suddenly his eyes darted down to my hands, hanging limply down from my firmly clenched shoulders. I suppose he saw the dirt on them, because wildly he grabbed at them and stared in stunned disbelief at my blackened nails. I cursed myself for not having washed them.

Aghast, he said, "H . . . how did you know? That's . . . that's what you came for—isn't it?" His voice suddenly turned bolder and stronger, and again he shook me. "Give it back to me! Give me back what you stole, you little thief!"

What happened next, happened so quickly, I can scarce remember the progress. I recall trying to shake loose of his grasp. I think I gave him a little shove, for my intention was to wriggle free and run. He stumbled backward, I think, in reaction to my shove. And before my very eyes, the overgrown grasses opened up, and he disappeared with a scream—a scream that echoed and grew fainter as it seemed to come from the bowels of the earth. I heard a soft, distant thud, then all was silent.

Stunned, I froze, thinking I had somehow imagined it. Then my foot touched the rotted old bucket, and I knew it was from an old well. And Goodman Corwin had fallen into its hole.

My heart sank. Fearfully I tiptoed closer, and my voice sounded like it came from a timid rabbit.

"G . . . Goodman C . . . Corwin? Are . . . are you there? Can . . . can you hear me?"

Silence. The only sound came from a small, tattered boy who appeared beside me. "Where's my Papa?" he asked.

Salem, 8 September 1692

They came last eve and dragged me away in chains. At first the charge was to be murder; now I think 'tis to be that of a witch. Goody Bishop is collecting the evidence.

The constable was the one to clasp on the irons. I stood, silent and numb, in the middle of the great room. A dozen eyes burned into me, gaping. Goody White elatedly announced, "I always said that child was peculiar!" Her tattered children, dirty thumbs in mouths, sleeves wiping at runny noses, stared at me with all the awe of watching a ferocious beast. Even Daniel rose from his sickbed and staggered to the top of the stair to watch me led away.

Papa turned from me, grimly. He said nothing. His clothes were dirty from pulling up Goodman Corwin's mangled body. Mama was weeping, her labor-ruddy hands brushing back tears. Mercy showed me the first sign of affection since my visions began, stepping tentatively forward to touch my hand. "Shall I ever see you again?" she asked in her small, whiny voice. I did not answer. I did not know, and I did not want to think. Mama's silent weeping grew to an audible sob.

Roughly the constable pushed me forward. The

chains clanged as I walked, my steps felt strange and heavy, and I wondered if the chains would dent the floor. I paused as I reached the door, turned and took one last look around, knowing I would never see the great room again. Then numbly I walked out into the dark night, my ankles already rubbing raw from the weight of the irons. I felt all those eyes upon me, burning into my back, as I was roughly lifted, then dropped into the waiting, rickety cart.

I was taken to Salem town, where I have never been, because the village's small prison already overflows with witches. An eternity that journey seemed to require, me lying like a heap of grain against the creaking slats, my hands tethered together with heavy chains, my feet bound by chains heavier still, and I gazed up at the coal black sky with its tiny white dots of stars and thought how still the night was. Only the creak of the wagon and the snorting of the horses broke the silence. I thought back to that day which seems so long ago now, when I watched this same rickety cart carry Goody Glover up to the gallows. It was the first time I knew the same fate was to be my own. The rutted road tossed me from side to side and back again, and occasionally I cried out in pain; but the constable continued on in his rapid, jolting pace.

Aye, so long that journey required, yet not long enough, for too soon did we pull into the square with its neat clapboard meetinghouse facing the courthouse, and too soon was I roughly led round to the back of the courthouse toward the prison, led by the constable's flickering lantern in the dark of night. The jailer was awakened, a burly, hairy, swarthy man who resented the intrusion upon his slumber.

"Eh?" he roughly grumbled. "What's the charge?"

"Witching," replied the constable, cryptically.

The burly jailer lit his lantern and peered down at

me, wondering, I suppose, if I were any different than the rest. I presume I was not, for he looked vastly disinterested, undoubtedly because he had seen so many, then he yawned an enormous yawn, shook the sleep from his eyes and gruffly shoved me through a door. The darkened corridor before me seemed vast indeed, but now I think it appeared so only because it was so black and dark, the flickering light of the lantern merely opening it up to be endless as we walked. My chains clanged and clattered with all their enormity in the black silence, and my pace was a shuffling one, requiring great effort against the chains' weight. On either side of the corridor were enormous doors, and I think there were either four or six in all. When we reached the fourth, the jailer took a long brass key from his belt, shoved it into an enormous lock, pushed the heavy door ajar, then pushed me in, me stumbling and falling over my heavy chains. Behind me I heard the door close and the key again turn in the lock, securing me inside.

The chamber was small and dark. Heaps of filthy rags lay strewn about, lit only by a dim stream of moonlight trailing through a tiny high window, which was barred, and as my eyes adjusted, I realized those filthy heaps of rags were people. Six or eight had taken the wooden benches which ringed the walls. The rest lay on the floor, as did I.

My first memory of the cell was the stench. The acrid smell of urine cut through my nostrils worse than any of Mama's boiling lye, and on top of it was the strong sickly sweet smell of darker human excrement. Two large, full chamber pots stood in the corner. Later I was to learn they are emptied once daily. Then, I wanted to wretch.

Not one of the piles of rags moved or took note of me. Slumber, I have so soon learned, is our only escape. There being no place for me to move, I laid in my own heap by the door, feeling the tears trickle down my cheeks, salty stinging tears, but I did not wipe them away, for they were my only comfort. And so I passed the night.

When morning came and that thin thread of moonlight became a small trickle of sun, making the chamber gray and hazy and viler still, I expected I would immediately be dragged to the courtroom, tried and hung; but I was not. Some, I have learned, languish and rot for fortnights and for months, while for others the end comes within weeks, and that is what makes the agony so unbearable. The not knowing.

For morning meal, we were brought a large bowl of suppawn which was watery and cold. I did not want to eat it, for we were all expected to eat from the same large wooden trencher, and my stomach heaved for all the filthy unwashed fingers which dipped into it. Some of those fingers were attached to a pile of rags which was no more than a pile of bones draped in tatters. I decided to force at least some of the unappetizing preparation down my throat for nourishment. The ensuing elimination of bodily wastes was too noxious to describe, for the poor quality of food, which is oft allowed to sit in the jailer's chamber until rancid and rife with flies, makes bowels run and stomachs turn in torture. The race for chamber pots after eating brings moans of agony from those who must sit and wait.

There are, in my small cell, two score exactly, and someone told me we are among the fortunate, for many have been carted as far away as Boston. I suppose the constable did not wish so long a journey in the middle of last eve. I wonder if Boston cells could be any more vile.

Most of the prisoners are older than I, being goodwives and ranging all the way up to the wrinkled and aged. There are two other children besides myself. One is a pale, mute little girl who stares at the wall, and I helped her pick the lice out of her hair. In demeanor, my neighbors are a bizarre lot. Some are cantankerous and mean and take open delight in their witchery, freely admitting their sins, and would have long ago been released for their confessions, save for the fact that they refuse to relinquish such practices, so are incarcerated to spare their victims, if such sparing is possible. They remind me of Goody Glover. Most are stunned or confused and do not at all understand why they are here. There are spinsters, who are considered "strange" due to their unweddedness, and indeed a few are decidedly strange, leaving no doubt as to why they are unwed. An elderly woman has been charged for the practice of medicine with doubtful results. Two goodwives have been charged for being incorrigible rails. Many have visions which order them to sign up souls for the Devil. A few are extremely low in intelligence, and I think that is the case with the two other children. The mute says nothing; the other babbles in some incoherent tongue. Of all of us, there are perhaps three who could have once been held up as a pillar of village or town, and those are the ones for whom I feel the most pity, for they have been brought here as the result of some envious neighbor who reported them the cause of some unfortunate occurrence for which they were hardly aware; and they weep softly for being torn whether to admit witchery and thereby gain their freedom or whether to be true to their souls and to God and maintain their innocence. The rest of us are misfits. We have never been popular, sought out for our advice, or been glibly charming at conversation. Only God knows whether our eccentricities threaten His teachings.

And so concludes my observations of my first day.

You, dear journal, I was able to conceal beneath my skirts before the constable arrived, and my current neighbors, paying little attention to anything, pay even less attention to some new little heap of chains who sits in the corner and writes. The locket still lies cold and concealed in my shift.

Salem, 9 September 1692

They came to ask me to confess to witching.

The jailer fetched me from my sordid little chamber, plucking me out from the small sea of rags by extending his long hairy finger toward me and ordering, "You there! You what come in evening last! Aye, you! The little one! Magistrate waits to see you!" He gave me a little shove as I reached the door, to exert his authority, I suppose, then shoved me again as I shuffled down the corridor. The quivering faces behind me relaxed as the door slammed with a jolt. My chains clattered against the wooden floor.

I was led into an antechamber, where, awaiting my presence, sat a town constable and a magistrate of the court. The magistrate did the talking.

"You are Rachel Ward?" he asked, tonelessly. A severe looking man he is, with sharp features and a crisply starched white collar which had been newly pressed, though I don't think the pressing was for the benefit of me. He appeared rather bored at first, having been through such proceedings so often, I presume. On the short wooden table in front of him lay a sheaf of papers, which crinkled as he thumbed through them. I suppose they referred to my charges.

"Aye," I said. "I am Rachel Ward."

His eyes peered up at me over the smooth rim of his eyeglasses. I don't think he liked my tone.

"You want to confess?" he asked.

"For what?" I said.

Suddenly his voice came to life. I could hear the harshness in it. "For entertaining Satan," he growled.

"Nay," I replied.

"Nay, what?" he demanded. "Speak up, girl! Don't answer me with cryptic words! Explain yourself! Do you or do you not wish to admit that you have been compacting with the Devil?"

"Nay," I repeated. "I do not wish to admit such a thing."

He eyed me long and hard, his gaze travelling over me from cap to toe as I stood small and chained before him. Probably, I think, he was trying to determine from whence I derived my haughtiness. Narrowing his gaze, he said, "Are you aware of the severity of your charges?"

"I have done nothing wrong," I replied. Which was not exactly the truth. I *had* stolen the locket, though I didn't think anyone knew that yet, for if they had, they would have searched me.

His bellow nearly made me jump. "Do you not admit you made the earth open up and swallow a man!"

"'Twas an accident," I replied, calmly.

"An accident! 'Twas a diabolic touch! Do you not admit you caused that well hole to appear?"

"I do not so admit. Someone else caused it."

"That someone being Lucifer in one of his deceitful guises! Assumed by *you!*"

"I know not who dug that well. It may have been Lucifer. It was not I."

"Do you deny being in covenant with the Devil?"

"Aye, I do."

"Speak up, girl! Explain yourself! Why do you deny sorcery with that fiendish Prince of Darkness?"

"Because I have done nothing wrong. I have done nothing which I have intended to bring harm to others."

"God hears your false tongue!"

"God is my judge in my intentions."

"Don't blaspheme His name, girl! Don't deceitfully use Him to erase your guilt! That, too, is the work of Satan! Aye, I have seen such tried by many before!"

"I do not intend blasphemy. Which is why I do not confess to falsehood. Were I to admit to witchery, 'twould be Satan guiding my tongue, not God."

The magistrate shook his head, a disgusted, heavy shake that told me my arguments had been repeated before him a hundredfold, if not more. Gruffly he conferred with the constable in whispered tones. Finally he straightened and turned his attention back to me.

"Are you aware, girl, that confessing can save you? If you repent of your compacting, the Lord will hear you and have mercy upon your tortured soul. Your chains will be loosed, and you will be spared from the gallows."

"My soul would still remain tortured," I said, truthfully. "For if not witching, I should be charged with murder."

My statement took his breath away. Harshly he accused, "Are you reading our thoughts, girl?"

"Nay, I merely speak the obvious. For if I am to be hung, I prefer it for something which nearest resembles the truth."

"Aha! So *murder* you admit?"

"Nay, sir. But murder is more true than compacting with Satan." Proudly, I then added what I also knew to be the truth. "I realize the village would have my preference reversed. For riddance of a witch purges souls and purifies the air and offers more promise than does riddance of a murderer."

The magistrate's sharp features purpled with anger. "Your tart tongue serves you poorly, girl! The Lord hears your proudness and shall strike it down!"

"Aye. So my mother has warned me."

"And has your mother also warned you a petition is being circulated to give yet further evidence of your witching? Do you know your neighbors add to that list? Do you know the list lengthens far beyond the sorcering of a well hole? Do you know those additions shall be marched up before you at your trial?"

"Nay, sir. I do not know of such a list. I have not spoken with my mother since my arrest." I did not ask what this list contains. Too well do I know how the most innocent of occurrences can be misconstrued as the touch of the Devil. I would learn soon enough all that would damn me and send me to the gallows.

"And now knowing of that list," continued the magistrate, harshly, "do you still not wish to repent?"

"I have nothing to repent for, sir."

"Jailer!" bellowed the magistrate, as he furiously began writing on the papers before him. "Return this witch to her prison! Let the Devil hear her conversation!"

Wearily, I shuffled back down the dank corridor, my chains jangling, wondering if I had made a mistake.

Salem, 10 September 1692, morn

Mama brought me some journey cake, but as I have no milk or beer to dip it in, I must consume it in dry mouthfuls. To receive it, I was again shuffled into the antechamber, having been once more searched out by the jailer's pointing finger, and each time one of us is so selected, all eyes stare up at that outstretched finger and quiver and quake, knowing not what awaits such selection.

Mama sat in a tall ladder-back chair, weary from her journey, her long dark skirts caked with dust, and upon her lap sat a small cloth covered bundle, which contained the journey cake. I was surprised to see her. I did not think she would come. Shuffling across the room, chains clanging, I took a seat in the chair beside her, grateful for a seat other than the floor. Removing her cap, Mama ducked her head to conceal a wince of pain, but since acknowledgement of that pain would have embarrassed us both, I pretended not to notice. Bitterly I thought that if it had not been for Mama and Goodman Glover, I would not be here, because Goody Glover would not have singled me out. My visions are where my downfall began.

I attempted to sit erect and proudly, so as not to

display any weakness; but it was a difficult task, because my bones ached from sleeping upon the cold floor, and already my wrists and ankles are rubbed raw and bleed. Mama sat equally proud, but there was a softness in her that I have not seen before.

"Do you fare well?" Mama asked.

"Well enough," I replied, coolly.

"And . . . and your quarters? Are they . . . suitable?"

I suppressed a sarcastic laugh, but I need not have. The sarcasm was evident in my tone. "The rats do think so. They are the only ones well fed. Though the lice do survive, as do the weevils."

Did I provoke guilt? 'Twas my intention, and apparently I was succesesful, for Mama again averted her eyes and gazed down upon her lap. "I . . . I brought you some journey cake," she said.

My chains clanged as I reached out for the bundle, but I did not open it. "Did you come alone?" I asked.

"Aye. Your . . . father works hard to prepare his countersuit against . . . Goodman English." We both knew she was lying. A vast heaviness settled in my chest. Even Papa has deserted me. With false brightness, Mama added, "But Daniel fares better. Afternoon last he was able to take food. Today he sits in the settle."

"That's nice," I said, dully.

"And Mercy," said Mama, vainly attempting conversation, "has been knitting you a shawl. She shall bring it to you."

"I don't think I shall be allowed it," I said, cruelly. "We aren't allowed any comforts."

"Well," ventured Mama, lamely, "perhaps we shall try, anyway."

Silently we sat staring at the small window, I trying to inflict punishment by my silence; Mama, I think, aware of my hatred, but pretending she was not.

Beyond the window I heard a bird chirping, and I could see the sun shining upon the green common; and all that brightness contrasted to my own wretched circumstances only fueled my bitterness, making my hatred grow stronger. I suppose I shall go to my grave having snuffed out every last trace of consideration toward me.

Mama said, softly, "Goody Bishop . . . she is circulating a petition against you. She . . . asks our neighbors to provide evidence of your charges."

"O?" I said, wondering how Mama felt about these proceedings.

"I . . . I pled with her against it. I . . . told her you were being misjudged."

"And her reply?" I asked, already knowing the answer.

"She . . . she said it was her duty. She said the village . . . must be purified of its curse. That it would be against God's will . . . to impede such purification."

Mama's posture remained straight as a rod, but her voice sounded small and beaten; and I wondered if she and Papa were yet speaking. I thought it ironic that her best friend was playing a major role in her family's destruction. I wondered if Mama felt the hurt of that betrayal. I think she did.

Formally, I said, "In the end, God shall judge us all."

"Aye," replied Mama. "So He shall."

"Her petition . . ." I asked, not being able to completely stifle my curiosity, "have many added to it?"

"I . . . don't know."

Again I sensed her lack of truth. "Undoubtedly a great many," I prompted.

"I . . . I'm not certain."

I wondered if Jeremiah had signed it. I considered giving Mama the locket to hand over to Jeremiah for hiding, but I decided against it, fearing Mama could not be trusted.

"I shall have to go soon," said Mama, quietly. "'Tis a long journey back." Rather lamely, she added, "I . . . I brought the horse."

"No matter," I answered, disinterestedly. "Already I hear the jailer to return me to my chamber."

She stood then, gazing after me as I shuffled across the room, walking slowly so as not to further chafe my ankles, which pain me with every movement; and even as the door opened, then closed, I felt Mama's eyes follow me. I wondered what she was thinking.

Salem, 10 September 1692, aft

This aft I was again singled out by the jailer's finger, and I had hoped above hope that 'twas Papa who had come to see me. How dreadfully mistaken was I!

Fearing, however, that something may be amiss, this being my second selection in the same day, when the jailer's hard eyes glared down at me, I swiftly pretended the discovery of lice in my shift; squirming in mock surprise, and giving a short squeal of fright, I bent over and unfastened a few buttons of my dress, causing the jailer to momentarily avert his eyes, at which point I hastily retrieved the locket and hid it in the nearest place I could think. In the mute girl's pocket.

"You, there!" bellowed the jailer, again peering down at me. For a moment my heart sank, fearing he had seen my action. But he had not, for he then bellowed, "Up with you! And no need to re-fasten those buttons!"

Too soon did I learn his meaning.

Again I was led into the antechamber, this time to find myself facing not only the magistrate, but a reverend and two frightfully prepossessing women. The magistrate spoke first.

"Rachel Ward. You are accused of being a witch."

"Aye," I replied, rather stupidly, because I wondered if he had forgotten he had seen me afternoon last.

Sternly, he said, "Do you still deny covenanting with the Devil? We provide you a last opportunity."

For a moment, I wavered. But my voice emerged clear and strong as I replied, "I am not guilty. I have made no covenant with Satan."

"You deny he has appointed you his servant on earth?"

My eyes darted from him to the women, who stared at me with such ferocity, I nearly quaked in my chains. "Aye," I replied. "I do." I wondered if I sounded as fearful as I suddenly felt.

"Then we must make an examination."

Dumbly I stared, not understanding his meaning. Is my trial to be now? I wondered.

One of the women spoke, her voice high and nasal, with an elongated nose that made her appearance rather like a crow. "Remove your clothing," she commanded. "We shall search to test your word."

Still not comprehending, I continued to dumbly stare, and my pause seemed to incense her.

"Have you no hearing, girl? Remove your clothing! We are to search for witch's teats!"

O God! I thought. Pray do not do this to me! Have I not always been Your faithful servant?

The constable unlocked my irons. How free I suddenly felt! How soothed were my wrists and ankles without their chafing weights! My eyes leapt toward the window. 'Twas blocked by the imposing figure of the magistrate. The constable guarded the door. I was trapped.

Again the crowlike woman snapped, "Girl! Unfasten your dress!"

Stammering, I asked, "Are . . . are the men to leave?"

"Have you something to hide?" she sneered, contemptuously. "Is there a teat grown to suckle the Devil?"

"Nothing . . . er . . . grows," I replied. "But I, uh, have never unclothed in front of a man. 'Tis sinful I am taught." Fervently I hoped my argument would sway them. It did not.

The crowlike woman retaliated. "And whom are *you* to speak of sin? You who do the work of the Devil. But if you do not do his work, then prove as you proclaim! Prove you have not been entertaining that which resides in the world of fire and terrorizes us with his evil deeds. Unfasten your clothing, girl! Display your innocence!"

My eyes met each one of the four gazes upon me resentfully, a meeting which searched for a glimmer of compassion, a meeting which communicated both boldness and a plea. But it had no effect. Arms crossed, four bodies returned my stare coldly. Slowly I began to unbutton. One by one, I pushed a button through its hole, no longer meeting their eyes, feeling a heat rise up inside me, knowing my cheeks flushed and my body shuddered, and I prolonged the undressing as long as I possibly dared; yet my prolonging did not appear to disturb them; they seemed to derive a strange sort of satisfaction from my hot humiliation. Only once did one of the women impatiently snap, "Make haste, girl. Do you require all aft to disrobe?"

Valiantly, I hoped when I reached my shift 'twould be sufficient, though I knew such hope was useless; too well did I know the procedure; too clearly did I recall the public humiliation of Goody Glover. Only could I consider it a blessing that my own exposure would be witnessed by four, not forty, not a throng. "The shift, girl!" the woman reminded. "Does the shift conceal what you wish to hide?"

Naked, I stood before them. I suppose because I am a child, they thought I was without modesty. Intently they approached, then poked and scrutinized every private part of me. Even the men did not flinch. Shame was left only to me. My small brown nipples stood pert and hard as if with chill, and my tiny bosoms coiled from their probing touch. Inwardly I writhed, every sense feeling their prying, examining fingers, intently searching for a third breast, which I knew they would not find.

How far I have come since that day I stood, as a child, witnessing Goody Glover. Am I still a child? I do not feel so. Though humiliation enveloped me with all its heat, I did not show it. I made myself stand erect as if wood, my eyes focused into thin air, pretending to neither see nor hear, pretending no existence of a touch, a frown, a disappointed sigh of futility. Birds chirped outside the window. I did not hear them. A bright sun streamed past curtains and made a white pathway across the floor. I did not see it. I willed myself to lack all emotion or sense. Only numbness met the rough prying hands as they moved over every crevice of my body. And when they were finished, when all stood back and rubbed their hands over their faces in disappointment, I slowly reached down, picked up my rumpled heap of clothing and methodically re-clothed.

The magistrate announced, "You are without an extra teat."

Tears burned behind my eyes, but I blinked them back. "I know," I said, proudly.

"Do you still deny you have bound yourself to the Devil?"

"I do," I replied.

"Then you shall be judged by a trial."

All this, I thought, yet nothing is proven. Shame and humiliation have absolved me of nothing. "Do you not believe your own search?" I asked, bitterly.

"A search proves nothing, unless 'tis fruitful," said the crowlike woman, self-righteously. "Not all of Satan's instruments are provided with means to suckle. You have been chosen to do his deeds without."

"So," I concluded, "searches prove only guilt. Not innocence."

"'Tis the *procedure,"* she maintained, and I knew it to be so. "The trial shall be your judge."

"God shall be my judge," I told her.

"Care of your tone, girl! Else you condemn yourself!"

"Already I am condemned."

"By *Satan,* you confess?"

"By a witch-crazed village," I said, coldly.

The magistrate fairly leapt at my words, stepping toward me as the constable clasped on my irons. "And do you now deny even the existence of witches? Has Satan bid you to blind others to his acts? Is your mission to convince us that Satan does not spread his fiendish sorcery?"

"My mission is the truth."

"Then speak it!"

"As you bid, sir. I think the truth is that Satan has not sent us witches, but madness. A madness which serves him just as well. I think he laughs at us from the depths of his Hell for the torment we have wrought upon ourselves. For in the end, 'tis the judges and juries which serve him, and they do so better than any instrument he could have devised."

The magistrate purpled. So choked with fury was he, his words emerged in bellowed gasps. "You say the *courts* are the instrument of the Devil?"

"Not by their intent, sir. Through their misguidance."

I thought his hands would shake the breath out of

me. Violently he gripped me by the shoulders. "I shall see you mount the gibbet, girl!"

"Aye, sir. I am sure you shall."

I spoke with resignation, yet with pride. For if the gallows are to be my fate, I shall go to them with a clear heart, and with a tongue which shall perhaps open a door and serve those who come after me. Perhaps that is how God intends me. Perhaps He has not deserted me but instead uses me to serve Him in a way which is not yet clear to me.

My examination was over. The jailer led me away in my chains while four gaping sets of eyes gazed upon me in fury.

Salem, 10 September 1692, eve

Goody Warren is incarcerated with me. I do not think I have yet recorded that. She, who is Eunice Flint's accused possessor, is highly advanced of years, quite frail of body, has a face which is an intricate web of wrinkles, and displays a queer habit of twitching her nose when she speaks, her conversation being frequently peppered with the memory of her lost children, of which there appear to have been many. Tiny yellowed caps and infant gowns are brought to her by her husband, and all of them she meticulously shows to me. Though peculiar, she seems harmless enough. I try not to think about my suspicions regarding Eunice's accusations. But I do think of them. So I feel sadness for Goody Warren.

She consoled me today after my humiliation.

"Did they search you, child?" she asked, when I returned.

Though I perceived myself as being in chill control, apparently my demeanor spoke otherwise. Inwardly I still writhed. Calmly I retrieved the locket from the mute girl's pocket, the girl remarking nothing for my actions, and Goody Warren affording me the courtesy of privacy for what oddities I displayed, such as concealing lockets.

Cryptically I told Goody Warren aye, they had searched me, and my sharp tone said I did not wish to speak of it further. I felt badly for my sharpness, however, when Goody Warren easily volunteered: "My turn was fortnight last. How disappointed they were when a teat was absent!" I felt even sadder for her then, sad for the indignities to which even this frail old woman has been subjected. Looking round me at all the dirt streaked faces on bodies which had not been washed for fortnights, nay months even, I thought of their husbands, their brothers, their sons, and I wondered how men could allow such humiliation to come to their women. Like caged animals we are in our tattered, filthy clothing, our treatment no better than that of some captured beast.

Stiffly I stretched straight my legs in a small unoccupied space and rubbed my bruised ankles. Dried blood stained my stockings.

Goody Warren, nose twitching, softly said, "Here. Put these little gowns beneath the irons. Helps the chafing. 'Tis what I've done."

"Thank you," I said, grateful for her show of kindness.

"I wouldn't offer to just anyone," she explained. "You're special. You remind me of my dead little Temperance. Died not three hours out of the womb. Such a little bit of a thing. Her face was much like yours."

Vaguely I wondered how one could possibly detect a resemblance between a mewling infant and a girl of thirteen.

Goody Warren then began chirping on and on about such nonsense as to whether Temperance had been prettier than Harriet, whether Simon displayed the greatest strength of character, whether Joseph might not have been a prosperous merchant, and so on, all of which made very little sense since not one child had progressed beyond the age of seven days. So I was startled when, in the midst of this confusing litany, she suddenly stopped short, peered over at me with her frail, wrinkled face and asked, "Are you afraid of dying?"

I did not know how to answer. Truthfully, I had not really considered the matter. My thoughts had taken me only as far as the gallows, which was to be quite a proud and heroic affair, with me standing calm and brave, the wind blowing through my hair and the sea of gazing faces downcast and remorseful for how they had condemned me. Thus, it was with much surprise when I suddenly realized: I don't *want* to die!

Gulping, I admitted, "Aye. I am afraid."

"Don't be," said Goody Warren, reassuringly. "'Tis swift, they say. The pain is scarce felt before 'tis gone."

That's about as far from the truth as anything I've heard! Too vividly do I recall how long Goody Lawson lingered! Too clearly can I see the snapped neck and the twitching feet of Goody Glover and all the others! And, with what was rapidly approaching hysteria, I knew the pain would be great indeed!

"And," continued Goody Warren, cheerfully, "think how peaceful when we reach Heaven. You *have* chosen Heaven, haven't you? Some think I shall go to the other, toward the blazing inferno and into the hands of Satan, but I shall fool them. I shall go to Heaven; and then I shall see all my babies. How blissfully happy I shall be then! Think of it, child. Think of all those blessed faces we have missed and shall finally greet!"

I could not think of a single face I wished to greet. Rather frantically, I said, "I don't want to die! I'm only thirteen!"

"But child, life on earth is but preparation for the greater things to come."

"There must be great things *here,* as well! I want to experience those things, too!"

"But not near so blissful as Heaven. Nay, not near so—"

"Once they were! Once I ran along the stream holding hands with Jeremiah! I laughed with Deliverance! Mama and Papa were happy! And the birds sang! And the sun was bright! And—"

"Calm yourself, child! Do, do regain some control. Else the jailer shall toss you into the dungeon. 'Tis a horrid jailer, isn't he? Does your mother not tell you of Heaven? Does she not tell you how you shall be angels together, that your souls shall be at peace forever?"

Miserably I said, "Mama cares nothing for me. Mercy is her favorite."

"And your father? Do you not look to the day when your father shall hold you forever upon his knees?"

I was feeling more desolate by the moment. "Papa . . . he seems to have disowned me."

"O," said Goody Warren, rapidly losing interest in my sorry story. "Well, then, I suppose you can come with me. To help care for the babies. You'll like Harriet. She reminds me of you. Or is it Temperance? Such a little bit of a thing when she was taken. Harriet, I mean. O dear, there goes Goody Cloyce again, screaming at the Devil. She thinks he tries to choke her, you know. Something about how she has not been a faithful servant. She confessed once, you know. But then she made some timber fall, and it missed its victim. So now both the Devil *and* the courts are angry with her. Her shrieks do echo against these walls, do they not? One can scarce get a moment's peace. Doesn't seem to disturb the mute girl, though, does it? Is her trance caused by the Devil, do you suppose? A pretty child, isn't she? Puts one in mind of my little Temperance. She died when she was but three days out of the womb, and . . ."

Pray, God, save me! I shall go mad in this prison!

Salem, 11 September 1692

Alas, Goody Warren was hung today. I feel terribly sad.

Salem, 12 September 1692

A day has passed with nothing to record save for rats, lice, watery suppawn, suffocating stench, matted hair, filthy face, dank air, bleeding ankles, the babblings of one of the children and the piercing, echoing shrieks of Goody Cloyce in her battle with the Devil. Oddly, even my visions have vanished. I have expected from moment to moment to hear Goody Glover's cackle ring triumphantly from these rafters, her large face leering down at me, bug-eyed, her drool and blood sliding down and wetting my shoulders; but she has not appeared. I can only suppose she has gained her triumph from where she has placed me.

Again I have been singled out by the jailer's finger. In the antechamber this time were led three girls whom I have never before set eyes upon. No sooner had they stepped through the door (I, all the while wondering if some mistake had been made, if 'twas some other person they had come to see), when all three girls immediately dropped to the floor with shrieks and howls of pain, one clutching her stomach, another an arm, the third, her leg. Amazed, I wondered what illness had so suddenly befallen them. Fleetingly I decided they must be prisoners, that they had been poisoned by the rancid suppawn, yet they wore no chains.

Through the door, the reverend from two afternoons past then appeared. Glaring at me, he demanded, "Do you afflict these girls?" Scarcely could I hear him through the tortured shrieks.

"What?" I murmured uncomprehendingly.

"Do you afflict these girls?" he bellowed, nearly rattling the building from its beams. "Does your wizardry cause them pain?"

Good heavens, I thought, stunned. Never in my life have I been noticed, much less caused such commotion!

"Touch them!" commanded the reverend, through the din.

Touch them? I scarce wanted to be *near* them, for fear such agony would befall myself!

"Touch them!" he again roared.

Gingerly I stepped forward, my chains banging against the floor. The first girl I could hardly reach, so wildly did she toss about in agony. Her feet flailed this way and that, and I thought I should be kicked black and blue were I to get nearer. But upon another roar from the reverend, I jabbed a finger forward, managing to make contact with her flailing foot, and upon my very word, she instantly stilled. Dumbfounded, I stared, unblinking. With one pitiful last groan, the girl sprawled wearily upon the floor, relieved to be rid of her pain.

"Touch the others!" roared the reverend.

Hesitantly I moved toward the second girl. Again, I feared having the breath knocked from me by a thrashing foot. But when my jabbing finger had the same stilling effect as upon the first, the girl emitting one last soft moan, I angrily marched toward the third, not surprised at all by her sudden calm.

Furiously I wheeled. "'Tis a trick!" I cried.

"Do you deny you are empowered to inflict pain?" demanded the reverend.

"I have not a whit of power over these little frauds!"

"And do you deny your touch can break your sorcery!"

"I deny all! Admit nothing! Should you wish to prove me a witch, you shall have to do so by honest means!"

The three girls quietly shook themselves out, rose and stood primly against the wall, appearing quite pleased with themselves.

Enraged, I turned on *them*. "What gain for you by such display? Do you think God blesses you for your deceitful ploys? Do you think He blesses your little blackguarded hearts for sending another body to the gallows?"

My words had as much effect as a drop of rain. The smaller one replied, quite priggishly, "God knows us as His chosen. We please Him with our purifying ways."

"Purifying?" I exploded. "'Tis blasphemy, I'll hold! And you can wipe those arrogant smirks from your faces! All of you, with your o'erweening opinions of yourselves! Not God's chosen you are, but instruments of the Devil!"

"Hear! Hear!" cried the reverend, shocked. "The Lord shall strike down such vile attacks upon His innocents! Confess, girl! Confess what has been evidenced! Once more, save yourself! I have pled with the magistrate to gain you one more chance!"

"Never!" I cried. "I shall never confess to that earned by tricks!"

"Nay, not tricks, but that caused by evil powers! Confess to them all, girl! Confess to all your evil deeds! Seek God's salvation!"

"Such seeking would be a lie! A lie in exchange for a

life lived under a cloud of witching! A life lived 'til old, while neighbors shun me! Nay! A better fate indeed to meet the gallows!"

"As you shall!"

"Nay! I shan't do that, either! Upon my word, I *shall live!* And not as a witch!"

"Jailer!" roared the reverend, startled by my threat. "Off this girl to the dungeon! She threatens escape!"

So now I write from the bowels of this wretched prison, sitting upon a damp earthen floor in gray darkness, with scarce room from wall to wall to stretch my legs, with no voice to hear but my own. For evening meal, 'twas bread, but I could not eat it for the weevils.

Salem, 13 September 1692

How close I once was to freedom! How miserable I am in this wretched prison!

Salem, 13 September 1692, eve

Mercy visited this aft. She came with Mama to determine if I am really a witch. Both were brought down to me in my dungeon.

I had hoped Mama would stay. So despairing did I feel, I wanted only to lay my head in Mama's lap and weep; I wanted her calm, capable hands to fondle my hair and pet my head; I wanted her strong, reassuring voice to tell me this summer had been merely a bad dream, that if only I were to close my eyes, I would open them to find myself in my own little four poster bed with its clean linens and soft, plump quilts. But Mama did not stay. She did not fondle my hair, nor touch me, and the sternness evident in her voice was neither reassuring nor comforting. "Mercy wishes to visit with you," said Mama. Then she was gone.

Timidly Mercy sat down beside me. She blinked her small brown eyes to adjust to the darkness. I was stunned that Mercy consented to be alone with me, much less allow herself to be locked behind the door of a dungeon. Fervently I prayed a rat would not scurry past and send her into a screaming frenzy, for how I would ever keep her from frantically climbing upon my shoulders for escape within my tight, dank quarters, I did not know. I could see her eying my chains. I felt like an animal.

Meekly, Mercy ventured, "I brought you a shawl. But the jailer wouldn't let me give it to you. He said people in the, er, dungeon aren't allowed gifts. 'Tis a very pretty shawl, though. I knitted it myself."

Clearly Mercy was still afraid of me. Her small figure huddled as far from me as possible, which, to be sure, was not far at all in such confined space, and her squinty eyes stared over at me, sizing me up. I said, "Keep it for me, Mercy. Someday I shall wear it."

I knew my words rang hollow. But it made me feel wretched indeed to see Mercy's look of amazement. So Mercy has given me up for lost. Why then did she come? Merely to add to my misery?

In her whiny voice, Mercy nervously said, "Some people say you're a witch. *Are* you a witch, Rachel?"

No one had ever asked me that question before. Oft have I been accused, but never have I been queried. I now leapt at the chance to finally explain myself, even if it was only to Mercy. Not even pausing to consider my reply, so certain was I of its correctness, I said, "Nay, Mercy. I am *not* a witch. But I did once fear so. 'Twas at Goody Glover's hanging—do you remember that, Mercy?"

"Mama made me honey bread afterward," Mercy said.

Leave it to Mercy, I thought, to remember only the treats received! In exasperation, I continued. "Well, Goody Glover stared at me in the most peculiar way. Andthat night when she came to haunt me—to *torment* me—I feared strongly that she would indeed take over my soul. For fortnights, I feared as such. How terrified I was that I would fall victim to the Devil. But now, Mercy, I know that I am *not* an instrument of Satan. And not only that, I think few of us accused are.

Leastwise, not so that we cast spells and evil omens."

Clearly Mercy did not believe me. "What about that day I found you in the barn?" she said. "When you were doing something with your blood and talking to Goody Glover?"

"Good Heavens!" I gasped, with a start. "How in the world did you ever remember *that!* I'd almost forgotten it myself! Pray, put it from your mind forever for what you are thinking! 'Twas only some trick I was trying. Some silly trick. And if you must know, it didn't work. She *still* came to haunt me!" If Mercy remembered *that,* I thought with a shudder, heaven only knows what else rambles round in her brain!

Mercy said, "I remember because Mama was fit to be tied. And I'm certain she said something about some spell."

Quickly I put a stop to such conversation with "Well, 'twasn't! So put it from your thoughts! Nay, Mercy. Like so many others, I am only the victim of everyone's fears and tragedies. Like you being so fearful of my fits. Sometimes I used to make up those fits to scare you—did you know that? Well, I did. 'Twas stupid of me, I now know. For look where it has helped land me. I have decided, Mercy, that everyone is searching for causes for their problems. 'Tis a convenient place to find such causes in people like me. I'm hardly the most popular person in the village, am I? Well, neither are most of the rest of the people accused. We're sort of . . . well, misfits."

Goody Bishop says you're peculiar," announced Mercy.

"To blazes with Goody Bishop!" I sputtered, angrily. "She thinks half the village peculiar! O Mercy! If only you could see some of the women in this prison! Some are so harmless, they couldn't hurt a fly! And some are so bereft of reason, they don't even know of what they are accused! True, a few do appear to court the Devil—

but out of pure contentiousness, I think. And *I*, certainly, am not amongst them!"

Mercy considered me a moment, her round babyish face screwed up in thought. Then she asked, "Why did they put you in the dungeon?"

"For being pert with the reverend," I replied, with a sigh.

"What did you say to him?"

"I told him I would live. He didn't like that. He wants to see me at the gallows."

"*Will* you go to the gallows?" she pressed.

"If the magistrate has anything to say about it, I shall. He's angry with me, too. For accusing his courts of being misguided. O Mercy, pray stop looking at me as if I were some ferocious villain! And pray, let's change the subject! If I must go to the gallows, I shall think of it then. Not now. Now I can only pray that God shall somehow spare me. He shall, shan't He? I haven't really done anything so wrong, have I? What happened with Goodman Corwin was all an accident. And what else can they accuse me of but my visions? And visions aren't a sign of witching. And . . . O do, do let's talk of other things! Tell me news of the family."

For some unknown reason my ramblings must have been reassuring to Mercy. Because to my profound amazement, Mercy edged closer to me, and in one of the few signs of tenderness she has ever shown me, she laid her small hand atop my chained one. Nearly did I break into a sob, so hungry was I for affection. Gratefully, I drew her toward me, laying her head upon my shoulder as I used to do when she was a baby, and though she showed an initial stiffening of reluctance, she allowed herself to be coddled. I patted her hair, as I so fervently wished someone would do to me, and we were like two young orphans sitting there in the darkness, nestled in each other's arms.

Stammering, Mercy confessed, "I . . . I used to be

jealous of you, Rachel. Because you got all Mama's attention with your visions. I . . . I'm sorry I was jealous. 'Twas mean of me."

Then I knew why she had come. Why she had consented to be locked up with me. Not to add to my misery, but to purge her soul of her guilt. I suppose she thought it would be her last opportunity, since my remaining days were numbered. How I hated her for that. How I hated every whiny little bone of her for even in the end thinking only of herself. But I knew what God wished me to do. So I decided to allow her her purification.

Glumly, I reassured her, "But you've always been Mama's favorite, Mercy. Always. Since the day you were born."

"I know. But for a while I thought you had replaced me. Does it bother you, Rachel? That you are no one's favorite?"

O the cruelty of children! And with what bite did her observation greet me! Choked, I asked, "Papa . . . does Papa ever ask of me?"

"O I forgot to tell you! His suit was morning last. The one with Goodman English."

"Morning last?" I exclaimed, suddenly sitting up straight. Swiftly I realized how the days have all run into one; yet how could I have ever forgotten such an important event as this! My heart hammered in fear as I pressed for the outcome. "What happened, Mercy? Did Papa win? Pray, say the mill still survives!"

"Papa lost," said Mercy, simply, in her childish whine. "I think he shall return to husbandry."

Like a clenched fist, Papa's devastation hit me, settling in my stomach like a piece of swallowed lead, and I could scarce believe Mercy's matter-of-fact relating of the news, as if she had no realization of its import. Such blindness in her selfish ways!

Shaken, I asked, "How . . . how is Papa? What does

he say?"

"Nothing much. I heard him talking to Mama, though. 'Twas right before Mama went to the Sibleys to ask for food. Mama doesn't know I know about *that,* though."

I could hardly believe my ears! "Mama?" I breathed. "Mama went to the Sibleys for *food?* Why, whatever for?"

"Because our stores have run low. I suppose because the Whites eat so much. And since Papa didn't plant much this year, with him being so busy at the mill and all . . ."

And expecting the mill to plentifully provide for us, I thought, miserably.

"But," continued Mercy, candidly, "Goody Sibley didn't give Mama anything. I think Mama's angry with her for that."

So proud, capable Mama with her stiff wall of reserve has been reduced to begging. And has been refused. I could only guess at the blow to her dignity. I wondered how the family would survive the winter.

"And Daniel?" I asked. "Can Daniel not hire out in return for provisions?"

Brightly, Mercy exclaimed, "O Rachel! How well Daniel does! One can scarce believe the miracle after he was so ill abed! But Prudence Cory is pledged to another. Did you know that? Not just courted, but pledged! The marriage is to be next Spring. And Daniel is in such frightful temper over it all, no one dares be near him! Why, afternoon last, he chopped wood for the Watts, and Goody Watts and Daniel got into such a horrid row, she chased him from her farm and said he was never to come back! Whatever is Papa to do with him? Yet Papa took Daniel's side of it—even though Mama dressed him down with words like that time you snapped at Goody Bishop. Remember that? Remember how angry Mama was? Well, add scores onto that, and that's how angry Mama was with Daniel!"

So our family falls apart like straws in the wind. How empty I felt. And how perplexed that Mercy could remain so oblivious. How I wish I had her blindness. Feeling multiples older than my years, I removed my arm from around her waist and wearily reached down the front of my shift.

"Mercy," I said, "I want you to do something for me. 'Tis a secret, and you mustn't tell anyone what I am about to ask you to do. 'Tis very, very important. And you are the only one I can trust. I *can* trust you, can't I, Mercy?"

Solemnly, her soft brown eyes stared over at me. Too many years of obedience had been ingrained in her to even consider violating a trust. Yet her obedience was first and foremost owed to Mama, and for a moment I wavered. Could I commission her with something I had risked—nay, *given*—my life for? What if she betrayed me? But I saw her expression grow grave with the expected import of what I was to impart, and I decided I would take the risk.

"Mercy, I want you to take this locket and give it to Jeremiah. You must not mention it to anyone else. Not so much as a word. And when you give it to Jeremiah, you must tell him that he must also keep it only to himself. Never must he hint of it to another soul. For if he did, 'twould bring great tragedy to someone close to him. You must tell him that. Emphasize it. So he realizes how important it is."

Carefully I placed the locket in Mercy's small hand and allowed her to hold it, which she did with great gravity and wonderment; then I placed it in her pocket, knowing she had sensed its importance.

"You must tell him," I continued, "that someday I shall explain it all to him. But I cannot keep it here, with me, because someone may find it. And if anything should ever happen to me . . . well, tell Jeremiah he should take the locket out to the woods and bury it in a very deep hole, so no one shall ever, ever find it. Can you remember all that, Mercy? Can you tell it all to Jeremiah, just as I have told it to you?"

Her whiny voice was so grating that for a moment I again doubted the wisdom of entrusting her with such an enormous mission. But, alas, I had no choice. There was no one else to whom I could turn. Having made my decision, I then attempted to put the matter to rest and tried to feel a sense of relief (which I did not) by changing the subject and asking Mercy to tell me about Bridget White and all her chaotic children.

Giggling, Mercy proceeded to relate to me all the antics that have occurred since I have been taken: how Bridget is as useless as ever with the chores, how the child with the mangled leg hops about with more energy than any three children with both legs, how, no matter how often washed, faces remain constantly dirty and how Daniel's screams are the only thing able to quiet such chaos. I continue to wonder why Mama contends with such mayhem, whose only contribution seems to be that of depleting our food stores. When the jailer finally came to fetch Mercy, I was weary from merely the hearing of such energetic encounters.

Feeling suddenly desolate and lonely, I watched Mercy stand, and I wondered if she would squeeze my hand again before she left, or if she would show some small sign of affection. She did not. I suppose she had doled out as much affection as she was capable.

Still giggling over the Whites, Mercy took one last look at me and, with her childish whine, observed, "You look terrible, Rachel! Like some old pig who's been wallowing in the mud! Only you're skinnier. Next time I'll try to bring you some corn cake."

I hope she does. I haven't eaten since morning last.

Salem, 14 September 1692

Two days I spent in the hellish dungeon until they brought me back upstairs to the normal prison. I suppose they needed to make room for someone else.

How sad to arrive back and have Goody Warren gone. How little did I realize the extent to which I had come to depend upon her disconcerting cheer and her distracting chatter; and, as she was my only friend in this miserable, dirty prison, without her, my cramped chamber seems oddly empty and desolate, despite its numerous motley heaps of chained rags which spill onto every bench and corner.

At midday, they came to take away the little mute girl, and a pall fell over the chamber, for fear we would not see her again. Though she speaks to no one, I think we all feel rather possessive toward her. Her large dark eyes and small white face stare vacantly at the wall, and what she thinks of, I cannot imagine. No one comes to see her. Never is a piece of journey cake brought, as is for the rest of us. And whether she has ever spoken, or always been mute, I do not know. Secretly I harbor the hope that I shall one day encourage her to speak. I was glad when she was returned.

Salem, 14 September 1692, eve

Word has reached us that Giles Cory has been pressed to death. A gruesome death, to be certain. Boulders were placed atop his body one by one, and after each he was asked to enter a plea against the charges the courts have levied against him. Each time he refused. Such refusal denied the court's right to try him, so yet another boulder was added. Until he died.

So yet one more man is added to all the women who are executed for witching.

Salem, 15 September 1692

Jeremiah visited me today.

I suppose I partly expected him. If Mercy had been faithful in carrying out her mission, as I suspected she would be, Jeremiah's curiosity would have plagued him, and he would not be able to allow me to go to my grave without learning of the secret which I carried. Yet that he came told me he does indeed expect me to go to my grave, else he would have waited for my return, and I found that realization vaguely depressing. Nothing else, I think, has made my circumstances seem quite so bleak. I wondered what Jeremiah would say when I told him what he had to hear.

He was standing in the antechamber, by the window, when the jailer led me in. How handsome he looked with the light streaming in behind him through the small leaded panes of glass. Had I ever said him gawky? His long, lean limbs held themselves with all the strength and posture of a man, and he appeared to have grown taller by at least a head since last I saw him. His smooth olive complexion showed the wispy hint of a beard, and I knew he would soon be shaving. Looking into that smooth, dark face, I desperately searched for signs of pleasure at seeing me but was disappointed to find not a trace. Only a grimace of pain did I detect, much like that I had seen on Mama, and I realized the shock of my own appearance.

Nervously I stood facing him, my wrists bound by heavy chains, as were my ankles, and I knew that my dress was filthy and torn, that my face and hands were dirty, that my once silky hair hung twisted, matted and unprotected by a cap which has long since gone to bind my bleeding wrists. I was a sorry sight indeed. Had I once fretted over a smudge of dust upon my skirts when Jeremiah called? How long ago that seemed. Self-consciously I raised my hand in a futile attempt to smooth out my hair, but then lowered it, for the clanging of my chains echoed in the still room and widened the gulf between us.

With as much dignity as I could muster, I anxiously said, "Hello, Jeremiah." My voice was that of an old woman.

"Hello," he murmured. I do not think he was conscious of his stunned stare, nor of the extremely discomfiting effect it had upon me.

"I, uh, seem to have misplaced my comb," I said, with a flustered, feeble attempt at humor.

I think in that feeble attempt, Jeremiah's heart went out to me, and he realized how much I suffered, for he moved across the room and came toward me.

"I have one," he said.

With his own wooden comb, he then began to untangle my hair, my heart all the while fluttering up into my throat; and while his combing pulled and pained me, I did not whimper, and the tears that filled my eyes were not of hurt. When finished, he took his clean white handkerchief, dipped it into a pitcher of water and cleansed my face and hands, and I tried not to show my nervousness. How vulnerable I felt! What is he thinking? I wondered.

"There now," he said with a kind smile, standing back from me. "You look more presentable to receive a guest." So he was trying to put me at ease.

Awkwardly I returned his smile. "Shall I provide my guest with my best chair?" I asked, pointing toward the two ludicrously uninviting stiff ladder-backs which stood starkly in the corner. Yet how inviting they seemed to me—who always made my seat upon the floor!

Jeremiah matched my false cheerfulness. "Thanks," he said, "but I prefer to stretch out my long limbs. Half the morn I've spent bouncing up and down astride a frisky horse. Come. Lounge beside me on the floor with our backs to the wall."

I did not tell him how those stiff ladder-backs looked like a feathery haven to me. Instead, I allowed him to lead me toward the spot he had chosen, shuffling in my walk and agonizing over every clang of my dehumanizing chains, those clangs seeming as loud as thunder. Jeremiah pretended not to notice. Sitting close to me, he casually drew up one knee and draped an arm over it.

"I should have brought some food," he said. "'Twas stupid of me. I, er, didn't think." I could tell he was as nervous as I.

"We are well fed," I lied. And because Jeremiah knew I lied, I airily added, "Only last eve, the jailer passed out cakes and wine. I declined, however, saying I remained stuffed from the afternoon's feast of quail and sugar buns."

Jeremiah chuckled. "So much feasting. Yet your clothes hang on you like a new sapling. Has the clothing grown instead of the girl?"

"Aye. My feasting made me a trunk, and I outgrew my original garb. I had to borrow these from one of the women. Any more weight I add, and I shall have to borrow something from that fat old jailer!"

"Make sure 'tis the clothing with the keys!" he laughed.

He meant it in teasing; but instantly it spoiled our little game, and the air hung heavy and quiet again, for I could not think of anything clever with which to reply. Too conscious am I of the humiliation of my irons, too raw are the sores on my ankles and wrists to treat my damnable tethers lightly, and as soon as the words were from his mouth, Jeremiah knew all this. Uncomfortable, he apologized, saying he seemed to be saying all the wrong things. That he wished he knew what was right.

"There are no right things," I replied. "Just conversation. The world is a strange place, is it not, Jeremiah?"

"Aye," he said, politely, not really understanding my meaning.

I explained, "Only last summer we chased each other along the river with nary a thought of witches or prisons. Now look at all that's happened since."

My words were gloomy, I suppose, and Jeremiah, uncomfortable with the gloominess, countered them with something more pleasant, being true to form in ignoring the unpleasantries of life. "You were quite a runner," he said. "Always faster than I."

I decided to go along with his distractions, simply because memories seemed infinitely more easy to discuss than the wretched present. And what followed became a brief nostalgic journey through our past. "I was faster," I said, "only because you let me. Remember how we used to have contests picking berries? I always won then, too, because you let me."

"Just as you always allowed me catch the most fish. By giving me the largest worms."

"Jeremiah!" I said, with surprise. "You weren't

supposed to guess that!"

"Do you think me without sight? Certainly, I guessed. You were never good at pretending—except for the time you feigned a broken ankle so I would carry you home and you wouldn't have to walk through the marshes. I thought I was such a hero! Until suddenly you climbed down and skipped to the door! I could have wrung your neck for the fool I felt!"

"What fun that was! But do you remember the time we were skating and I fell through the ice? You really *were* a hero then!"

"And laid abed a week with sassafras tea for it."

"As was I. O Jeremiah! Remember how you used to tease me? All those times you chased me with lizards and snakes . . ."

"With you howling and scurrying up trees!"

"And remember when you drank all that beer with Deodat Easty? Both of you as sick as poisoned magpies! And I sat with you for hours, plying you with herbs, 'til finally you were presentable enough to return home. What a whipping Mama gave me for missing my chores!"

"I *was* almost poisoned when you first were learning to cook. Remember those sugar buns you brought me? I thought I'd never eat again! Whatever was wrong with them, anyway?"

"Salt."

"Salt?"

"I accidentally dropped the salt box into the batter. It didn't seem so bad at the time."

"And you didn't sample before giving as a gift?"

"Nay. They looked too pretty to waste with sampling. O Jeremiah, remember the time I was collecting the eggs and dropped the basket and broke every last one of them? I was in tears for what Mama would do, and you brought me some of yours. You were always watching out for me, weren't you?"

"And remember the time the cow kicked me? I couldn't walk for weeks, and every day you came to help me with the milking. You watched out for me, too."

"And remember when we took Papa's horse without telling and rode practically as far as the moon?"

"I sure do. We got ourselves so lost I thought we'd never return. Your father threw a fit for our cavortings and almost bid me never see you again!"

"He didn't only because you presented him with that lovely pipe which you had intended for your own father."

Tears began glistening in Jeremiah's eyes, and it was with touching sentiment that he sighed, reached over for my hand, and said, "Ah, Rachel! What lovely times we've had, have we not?"

My heart was in my throat. I wanted to sob, and my voice trembled as I replied, "Aye. We have."

"I wish . . . I wish we could do them all over again."

By his words, I knew he was certain we would not. I felt more miserable than ever. I wanted to tell him, "We *shall* do them again! And they shall be even better than before!" But I did not tell him. Because I was no longer confident.

Hesitantly he asked, "Do . . . do you still have your visions?"

"Nay. Goody Glover has deserted me." I almost added "also," but thought better of it. I did not want to be bitter. Not when I knew not what lay ahead of me. I wanted to be calm and stoic and unthinking. I said, rather absently, "Perhaps they were only my imagination, after all. Just as Papa always said."

"I wasn't very understanding about them, was I?" Jeremiah said. "I'm sorry about that. 'Tis just that they . . . well, they frightened me, because I didn't know what to expect. I've been thinking about how I've acted Rachel, and I'm not very proud of it. I should have been stronger than that. Will you . . . will you forgive me?"

So, I thought, heavily, Jeremiah too comes to ease his conscience, just like Mercy. How many others will come to ogle me in my tatters and chains so they may depart with lighter hearts? I tried to keep the sting and disappointment from my voice as I said, "That's alright, Jeremiah. I forgive you." But I did not. And he knew it. Yet no words could put back together what had already been broken.

Feeling suddenly sorry for myself, I said, "I've made such a mess of things, haven't I?"

"Nay! Nay!" said Jeremiah, quickly, but I knew he was just being polite. How I yearned for sincerity in his denial.

"I was going to run away," I told him. "I had wrapped some things in a shawl, and I was going to head north, someplace where there aren't any witches or trials or accusations. But then . . . well, other things happened." I did not elaborate upon those other occurrences. "Strange," I added, "I might have been on some empty road at this moment."

The absurdity between my daring plans and my present circumstances was lost on him. "How would you have fared?" was all he asked. "Where would you have lived?"

I shrugged, neither knowing nor caring of the answers to his questions. "Perhaps I would have become like Bridget White, and gone door to door begging for shelter." Then, with a short laugh, I added, "Nay! 'Tis a terrible thought, is it not? No matter. God would have taken care of me. He probably would have hired me out to some needful family."

With no more than idle curiosity, a reaction which pained me greatly, Jeremiah asked, "You would have gone by yourself?"

"Aye." I nodded. "Just me and— Just me."

Suddenly his interest grew alert. Finally I had touched a chord of emotion. "Just you and who?" he pressed.

I don't know why I told him. Perhaps I wanted to break through his placid demeanor. Or perhaps I was searching for sympathy. Perhaps in my childish manner, I thought if I made clear to him my desperation, he might once again like me and protect me as he had for so many years. What error lies in seeking love out of pity! But then again, perhaps I told him simply because I had always told him everything important.

"Just me and the babe," I finally replied, and I looked directly into his eyes as I spoke, to determine his reaction.

He was stunned. His jaw dropped, and he gaped.

"I am with child," I repeated, and, upon reflection, I think I repeated this fact more for my own benefit than for his, for so peculiar is the idea still to me, that yet I have difficulty believing it.

"Whose . . . whose is it?" he asked, and for a moment his voice returned to the high pitch of a boy, a pitch that nearly made me smile for how at odds it was with his manly posture.

"I was defiled," I told him, and again I waited for his reaction. Then, to make certain he understood, I said, "Someone forced his way with me."

Incredulous, Jeremiah asked, "Who? How?"

"'Tis of little matter." I had no intention of amplifying upon my horrid memories. Besides, not at all could I bear to reveal my defiler as being the weasely, repulsive form of Goodman Glover. Rather would I prefer Jeremiah to think it one of the boys—even homely Joshua Snow!—than the disgusting figure of Goodman Glover.

"But why did you let him?" Jeremiah demanded. Clearly he did not at all understand.

Emphatically I told him, "I didn't. I couldn't stop him. I didn't realize what was happening until . . . well, until 'twas too late."

Vast indeed was the difference betwixt the reaction I yearned for and Jeremiah's gape. Not pity but stupefaction was written into his face, and slowly I was beginning to realize I had committed a blunder.

Still incredulous, Jeremiah asked, "Why didn't you tell someone? The constable? Or the reverend? Reverend Parris would have had him arrested!"

'Twas the one question I should have foreseen, and did not. How I despised my thoughtless tongue! "I . . . I couldn't." I cringed at how evasive I sounded. "There . . . there were other reasons."

"Such as?" he demanded.

"I can't tell you," I said.

He shook his head then, staring at me as if I were someone he did not recognize and was attempting to, like someone who comes upon a face in the road that was once encountered and could not be placed. Then, frowning, he rose and went to stand at the window, his back to me. How tall and wiry he was. I wondered what he was thinking.

Nervously I told him, "No one knows about the babe save for Mama and me. Even . . . even *he* doesn't know about the babe. So . . . well, I'd appreciate it if you didn't speak of it until . . . well, until whatever happens."

"Why did you tell me this?" he suddenly asked. His back remained to me, and his voice was low and angry.

"I . . . I don't know." With every breath, I regretted my impulsiveness, and had I been able to cut my tongue from my throat, I might likely have done so. Too well should I have realized Jeremiah's conservative nature. Yet weary was I, too, of how I could never share with him my deepest troubles. Tiredly, I said, "I'm sorry I told you. Perhaps we could just forget it, and—"

Harshly he interrupted. "Did you not know how it would make me feel?"

Fervently I searched his tone for evidence of that feeling, but beyond anger, I could not determine it. If only he would face me!

"Nay," I finally answered, and I wished it were an hour prior and I could turn back the clock and do things differently. "Couldn't we just pretend I didn't tell you about it? 'Twas a mistake Jeremiah. I shouldn't have said anything. Pray, don't think ill of me. Not now, Jeremiah! Not at the end!"

Abruptly he sniggered, a high, jarring snigger. "What a dolt you must think I am! All those times I awkwardly kissed you . . . and all the time you were with child!"

Horrified, I cried out, "Nay, Jeremiah!" Too keenly was I now aware of the enormity of my blunder. My chains jangled as my hands flew to my face and I pled, "'Twasn't at all like that, Jeremiah! I wasn't with child then! Truly I wasn't!"

His sarcastic laugh crushed me. "O? 'Twas afterward, then, that you smiled and mocked me?"

O God, I prayed. Please don't let him hate me! "I never mocked you, Jeremiah! I swear it!" Frantic, I wanted nothing to spoil the memory of our innocent kisses. "Your kisses meant a lot to me! I dreamed of them! O Jeremiah! How in love with you I was!" And still am, I wanted to add, but did not.

He turned then, and his face was distorted in a sneer that wrenched my heart into painful slivers. Yet my pain had been self-inflicted; no one was to blame but myself, and my own oafish bungling. Perhaps Bridget White is correct. Perhaps I am a peculiar child.

"Mercy brought me a locket," said Jeremiah, abruptly. I knew his politeness had ended. 'Twas that politeness which had prevented him from asking about the locket initially, his attention to proprieties dictating that he begin by demonstrating his concern for me and for what had once been shared betwixt us before proceeding to his real mission. From his impatient shifting of weight from one foot to the other, I also knew that he was anxious for our meeting to be over.

Nervous and shaking, I was now not at all certain of the wisdom of proceeding. What had once seemed so noble and sacrificial, now seemed naive and folly. I found myself regretting everything about the locket. I wished I had buried it in a corner of the dungeon and had let it lay for whoever might have discovered it, let it lay for some wretched prisoner who might unearth it and therein bequeath it to her children in her one last desperate act before the noose. I wished I had never gotten involved. I wished I had never stolen it!

Yet, searching further inside myself, I knew I could not have buried it. I knew I had to tell Jeremiah the truth of what lay within, for if I did not, I knew by some sixth sense that someday even greater disaster would befall. Sufficient disaster had already been experienced.

Taking a deep breath, I steeled myself and said, "Inside the locket, Jeremiah, is an inscription. I shall tell you what it means and how I came to learn about it."

Methodically I began unthreading the whole entangled story, trying to keep my voice calm and toneless so as to lessen the shock; and Jeremiah did not interrupt me, but listened in silence, his color graying and turning to ash, his dark eyes widening then narrowing, his chest barely moving with breath, and too clearly did I feel the jolt my words were producing. O if only I could have spared him! And when I finished my tale, I understood exactly the reason for Jeremiah's reaction.

He blamed *me* for the tragedy. Because I was the messenger.

"I don't believe you!" he cried.

Quietly I said, "'Tis true, Jeremiah. You must realize it before others do." I had to impress upon him the danger.

"'Tis a lie!"

"O that it were."

"You've made all this up!" he screamed. "You've made it up to get back at me for how I've treated you! This and that other story, too!"

The acid in those words stung like hot lye for the knowledge that Jeremiah would consider me capable of such vile retaliation. But still I kept my voice calm. "I would not say such things to hurt you," I said. "I do it only to warn you. For when the truth becomes known, 'twill bring great tragedy. You must prevent that, Jeremiah. You must figure out a way. Please, Jeremiah. Please listen to me, and think."

Still he did not believe me. "'Tis a monstrous thing you do! How could you have thought up such a diabolical lie? Aye, that's it! 'Tis the Devil speaking! You *are* a witch!"

With that, his lanky limbs immediately sprang into motion, and he flew from the chamber. I watched him in horror as he threw wide the chamber door and cried out, "The Devil! The Devil's in there, jailer! Speaking with his malevolent tongue! God spare me from such wickedness! Silence this Satanic power that grasps for us all!"

In moments, the jailer came to get me, as I sat there drained and weary. 'Tis out of my hands now, I told myself. The future is for Jeremiah to decide. I wanted to feel a sense of release. I did not. I still felt troubled. Jeremiah had believed nothing I said.

Salem, 16 September 1692

My trial, I have learned, begins on the morrow. I confided to the mute girl that I am frightened; but she did not reply, and I do not know if she heard me. So thin is she that I have decided to give her some of my journey cake next time Mama brings some. If Mama ever again does. The nights have grown chilly, and dearly do I wish I had Mercy's shawl. I wonder whom Mercy shall give it to. Pray, God, guide and watch over me.

Salem, 17 September 1692, noon

I awoke this morn quite hopeful. The suppawn in the large trencher brought by the jailer was not so watery as usual, which I thought to be a good sign. And our bread did not have weevils.

The mute girl's teeth were chattering from the cool night, so I put my hand on her arm to comfort her; but she did not acknowledge me. Such a thin, pathetic thing she is, with dark circles rimming her vacant eyes. I wonder if there is a mind left behind that glazed stare. The only time that glaze disappears is when she is sleeping, and then she looks so soft and at peace that I sometimes wish God would show His mercy and take her when she is most serene. I slid my hand down into her small shivering white one and spoke to her, telling her it was the day of my trial and asking her to pray for me, telling her that I have not a friend at all left in this world, and it would make me feel ever so much stronger if she were to offer to be my friend. Alas, she gave me no response. I suppose she has her own troubles to occupy her. Perhaps that is why she has retreated from the rest of us, into her own private refuge.

I was still attempting to make contact with her when

the jailer appeared. As I shuffled around the heaps of rags, one of the women murmured, "God be with you," which I thought to be another good sign. Turning quickly, I wanted to thank her, but could not determine the source, for all faces were turned away from me. I was heartened, however, knowing that someone cared.

First being led through the corridor, through the antechamber, then through another corridor, finally I was brought through a door which opened into the court chamber, my chains all the while banging against my ankles. Behind two long, highly polished tables sat what I was soon to learn were the Chief Justice, six magistrates, and several reverends—all, I thought in astonishment, to decide the fate of small, insignificant *me!* And witnessing the event would be an audience completely filling a half score or more benches, an audience which included faces vastly familiar to me yet suddenly so unnervingly foreign.

What a shock to find a chamber so heavily peopled. Swiftly I began sorting through what seemed a blur of faces, fervently trying to single out one with some glimmer of compassion. Alas, all were exceedingly somber and grave, some even hostile. So I braced myself for what was certainly to follow.

I was not allowed to sit. The Chief Justice bade me stand sideways at the front of the chamber, alongside the end of the imposing length of table and positioned such that I would face both the magistrates and the audience. A constable sat beside me—as if with scores of eyes upon me and my limbs bound by chains, I might even consider flight.

Dishearteningly, I saw one of the magistrates to be the severe looking one with sharp features and stiff white collar who had previously searched me for witch's teats. He glared at me. Beneath that glare was fervent dislike. Then he spoke with all the ferocity of fire, asking whether I now wished to confess (which I did not), whether I admitted entertaining Satan (which I denied), and whether I did not now wish to make my peace with God by apologizing for countenance of the Devil (to which I replied I had already made my peace).

Such answers sat ill with him. "The court shall proceed!" he bellowed. The resounding bang of his gavel nearly sent me leaping through the ceiling.

Nervously I tried to focus on the maze of faces and was able to pick out Mama in the first row, betwixt Mercy and Daniel. She looked solemn and weary, older by years than only this past spring. And though I gazed at her with desperation, she showed me no sign of encouragement; nor did Daniel, who sat grim and foreboding. Papa, I realized with vast disappointment, was not beside them. So Papa will not come to my trial. I wonder if he shall come to my hanging.

Goody Bishop sat perched in the audience, looking pious and self-righteous as always; and I also saw Goody Corwin, Bridget White with her throng of filthy children, the Englishes, the Disboroughs, Phebe, Abigail, Ann and her mother, Deliverance, Jeremiah's parents (alas, no Jeremiah!), the three girls whom I first met in the antechamber, Goodman Glover and a host of others, most of whom I cannot or choose not to recall. I wondered who was for me, and who was against. Glumly, I thought probably none of the former and all of the latter.

With no little surprise to me, Goody Corwin was called as first witness. I knew she would be. I had prepared myself that the onset of the trial would be the worst, with the most damaging testimony, so I was anxious merely to be on with it and have that portion to be over, so we could proceed with testimony in my favor. Little did I know how bad the testimony would be.

Goody Corwin—now Widow Corwin—rose, stepped forward and appeared sufficiently distraught over her lost husband. Nay, 'tis unfair of me. I am certain Widow Corwin is indeed distraught, as was the small, tattered son who clutched tightly onto her chapped hand, the same small, tattered son who stood beside me at the old well hole, asking, "Where's my Papa?" The remainder of her shabby ten children remained seated and squashed one into the other on their wooden bench. I was going to be in for a bad time of it. I tried not to think how all were now without husband and father.

Tears began streaming down Widow Corwin's leathery face as she pointed toward me and sobbed, "That's her! That's the specter of the Devil who took my husband! Made the earth open up and take him, she did! My poor beloved Thomas! Now 'tis only me—all alone in this world—to feed my children. Thomas was such a good husband—good and true! Never hurt a soul! Then he was taken by that girl there who assumed the spirit of Satan!"

Such fervent tears spilled easily and suddenly. Too suddenly. A vague sensation of something rehearsed indicated itself to me. And no sooner had I had such sensation than the weeping Widow looked despairingly down at her son whose face also began to screw up into a wail. Sighing, I tried not to be heartless. I told myself Widow Corwin had indeed loved her husband, and those tattered children will now indeed be without father. Wrestling with my conscience, I tried to feel responsible.

To me, the Chief Justice gruffly said, "Rachel Ward? How do you reply to this charge?"

Nervous, I tried to find my voice, but what came out was a small squeak. "'Twas an accident, sir."

"An accident? An *accident* the earth suddenly

opened up and a hole appeared?"

"It, er, didn't exactly open up, sir. You see, he stepped back from me and—"

"He? He, who? Be specific, Rachel Ward."

"Goodman Corwin, sir."

"The husband of the woman before you?"

"Aye, sir."

"And Goodman Corwin stepped back, and you made the earth open?"

"Not exactly, sir. You see, I—"

"Did you and Goodman Corwin exchange harsh words before the earth opened?"

"Well . . . aye, sir, I suppose—"

The tattered son said, "She were screaming at my Papa!"

The Chief Justice said, "And why were you screaming, Rachel Ward?"

"I wasn't exactly screaming, sir. We were arguing. Well, not exactly arguing, either. You see—"

"Be specific, Rachel Ward! About what topic were those harsh words exchanged?"

"Er, well—"

"About *what,* Rachel Ward?"

"You see, sir, he thought I had stolen something from him."

"He? Goodman Corwin, you mean?"

"Aye, sir."

So intimidating was his constant interruption and harranguing of me that my head began to spin and I could scarce keep my thoughts aligned. I am certain that was his intention. Taking a deep breath, I tried to regain my control so as not to trip over the next crucial part.

The Chief Justice demanded, "And *what* did you steal from Goodman Corwin, Rachel Ward?"

"I didn't really steal, sir. I only—"

"Why did Goodman Corwin *think* you stole something?"

"He . . . he was mistaken, sir."

"About *what,* Rachel Ward? About *what* was he mistaken?"

"About . . . about nothing really, sir. You see, I didn't really steal anything. There . . . there was some necklace—"

A wailing Widow Corwin suddenly screeched, "The locket? So that's where the locket went! All this time I've been blaming the children!"

The Chief Justice demanded, "Did you steal a *locket,* Rachel Ward?"

Swiftly I snuck a glance toward Jeremiah's mother, holding my breath. She appeared to be without recognition. Hesitantly I ventured, "Well, there was something of a locket, sir."

Again Widow Corwin screeched. "'Twas a beautiful locket! A gold locket! 'Twas to be our fortune! Make her return it! Make her return that which is mine! And for which she opened the earth to send my poor beloved toward her Hell!"

Mama looked ashen. Her daughter was not only a murderess, but a thief. I dared not look at her. The Chief Justice raged with this new evidence of my guilt.

"Return the locket!" he bellowed.

"I . . . er . . . don't have it, sir."

"Where *is* it, Rachel Ward?"

"I . . . er . . . threw it somewhere in the river," I lied.

Widow Corwin let out a heart-rending wail. The chamber echoed with it, sending shivers up my spine. The Chief Justice waited until her horrendous wailing lessened to a disconsolate sob. Then he concluded with: "So, Rachel Ward. You stole a locket from the now deceased Goodman Corwin—stealing being a clear example of entertainment of the Devil. And when

Goodman Corwin confronted you with your theft, you then summoned up your diabolical powers and made the earth open to take him toward your fiery inferno. Do you deny all this, Rachel Ward?"

Scores of faces stared at me, waiting. It was no use to deny the part about the diabolical powers, nor of anything else, either; denial would only lead to further discussion of the locket. Fortunately, Jeremiah's mother still appeared oblivious. Before me, a distraught Widow Corwin stood with shoulders hunched and hands covering her face, disconsolately weeping. The small boy beside her looked white and frightened. I knew this part had not been practiced. I decided the locket had been the one thing Goody Corwin had depended upon to provide for her now fatherless children. In a small voice, I finally said, "I'm sorry, Goody Corwin. I didn't mean this to happen."

Ferociously she jerked her head upwards toward me, eyes red and swollen, and cried out, "You! You are a witch! A witch sent from Satan to destroy me and my family!"

I think she truly believed what she said. I replied nothing. There was nothing I *could* reply. Gloomily, I glanced over at the scribe who was furiously recording the proceedings. Someday, somewhere, someone shall read his recorded proceedings and know why I was convicted of being a witch. Yet they shall know nothing of the truth.

The Chief Justice then adjourned the Court for a few moments, to allow the scribe to complete his recordings, and to allow a pitcher of water to be passed round the chamber. I was not offered any. Nervously I looked at Mama, hoping she would smile or show some sign of encouragement, but her expression was without emotion. Stoic. I wondered what *her* testimony would be. A sad tale, indeed, when one is sent to the gallows by one's own mother. Goodman Glover sat eagerly forward on his bench, his small weasely face gleaming, and I wondered if Mama noticed Goodman Glover's presence and what she thought of it. So much tension and heartache sat under that roof.

Next to testify when Court was resumed was Goody Bishop. Her form seemed to stretch as tall as a steeple, and her angular face was set and confident; she had all the posture of a woman on an exalted mission. Hastily she strode forward.

"Let it be known," said Goody Bishop, addressing the court before the magistrate even gave the order to proceed, "I take no pleasure in instances such as these. Too fervently do I wish we were without witchery. But as one of God's most fervent servants, I feel it incumbent upon my person to assist in halting that which has become a pernicious influence upon us."

How self-righteous she was! As if God had appointed her and her alone to purify His world! Bitterly I noticed she did not glance toward Mama as she made her little speech; nor did Mama look at her in return. I wondered if Goody Bishop realized that by her betrayal, and its consequences, she was sacrificing the £21 loaned to Papa—a sum which would now be a long time paying without the mill. Perhaps she does realize it. Perhaps 'tis just further indication of her fervent belief in her cause. I wonder if she sees herself as a martyr.

The magistrate who so despises me spoke—the one with the sharp features and the stiff collar. Unimpressed by Goody Bishop's devout little display, he impatiently asked, "You have evidence, Goodwife Bishop?"

"Aye," replied Goody Bishop, drawing herself up to her full height. "A poppet of the accused was found under another witch's bed."

"A poppet placed by another," corrected the magistrate, "is not evidence of witching. Do you have other evidence, Goodwife Bishop?"

Undaunted, Goody Bishop said, "I have reason, your Excellency, to believe the accused herself placed that poppet under the witch's bed. And other poppets, as well!" Her bright eyes fell on Goodman Glover, and I started. Instantly I guessed what lies *his* testimony would hold.

"Your reason for believing such?" demanded the magistrate.

"I shall leave that to others to report," replied Goody Bishop, simply.

The magistrate's color was rising, and I felt a ray of hope as he snapped, "You shall confine yourself to your own evidence, Goodwife Bishop. Now do you, or do you not, have testimony against the accused?"

"I do, sir."

"Then tell it!"

"I have witness to the accused's speaking in foreign tongues, sir." At first I was completely mystified as to her meaning, and thought surely she had been caught in yet more hearsay, until she went on to explain: "The accused also rides brooms, sir. I saw her with my own two eyes. Aye, I did. The accused was riding round her pasture on a broom and yelping in some very foreign tongue, which I am certain neither you nor I nor anyone else in this chamber would recognize!"

Amazed, I knew in a moment of what she spoke. 'Twas the day I frolicked in the pasture with our new colt and was entertaining Jeremiah. Yet no sooner did I instantly open my mouth to explain, than the magistrate demanded, "Rachel Ward? *Have* you ridden a broom?"

"Aye, sir, but—"

"And were you yelping in some foreign tongue?"

"'Twas not exactly a foreign tongue, sir. 'Twas—"

"Was it the English tongue?"

"'Twas an animal tongue, sir. I—"

"An *animal* tongue, Rachel Ward?"

"Aye, sir. 'Twas—"

"Proceed with your testimony, Goodwife Bishop."

Eagerly Goody Bishop continued. "The accused reads thoughts, sir. Oft has she known what I was thinking before I even spoke it!"

"Is this true, Rachel Ward? Are you capable of reading thoughts?"

"Only of minds like glass!" I snapped, knowing such tartness brought me little gain; but so frustrated was I over the magistrate's concerted intimidation of me and of my lack of opportunity to explain myself, I could not help it. Instantly I regretted such folly. The magistrate already had me convicted.

Acidly, he instructed, "You shall confine yourself to aye or nay, Rachel Ward. Is that understood?"

"Aye, sir."

"Now then, Goodwife Bishop. Proceed."

She had saved the best for last. Eyes gleaming, back erect, Goody Bishop reported, "The accused stumbles over her prayers, sir. Oft. Even in Meeting. Her mother has heard her, as well—as have I, with my own two ears!"

Caught, it would have been futile to deny. 'Twas the one accusation I knew to be true, and its reason (my visions) would meet with little compassion. Fervently I glanced toward Mama for assistance, but her gaze was maddeningly directed to her lap.

"Rachel Ward," bellowed the magistrate as I jumped, "*have* you stumbled over your prayers?"

"Aye . . . aye, sir," I stammered.

Satisfied, the magistrate's sharp voice rattled the chamber as he summed up my transgressions. "Rachel

Ward, you have admitted to riding a broom, speaking in a foreign tongue, reading minds, and stumbling over prayers. What powers the Devil doth hold! Thank you, Goodwife Bishop. You have been exceedingly helpful."

"As a faithful servant of our Lord, sir."

"Aye, Goodwife Bishop. The Lord blesses His servants."

"Thank you, sir."

"You may be seated while the next witness is called."

How pious was Goody Bishop! How I hated her for that piety and its misdirection!

Spirits ebbing, my body felt weak from standing. Swaying, I thought for a moment I might faint. But then a voice shot through the chamber: "'Tis the Devil trying to save her! He tries to take her from her trial!" 'Twas the voice of Goodman Disborough. Immediately I snapped to attention. Silently I vowed that if I turned to stone, I would neither faint nor move nor give one small further whit of cause for accusation. Because somehow I must prove my innocence.

At the magistrate's beckoning, Simon English stepped briskly forward, his stubby legs scurrying, and it was with renewed confidence that I straightened to face him. 'Tis not enough he has ruined Papa, I thought, bitterly. Now he shall try to ruin me, as well. I wondered how.

Another magistrate spoke, this one with silvered wig and an iron tongue. "Goodman English? You have testimony?"

"Aye," replied Goodman English eagerly, and I was equally as eager to hear his accusation to learn what it would contain. I had not long to wait.

He said, "'Twas first started when I entered into argument with the accused's father. 'Twas at his mill. During that argument, the accused glared at me, and on the way home, my cart crashed and nearly knocked me dead. Killed one of my oxen, too. And demolished my cart."

'Twas my first real surprise. I had entirely forgotten the incident and was ready to explain how Goodman English had beaten his oxen mercilessly when the Magistrate demanded, "Rachel Ward? Did you glare at the testifier? Immediately after which his cart crashed?"

"Aye, sir, but—"

"Excellent testimony, Goodman English."

"O there's more, sir. Sometime after that, when I was engaged in a suit against the accused's father, a most mysterious storm blew up. Out of nowhere. You might remember it yourself, sir. And lo and behold, it took my roof!"

"Rachel Ward? Do you convene with the elements? Do you serve up storms?"

"Nay, sir, I—"

"Do you deny a violent storm arose? And that it took Goodman English's roof?"

"Aye, sir. A storm did arise, but—"

"I do not presume you to admit to spells upon the elements. Unless, of course, you wish to confess to being a witch. *Do* you wish to now confess?"

"Nay, sir, I do not, but—"

"Thank you, Goodman English. 'Tis excellent testimony. Excellent testimony, indeed."

"But there's more, sir."

"More?"

"Aye, sir. I didn't put it in the deposition, but there's one more."

It was then that I realized the magistrate read from a petition, thereby knowing who each testifier was to be and what he would testify. My heart began to sink. Without being told, I knew it to be the petition circulated by Goody Bishop. I also knew it would be quite thorough.

Goodman English continued with: "The other thing,

sir, is that the accused made my crops fail. After her father's mill shut down, by my bringing suit, my crops immediately withered and died. 'Twas most peculiar. I didn't put it in the petition, sir, due to the fact that it had not yet occurred."

"Rachel Ward? Have you made this husbandman's crop to fail?"

It was useless, I knew, to explain that Goodman English is a terrible husbandman, or that I had not even known of the mill's closure until after its occurrence. But at least I could attempt to deny the charge; I could at least enable the scribe to enter it into record.

"Nay, sir, I—"

"I do not expect you to admit to such covenanting. Be it so recorded, Scribe, that the accused has caused the testifier's crops to fail. Thank you, Goodman English. The court shall now adjourn for midday meal. It shall resume again at half past one."

So now I write from my cell with my dry slices of bread while others feast upon turkey legs and rabbit. Since there is no one else to talk with, I have related some of what has happened to the mute girl, with my putting on a false face and telling her that the situation shall improve, that this morn, facing my enemies, was the presentation of the most damaging testimony. This aft shall opportune those favorable to my cause. Sliding my hand into her small white one, I asked her to provide me strength and to think of me while I stand alone and solitary against my accusers. For a moment I thought I felt the slightest tremor of fingers. Excited, I told myself the girl was going to show me some sign of a bond between us. Alas, her eyes communicated nothing. And as the tremor was only momentary, I decided it was merely the result of my imagination and my fervent need for compassion. So it shall again be just God and I battling my accusers when court resumes.

Salem, 17 September 1692, aft

My hope for favorable witness was immediately dashed when Daniel was called to the fore. Slowly, precisely, Daniel rose from his seat on the front bench, making no display of hurry, and in his measured movements I could sense all the years of building hatred and resentment.

A magistrate's voice rang out, this one from the magistrate with the white wig which glistened like snow against his black robes. "Daniel Ward? You are brother of the accused?"

"I am, sir," replied Daniel, formally.

"Present your testimony."

"I wish to testify, sir, that the accused has wrought disharmony within our family. She has caused bitterness, discord and extreme dissension by her recent actions. Prior to such actions, only peace and serenity reigned."

Daniel's reference to me as "accused," rather than "sister," stung, as did such public renouncement by a member of my own family, despite my contempt for that member.

The magistrate said, "Rachel Ward? Are you aware that domestic disharmony is against nature and dishonors God?"

"Aye, sir," I murmured. "I am."

"Do you wish to speak in your defense?"

Finally an opportunity to speak out! Yet I was caught without defense. Defense would dredge up days, weeks and months of private sufferings which were best kept private. Hopelessly I glanced toward Mama, but her gaze remained blank, telling me nothing. Finally, I murmured, "Nay, sir. I do not."

The magistrate said, "Continue, Daniel Ward."

There's more! I thought, gloomily.

Daniel said, "The accused caused my father's prized cow to die, suddenly and without explanation. The accused petted the cow, and not two hours later, the cow died."

Buttermilk! So Daniel knew! All this time Daniel knew without speaking! Or was he only guessing . . . ?

The magistrate said, "Rachel Ward? Have you a defense for the demise of your father's cow?"

I said, "I . . . I didn't mean it . . ." and I hated myself for my stammer.

Daniel's eyes glittered with revenge. He said, "The accused also caused to befall me a most peculiar illness, of which no explanation exists, an illness which occurred immediately after a harsh exchange between us. For days did I lie ill, to recover just as mysteriously upon the accused's arrest—which broke her evil spell."

Surely my ears deceived me! Was Daniel accusing me of even his illness? Terrible thoughts began to race through my head, thoughts that rankled and raged, and from somewhere within the depths of my deep-seated mistrust of this half-brother I never liked, I wondered if he had planned this all along. If he had never truly fallen ill, but had merely feigned such illness to pound another nail into my cross.

The magistrate demanded, "Rachel Ward? Did you

exchange harsh words with your brother?"
"Aye, sir."
"And immediately afterward did he fall mysteriously ill?"
"Aye, sir."
"And did he then mysteriously recover upon your arrest?"
"Aye, sir. He did."
My guilt appeared as evident as the vengeful smirk upon Daniel's curling lips. Daniel had left me without recourse. Nothing could release me from the trap he had so carefully set, and I hated him.
The magistrate said, "Continue, Daniel Ward."
Daniel replied, "The accused also caused my affianced to stop loving me. The accused did so out of spite for my happiness."
Resigned, I could see all tables rapidly turned against me; so when the magistrate said, "Rachel Ward? Did you cause your brother's affianced to turn from him?" I said, calmly, "Aye, sir, I did." For in a way, I suppose I had.
"Continue," instructed the magistrate to Daniel.
"Lastly," said Daniel with satisfaction, "the accused caused my father's mill to fail."
"That's not true!" I cried, suddenly.
But Daniel's further explanation left me again in error. He said, "The accused's influence caused my father's suit against Goodman English to be lost. The losing of such suit now sends my family into poverty and despair. The accused did all this, your Excellency, out of spite, because she has never been a favored child."
Of all the testimony, this is the one that hurt the most. Even Papa's ruin I was to accept. And while all that Daniel said had foundation in truth, I knew its truth was twisted and distorted; for while I may have

unintentionally been a contribution, I had never set out to be so, and I still love Papa dearly, despite his disownment of me for all I have caused.

The magistrate said, brusquely, "Rachel Ward? Did you cause your father's mill to fail?"

Dejected, I hung my head. "I . . . I did not intend it, sir."

The magistrate said, "Daniel Ward, you may be seated. Next witness, pray step forward."

Returning to his bench, Daniel's stride was confident and victorious, and I despised him with all the breath within me for how he had made me appear. Were I truly a witch, I would have bid all the forces of Hell and Satan to strike him dead, and I did not feel an ounce of hesitation in such thoughts. Nay, I even wished I were indeed a witch, so I could make it so. And I think Daniel knew it.

Goodman Disborough was next, and his testimony was mercifully brief, for I did not think I could endure much more. His bearlike form stood at polite attention as the magistrate instructed, "Goodman Disborough. Advance your testimony."

Coughing to clear his throat, Goodman Disborough's voice emerged deep and husky. "The accused caused a mysterious fire to burn down my house," he said. "And this burning happened immediately after I refused her father a loan of a sum of money."

The magistrate said, "Explain the mysteriousness of the fire, Goodman Disborough."

"Certainly, your Excellency. I was burning brush when a spark suddenly traveled across marshy fields and wetted grass, and directed itself immediately toward the house. All the village remarked upon its peculiarity, since it followed fortnights of continued rains. The field was unusually muddy, you see."

Nervously he fidgeted with the brim of his hat, which was held awkwardly in front of him, and I wondered if he felt guilty for all the times Papa had helped him; yet in Papa's one request, Papa was refused. Bitterly, I recalled how Papa had even assisted at the house raising. I wondered if Goodman Disborough felt guilty about that, too.

The magistrate bellowed, "Rachel Ward? Is this another example of your covenanting with the elements?"

"Nay, sir, I—"

"Did your father request a loan from the testifier?"

"Aye, sir. He did."

"And after refusal, did the testifier's house immediately and mysteriously burn?"

"Aye, sir. It did."

"Thank you, Goodman Disborough. Next witness, please."

By now, I was resigned to not only listening without explanation, but also being trapped by gnarled words and twisted events, all of which I was without defense. I could only hope my redemption would come when finally someone spoke in my favor. If someone did.

Next was Bridget White. It was with disgust that I watched her enormous, slovenly figure trot forward, her limping son in tow, and I knew without doubt what Goody White would present as evidence. But I was wrong.

The magistrate said, Goodwife White? You have testimony?"

"I do indeed, sir." The filthy child beside her rubbed his sleeve across his runny nose. Bridget White said, "I was in my cart one day, sir, near to where the accused and her mother was washing clothes, when all of a sudden the horses got spooked by something, run off the road they did, and turned the cart upside down. All was in the most frightful mess you ever did lay your eyes on, with horses bucking and children screaming, and me all the while trying to get that weighty cart off this little one here. And me, a big woman, couldn't for the life of me move that cart! Then all of a sudden, the accused appears in the middle of the road, standing in her *shift,* mind you, like some *ghost,* and water running off her like a drenched rat. Well, hardly could I collect my wits about me over such an amazing sight when suddenly the accused walks over to the cart and lifts it, pretty as you please. With nary a struggle nor breath. Such an unnatural show of strength, I still can nary believe. You'd have to have seen it yourself to believe it, your Excellency."

'Twas my second major surprise. So certain was I that Bridget White would claim me responsible for her child's mangled leg, and so ready was I to leap to my defense by claiming rescue, that all I could do was gape, wide-eyed and disbelieving. Again I was bereft of defense. Bridget White had told the truth, startling as that might be.

The magistrate said, "Rachel Ward? Did events occur such as Goodwife White testifies?"

"Aye, sir," I said, in amazement. "They did."

"And did you show display of unnatural strength?"

"I hardly thought of it at the time, sir, so anxious was I—"

"Did you, or did you not? Answer aye, or nay."

"Aye, sir. I did."

"Thank you, Goodwife White. Before the next witness, the court shall have brief recess for tea. All return to the chamber in one hour."

So now I again sit back in my cell, once more recording feverishly, and just as feverishly wishing my recordings could replace those of the Scribe's. Greatly do I fear history shall show me guilty of my crime with no knowledge of the truth. Future generations shall read the court's testimony, not only for me but for all the others so accused, and they shall remember our village as beset by Devilish forces which have risen up and reigned with terror over once serene hearths and pious hearts. Pray, God, how can I make known what truly occurs? How can I leave witness that words can twist and events can become so misconstrued and that the two together can result in anything seeming possible if truly desired?

I have considered making my own recordings known, to proffer them up as evidence of my innocence, which was my original intent when I began this journal. Yet now my writings contain so many secrets which would only bring even further destruction and tragedy. Nay, I cannot show it. For even were it not to plant seeds of further unhappiness, too well do I see that even my own words can be distorted.

Alas, I must go. My jailer comes for me.

Salem, 17 September 1692, eve

The third round of proceedings filled me with even greater sense of abandonment and showed me just how dire my situation has become.

Phebe Edwards was called to the fore, her smashed hand neatly wrapped with clean white muslin, so as not to detract from her pretty appearance, and her blond curls had clearly been meticulously arranged so as to spill entrancingly from the front of her cap. Undoubtedly Phebe had spent all tea-break grooming herself for just such an angelic appearance. Positioning herself so the light from the window shone most advantageously upon her, she smiled invitingly, and I knew her testimony would be without mercy.

One of the magistrates said, "Phebe Edwards? You are friend of the accused?"

"Friend!" I thought, incredulous. Were I to have friends such as this, I would need no gallows!

Primly, Phebe said, "Aye, sir. I am."

I could have wrung her neck for how sweet she sounded.

The magistrate instructed, "Proceed with your testimony."

Phebe's voice was musical and clear. "Well, sir, the

first I noticed of her witching was when she fashioned a crystal ball."

"A crystal ball, witness?"

"Aye, sir."

"For what purpose?"

"For portending the future, sir."

"Rachel Ward, do you fashion crystal balls for portending the future?"

Lamely, I replied, "Well, sir, I—"

"Do you, or do you not fashion crystal balls? Aye, or nay?"

"Aye, sir. I—" It killed me to see Phebe's victorious smirk. O that I could have related her own eagerness to have me fashion such a device! That she stood here now was only due to her displeasure with the results!

The magistrate asked, "And how did the accused fashion her crystal ball?"

"With an egg, sir," said Phebe, primly. "And a glass bowl."

"Rachel Ward? Did you fashion a crystal ball with an egg and a glass bowl?"

"A *crystal* bowl," I snapped, irritated. Phebe smiled.

The magistrate glared at me. Then he said, "Proceed, Phebe Edwards."

"Well, sir," said Phebe, "the next time I noticed her powers was at the Disborough house-raising. The accused was quite jealous of me for the attention paid to me by someone she wished for her own intended. She called me a 'gurley-gutted Devil'." An audible gasp rose from the chamber. I didn't care. I regretted not one whit what I had called her, and I would have liked to have called it again—right then and there! "And then," continued Phebe, sweetly, "very soon after, while I was watching the framing, one of the ropes most mysteriously slipped and caused my hand to be crushed." With a heart-rending tremor of lips, Phebe proceeded to hold up the evidence. Even the magistrate was touched.

Recovering himself, the magistrate bellowed, "Rachel Ward! Did you verbally attack your friend by calling her a gurley-gutted Devil? And immediately afterwards, was her hand mysteriously crushed?"

If I could have crushed *both* hands, I thought with a fury, I would gladly have done so! Glumly, I murmured, "Aye, sir. I suppose—"

"Phebe Edwards," said the magistrate, with sudden softness, "please be seated. Thank you for your testimony. And now next to testify is Abigail Watts."

A smile passed betwixt Phebe and Abigail as their paths crossed, and I seethed with anger. Too clearly could I see my future unfolding, all caused by small minds, vindictive dispositions and my own life-long neglect of courting favor. Scarcely could I wait for Abigail's testimony.

Preening, Abigail took her place in the exact spot Phebe had vacated, and by the pleased flush on her homely face, I knew she had not slept all night for her eagerness to be the center of attention. Abigail, who always walked in Phebe's pretty shadow, finally had her own opportunity to shine, and it went without saying that she would make the most of it. When the magistrate instructed her to proceed with testimony, Abigail paused just the slightest moment for effect, undoubtedly to insure all eyes and ears were hers and hers alone, and what she then proceeded with was the most astonishing story.

"The accused, sir, constantly appears to me in my rafters, demanding for me to sign my soul to the Devil. She is quite mean in her demands, sir. Sometimes she drools all over me. And she has this wicked laugh that sounds like a shrieking cackle."

My story! My story of Goody Glover and borrowed to now become Abigail's! Once again my wretched visions had come to haunt me!

The magistrate said with concern, "And does the accused present you with threats?"

"O aye, sir," agreed Abigail, readily. "Quite vehement ones. Once she said she would slit my throat if I did not sign Satan's book. Sometimes she fights with me. And once . . . once, she even bit me!"

Slowly Abigail rolled up her sleeve to display a perfect set of teeth marks. And so effectively had she gauged her timing, that the chamber immediately broke into audible gasps and pitiful moans, such gaspings and moanings creating so much disturbance that the magistrate had finally to bang his gavel and command a call for order. I wonder how long it took Abigail to concoct this story. And whom she had coerced into biting her. I know Abigail does not have the nerve, nor the creativity, to have done it herself.

With much satisfaction over her effect, Abigail then calmly re-took her seat, pausing from time to time as she passed each bench to further display her badge of teeth marks to a gaping, curious audience. And by the time she had finally re-seated herself, I knew without doubt I was convicted, sentenced and hung.

Next called to witness, and paraded before me, were the three girls whom I had first encountered in the antechamber, their testimony naturally giving further seal to my supernatural powers, none of which did I even attempt to refute, so clear were the odds against my favor. Thus, it was with rising hope that I heard Deliverance called to testify. Such hope was swiftly shattered.

"You are Deliverance Porter?" asked the magistrate.

"I am, sir," replied Deliverance. Her lips were solemn. I remembered how they looked open in laughter, and it was with a wrenching ache that I recalled all the fun we had once shared.

The magistrate said, "You are friend of the accused?"

"Since childhood, sir."

"A good friend?" prompted the magistrate.

"Her *best* friend, sir."

Deliverance did not look at me, and as fervently as I tried to catch her glance, her eyes fell only upon the magistrate who questioned her. It was my first sense of foreboding.

The magistrate asked, "You have witness to the accused's character?"

"I do, sir."

"Proceed."

"Well, sir, Rachel has always been different from other people. She does not make friends easily. For a long while I felt honored that I had been selected by her to be a friend, for she had so few of them. Recently, though, I have come to realize that I was not so much specially selected as fallen victim by default. You see, sir, I was the only one who *agreed* to be her friend. No one else seemed to like her."

It was with sadness that I realized how little my friendship had meant to Deliverance. All those times we had frolicked and played together, sharing our innermost secrets, I now knew meant nothing at all. Like petals from a dying flower, they had served their purpose and were allowed to fall to the ground, thence to wither and fade. Never again will I trust to others my thoughts and dreams; and my tongue, always closely held, shall be closer still.

The magistrate said, "And why is the accused unliked?"

"I think, sir," said Deliverance, carefully, "'tis because she cares nothing for what other people think. Thus, she does not attempt friendliness or conversation. Nor, when she does speak, does she soften her tongue. She seems simply to say what fills her mind, regardless of its effect upon others."

I remembered then, how starkly opposite Deliverance is from me, how fervently Deliverance courts and needs other people's approval, and how she had once complimented and envied me for my solitary nature. So I understood, then, exactly why Deliverance renounced me. Renouncing secured approval; defending would have defied it. In that one moment, I saw Deliverance's character more clearly than I have ever seen any other. Deliverance cares what people think of her, but she cares not for other people in return.

With a great emptiness did I watch her return to her seat, and the hollowness in my heart was one from which I knew I would never recover. My understanding of her motives neither comforted me nor improved my sad despondency.

With one last breath of hope, I watched Ann walk forward, her small, sweet form pausing quietly beside the table, and so desperately did I need that sweetness that I wanted to run and hug her and bury my face next to hers in sobs to erase my estrangement. Surely Ann would defend me. Surely Ann, who had once turned on all the others like a ferocious lioness, would do so again in my hour of need. But she did not.

She glanced at me, though only briefly, and in that glance there was such pained sorrow that my rising spirits evaporated like mist.

The magistrate said, "You are Ann Sibley?"

"Aye, sir," replied Ann, softly.

"And you have testimony?"

She winced. My heart went out to her. I knew, then, that Ann did not wish to say that which she had to, and I wanted to calm her by reassuring, "That's alright, Ann. I understand."

The magistrate directed, "Proceed, please."

With obvious discomfort, Ann said, "Well, sir, 'twas

after the fortune telling incident that has already been described. The egg which was used by Rachel, sir, was tossed upon the barn floor, and my pet lamb lapped it up. And very soon afterward, sir, that lamb suddenly died. He was such a sweet lamb, sir. I did so dearly love him."

O please, no! Don't hold me responsible for that, too! Not for Ann's lamb!

The magistrate said, harshly, "Rachel Ward? Did the testifier's lamb die after lapping the instrument of your portention device?"

"I . . . I suppose it did, sir."

He instructed, "Proceed with your testimony, Ann Sibley."

She was trembling. "Well, sir, not long after, Rachel pled with me to mix her blood with mine."

To be blood sisters, Ann! Because I liked you so much! Not to taint you!

The magistrate said, "Rachel Ward? Did you plead with the testifier to mix your diabolical blood into hers?"

Miserably, I nodded. "Aye, sir. I did."

He said to Ann, "And did you do as the accused pled?"

"Nay, sir. I . . . I did not."

"And what happened then?"

"Well, sir, you see, she . . . Rachel, sir . . . appeared in the form of a bumblebee and rose up and stung me."

Much as I wanted, I could not despise Ann for what she accused. I know she said so from the belief that her words were correct and proper in the eyes of God. And it is with great despair that I realize Ann truly does believe me a witch. Yet even so, her testimony came with extreme reluctance, and I wondered who prompted her witness. When I saw her solemnly take her seat, I knew. Her mother nodded at her in approval. I remembered, then, how Mama in all her dignity had gone to the Sibleys to beg for food, yet had been rejected. Goody Sibley feels guilty about that rejection. Now she can rationalize it. She can delude herself by saying her rejection is justified becaused in the end 'twas only for the family of a witch. Ann will not recover, though. Ann's heart is tremulous, and she shall always recall this day and regret it, even when matured and old. I wish I could spare her that. I wish I could tell her that what she did was with a heart pious and Godly, and I shall never hold resentment. But I cannot tell her. For I know there shall be no opportunity.

So the first day of my trial has ended. So many have testimony that it requires carriage over into another. Has an accused ever been presented with so many eager to speak in disfavor? If the morrow holds a ray of hope, I cannot think from whom it might be. I told the mute girl that all is lost, that soon there shall be another heap of rags sleeping beside her. When I gave her half my evening bread, having decided my own strength not being worth sustaining, to my immense surprise, her hand squeezed mine. Aye, 'twas only a fleeting squeeze! But 'twas there, I swear on God's Good Book! Pray, God, let that be the ray of hope for which I so yearn.

Salem, 18 September 1692, morn

When the jailer came to collect me, one of the women again murmured, "God be with you," but again I could not determine the source of the voice, for as I turned, all eyes were once more averted from me. So my only comfort was the knowledge that someone cared. I do wish, though, that she had revealed herself. Sorely do I need a touch or some small physical gesture to provide me courage.

In the second row of the court sat Jeremiah, his tall, dark form seated intensely forward on his wooden bench, and when I entered the chamber, my heart gave a short lurch of encouragement. Jeremiah had come. He had not abandoned me. Yet almost as quickly as I saw him, I realized the space beside him lay vacant, his parents being starkly absent, and that absence suddenly weighed on me and made my heart sink again. Why were his parents not there? Had something been revealed in my yesterday's exchange with Goody Corwin, some small spark of memory which had lit in the mind of Jeremiah's mother, causing her to recall the locket and his father to guess the truth? Or had Jeremiah simply told them?

My mind trembled with dismaying thoughts regarding my presumed expectations of Jeremiah's shattered family, but I had scant time to ponder this development, because the first to be called as today's witness was none other than Goodman Glover. Who presented me even greater cause for concern.

His weasely, stoop-shouldered figure shuffled to the fore, and I wondered if as usual, he had been drinking. I prayed so. For it would weaken his testimony and damage its credence. His one good eye rested upon me, sending my flesh crawling as if with spiders, and I dared not even think of what he would testify. Anxiously I glanced at Mama. Her expression was impassive, betraying neither fright nor agitation, so I took a long, deep breath and waited.

The silver-wigged magistrate led the examination. "Goodman Glover?" he said. "You have testimony?"

"Aye, sir. I do."

"Pray, proceed."

The witness's thin lips curled into a smile. Maliciously he savored each word before it was spoken. "The accused," he said, eagerly, "likes watching naked boys. I catched her, I did. Down by the river. When the boys was swimming."

Undoubtedly he felt my humiliation, delighting in the swift, hot color which flushed my cheeks, such flush deepening with the shocked intake of breath echoing from the chamber. Even the magistrate's voice was reproving. "Rachel Ward?" demanded the magistrate. "Do you watch boys swimming unclothed?"

Gluing my eyes to the floor, I dared not learn Jeremiah's reaction. "I . . . er . . . once I did," I mumbled.

"Speak up, Rachel Ward!" ordered the magistrate. "Aye, or nay?"

"Aye, sir."

"Proceed, Goodman Glover."

"The accused fornicated with me." Two beady eyes gleamed, and my head shot up so swiftly, I felt my neck jerk.

"I did not!" I hotly replied. "You defiled—!"

"Begged to join her body with mine," Goodman Glover maintained.

"A lie! 'Tis a lie, you grotesque man! You're the one who—"

"Kept begging me, she did," he interrupted, calmly. "Left me notes, too."

Mama moaned softly as I screamed, "You left the—!"

"And when I refused, she laid her hands on my private parts and—"

"You're a vile, ugly man!"

"—and she squeezed them."

"I squeezed them because—!"

"And she did all this because she wanted to be my wife."

"Never!" I shrieked.

"That's why my wife came to her in visions. My wife knew what the accused wanted."

"I did *not!*"

"She and my dead wife used to cast spells together."

"A lie! A lie!"

"I watched 'em."

"I didn't!"

"Made poppets."

"Nay!"

"Stowed 'em under the bed."

"Nay! Nay!"

"Goodman Bishop found 'em after my wife was convicted. Ask him. He'll tell you."

"You're a vile, filthy man, and I hope God strikes you dead!"

Somewhere in the midst of this ghastly turmoil, I

became aware of the magistrate banging his gavel for order. I could feel the hard grasp of the constable physically restraining me from tearing Goodman Glover from limb to limb, could see tears spilling down Mama's cheeks, could hear the audience clucking and swooning. Yet all this while, Goodman Glover remained calm and unperturbed, his malevolent smirk never fading. How I wanted to smack him! How I wanted to cry out with the explanations to unravel his whole sordid tale! But I could not. Because explanation would lead to his reason for blackmailing me. Whether that blackmail has foot in fact, I do not know, but even in my fury, I knew my own life would not be saved by taking others. All I could do was maintain him as a liar.

The magistrate snapped above the din, "What say you to these accusations, Rachel Ward?"

"I deny them!"

"All?"

"Every last word!"

"The poppets?"

"The poppets are a figment of this repulsive man's imagination!"

No one believed me. One more nail had been pounded into my cross. I no longer cared. Only did I yearn for release from my torture.

Slowly Goodman Glover slinked back to his seat. Mama's color had turned to ash, and though she sat staunchly erect, one hand brushed away her streaming tears. Mercy, wide-eyed and clearly frightened by these proceedings, was then called to the fore; but so terrified was Mercy that her whine was barely audible, and the magistrate had finally to call court into short recess so everyone might collect themselves. Which is why I sit recording when it is not yet noon. And shall be vastly relieved when finally this day is over.

Salem, 18 September 1692, noon

Mercy looked like a snared rabbit when Court resumed. The Chief Justice asked, "Are you Mercy Ward, sister of the accused?"

"Aye, er, aye, sir." Though an octave higher, Mercy's voice was still barely audible. An imposing situation, indeed, for a child of eight.

"Proceed with your testimony."

Tentatively, Mercy asked, "Am I, er . . . am I to tell about the blood?"

"Aye, Mercy Ward. Tell as you previously told the constable."

"O," she said, her thoughts obviously in disarray. "Well, er, you see, sir, one aft we were looking all over for Rachel—Mama and I, that is. Mama and I were the ones, er, looking for her. Aye, I suppose it was both of us. Then I, uh, finally had the idea to look in the barn—that was after I, uh, searched in the kitchen garden, sir, and the—"

"Pray, stick to the pertinent facts, Mercy Ward," ordered the magistrate.

"O. Well, er, I guess you want to know the part about the barn. Is that the part I should tell? Well, you see, that's where I, uh, finally found her. Rachel. In the barn. In the loft. And . . . and she had Mama's sugar bowl, only she had taken all the sugar out, and . . . and she had cut herself—with Papa's scythe, she said—and . . . and with the blood and the sugar bowl she was making some sort of crystal ball. I guess it was a crystal ball. 'Twas something I think to, er, tell the future. At least that's what she said. Isn't that how it was, Rachel?"

Two wide, appealing brown eyes gazed to me for confirmation, yet all I could do was inwardly groan and manage a weak affirmative nod.

The Chief Justice asked, "Rachel Ward? Do you admit to your sister's testimony?"

Feebly, I agreed. "Aye, sir. It was as she tells it."

The magistrate then ordered, "Continue, Mercy Ward."

"You mean, er, the part about the pact?" asked Mercy, timidly.

"As you told the constable," reminded the magistrate.

"O. Aye, sir. Well, uh, when Rachel was making this crystal ball—the one I told you about—she was talking to Goody Glover. She was making some sort of pact with her. It was a pact, wasn't it, Rachel? Isn't that what you called it? See, sir. That was it. And she did it lots of other times, too. I heard her. Really, I did. But I never saw Goody Glover."

Mercy, docile as always, followed instructions to the letter, eager to be both helpful and truthful, yet I could not help but feel irritation at her lack of insight as to the impact of her testimony or of its import.

The Chief Justice said, "Rachel Ward? Did you make a pact with a known witch? With someone a declared instrument of the Devil?"

"Aye, sir," I said, wearily, "I did."

"You may return to your seat, Mercy Ward. I now

call your mother."

At last the time had come for Mama. Despondent, I resigned myself for the last nail in my cross. But, curiously, Mama rose to plead, "Begging the court's generosity, sir. I would ask to be the last witness. Pray, grant such wish as the accused's mother." A butterfly of hope fluttered in my breast, but I forced myself to calm it, not wanting to provide myself any false expectations.

So then Jeremiah was called—he was to originally be the final testifier—and while I searched his grave expression meticulously, in it I could not detect a sign of the nature of his testimony. Clearly, though, he was still shaken by the news I had related to him and, I presumed, by the testimony advanced by Goodman Glover. I tried not to think about Goodman Glover.

The Chief Justice said, "Jeremiah Moore? You are a friend to the accused?"

Jeremiah's voice was solemn. Staring directly at me, he said, "Aye, sir. I am."

The Chief Justice said, "You have testimony?"

"Aye, sir. I do."

I held my breath. My gaze was locked into Jeremiah's. Fervently I prayed. Jeremiah was my final hope.

The Chief Justice ordered, "Proceed."

"I wish to speak in her *defense,* sir," advanced Jeremiah, clearly; and so suddenly filled with emotion were my eyes that I had to lower them, for fear I would weep. "The accused is misjudged," continued Jeremiah. In his sureness and certainty, I found warm comfort. "I have heard testimony of her character, and it is in gross error. Not friendless, but a good friend, is she. A loyal friend. A friend who would even—" His voice caught, so I looked up at him, which gave him courage to proceed—"a friend who would even risk her life for another."

The Chief Justice said, "Pray, explain your statement, Jeremiah Moore."

"Nay, sir. I cannot. But I presume my own character to be above reproach. So if it be so, let my character stand as testimony to the purity of the accused."

"No character is above reproach in these times," reminded the Chief Justice, harshly.

"Aye, sir. 'Tis so. 'Tis so for all of us in this chamber. That is why I beseech you to listen and know that the evil in us all far surpasses that of the accused."

Startled, the Chief Justice demanded, "Do you advance the accused's evil to be less than the court's?"

Take care, Jeremiah, I breathed. Pray do not convict yourself, as well. Too easily can one be bound in chains and tossed into Hell.

"I advance, sir," said Jeremiah, firmly, "that the accused has no more potential for evil than do any of us in this chamber. And I think, sir, even less. She is *not* a witch. She is my friend, and a truer friend I defy any of you to present. A witch would not protect another selflessly. A witch would not aid another in need, as Rachel Ward has done for me. Aye, so Rachel Ward has done often in my life. And a witch would not proffer such aid while asking nothing in return—save for appreciation. Which I now publicly acknowledge."

Thank you, Jeremiah. Thank you for that acknowledgement. 'Tis too late, but not too little, and it shall comfort me on my walk to the gallows. This one moment shall erase every trace of bitterness and pain from all that has happened, and God in heaven shall bless you, as shall I when soon He receives me. All this I told to Jeremiah through my gaze, and I think he heard me.

The Chief Justice said, tonelessly, "You may be seated, Jeremiah Moore." He was unimpressed. Nothing of the fluttering within my own breast was detectable in his, or in any other of my jury. "I now call the accused's mother," said the Chief Justice, clearly anxious to be over with the proceedings.

No longer did I care what Mama would say. I had had my taste of salvation, and nothing more could perturb me. How surprised I was to see Mama visibly upset, and how startled I was to hear her voice tremble. Poised Mama with her cool reserve was in a state of emotion, which I was soon to understand, and what followed next was even more startling than the testimony of Goodman Glover.

The Chief Justice asked, "Martha Ward? Are you mother of the accused?"

"I am," answered Mama, fighting for composure.

"And have you testimony?"

"I do, sir." Even before receiving the order to proceed, Mama launched into her testimony. "My daughter is no more a witch than I, your Excellency. Aye, she was once possessed. Plagued by the vision of that evil man's now dead wife—that man there, in the third row, to whom I point. But I shall explain more of him later. Pray, sir, hear me out. All the testimony that has been entered into this court—there is logical reason for every piece of it. Reason way beyond witchery. Prayers are stumbled over as result of a young girl's imagination. Foreign tongues—if that's what they be—are merely the incoherent babblings of a child the victim of terrifying visions. Crystal balls? What girl in this room has not engaged in fantasy over the identity of their future intended? As for mysterious storms, not only Goodman English's roof was taken, but fences and stables of many another villager. Pacts with a witch? Nay, pacts with visions to halt tormenting her and return to her her sanity. Pray, sir, hear me! Do not avert your head in disinterest! Aye, I *am* her mother!

But who to know the accused better than one who gave her breath and watched that breath continue hour by hour? All of you, give me your ears! Verbal attacks upon others? Which one of you has never vented anger? Which one is innocent of a glaring gaze or sharpened words? Are we all to be responsible for misfortune befalling one to whom our anger has been directed? I challenge you! Turn to a neighbor with whom you have ever entered argument, then say that neighbor is a witch for what misfortune has befallen you! Hear my words—all of you! And think in your hearts whether you yourself could not have been equally accused!"

So still was the chamber, breath would have echoed like a felled tree. For the first time since my arrest, hope burned like a bright ember. And, of all places, it came from Mama! Uneasily everyone shifted on their benches. Even the imposing length of magistrates took note. Would I—miracle of all miracles!—be acquitted? Had Mama's words struck a chord of sufficient doubt? Only Goody Bishop sat undaunted and erect.

A small frown of pensiveness creased the Chief Justice's brow—a pensiveness which sent me into an elated spin. Quietly he asked, "Is your testimony complete, Martha Ward?"

Mama, weary, wan, but not yet spent, continued. "Nay, sir. I have one more thing."

"Proceed."

"The most damaging testimony to character was that advanced by Goodman Glover. None of it had truth. Pray, listen while I explain the motives of this vile and wicked man. Once—before I was wed—I was in a state of being penniless, destitute and without dowry. No one would have me. Thrown into debtor's prison was I, along with my parents; until eventually, through the court's foresight, I was released to earn a means to pay off our debt, and through that means I fell into the clutches of this repulsive man, for that is when I came to Salem as a servant. Servant to Jacob Ward and his wife. Friendless, with every pence saved to secure my parents' release, I fell under the silky tones of Goodman Glover. Having fallen under such tones, I met him in the woods, as he has accused my daughter. Such secrecy was at his own request, it not being suitable for a servant to receive a formal caller. Why did he not tell all this in his testimony? Because he would not admit to the crime of inveigling my affections. And so despondent was my spirit during the time of those meetings that I allowed him to caress me. Nay, exceed caress. Not even to my husband have I admitted this regrettable story. For no sooner had I realized my mistake, than my master's wife died, and my master, in all his goodness and mercy, took me as his wife. Penniless and indebted as indeed was my condition. So you see, for all of this, Goodman Glover has never forgiven me. For a rejection not able to admit, he could take revenge only through my daughter."

Drained, Mama leaned against the table, the chamber hushed and stupified by such self-imposed humiliation. Wretched, I cursed myself for every evil thought I had ever directed toward her. I myself would never have had courage for such sacrifice—nay, I was not even a daughter worthy of it. But all is not finished. For what happened next was nothing short of astounding.

With one last surge of strength, Mama straightened, took a deep breath, and again stood erect before the chamber. Her voice was controlled yet full of emotion.

"There is one more thing I must tell this court," she said, "and I must tell it so the court may recognize this man for the vile creature that he is, so the court may realize his despicable nature and the depraved accusations he makes against my daughter; and in realizing so, the court may thus have mercy upon my daughter's tortured soul for the vileness he has made her suffer. That thing I must tell is the reason I wed my husband so young and so swiftly. I was with child. My husband, to whom I owe beyond any means of appreciation, rescued me not only from debtor's prison, but also and unknowingly, from the state of unwed motherhood. And the father of the child I carried was that depraved man in this chamber, Goodman Glover."

Mama did not move. Her erect posture swayed slightly, her head turned so that her gaze fell upon me, and in her tear-filled eyes, I read a plea. "Forgive me," they begged, and they spoke of love, and caring and sorrow. But so loudly did my ears ring with my pounding heart, I could scarce hear their meaning. Goodman Glover was my father. Only three people in the chamber knew the full import of that admission—Mama, Jeremiah and me. It meant I was carrying my father's child.

My blood drained from my head and turned to ice, and I felt my jailer catch me as I staggered, my clanging chains deafening the roar within my ears. Then suddenly, from the depths of the stupified chamber, a voice shot out like a cannon, a voice which was distinct, confident and nasal.

"How did that first wife die?" it demanded.

'Twas Goody Bishop. And the unexpectedness of the question sent Mama jerking her head back with a start.

"Why . . . why from a fever," answered Mama, in confusion.

"It's cause?" demanded Goody Bishop.

"Why, I . . . I don't know."

"Swift and unexplained, was it not?"

"I . . . er, why, aye. 'Twas."

"And did you not ply her with potions?"

"I . . . I gave her some herbs. She was a rather frail woman, and—"

"And did you not sit beside her bed and chant?"

"Psalms. I . . . I used to—"

"Psalms only, Goodwife Ward? Did you not chant other things, as well?"

"I . . . uh . . . aye, there were some small tunes from my childhood . . ."

Goody Bishop's eyes glittered with piety and justice. "Did you not, Goodwife Ward, cast a spell upon your master's wife? Did you not ply your herbs and chants to cause her sudden death? Did you not ply those herbs and spells to provide you a husband for your bastard child?"

No sooner had such stunning accusations been made than Goody Bishop wheeled to face the Chief Justice. "Hear me, sir! One witch has begat another! A silver tongue that wheedles a guilty daughter's innocence is the self-same silver tongue which caused a wife to die to provide a husband! Does anyone present not remember the unexpected death of the first Goodwife Ward? Was anyone here not stunned to learn Jacob Ward had wed his debt-ridden servant?"

Daniel colored purple. His face was twisted in hate so vicious, he was capable of slaughter. In the next pandemonious moments, Daniel leapt to his feet and angrily cried, "I remember! I remember! This woman killed my mother!" Mercy, terrified, screamed, "Mama! Mama! I want my Mama!" The entire chamber was on its feet, the gavel of the Chief Justice banging futilely, and before my very eyes, Mama, aghast and sobbing, was dragged through the door by a rough constable, while a frantic Mercy was restrained by Daniel. In moments I, too, was dragged from the chamber, into the antechamber, there to await decision upon my trial.

So I have sat, throughout the entire noonday meal, in this antechamber, detained while my fate is decided, a fate to which I am resigned, while wretchedly I attempt to make sense of this sickening disaster. So tumultuous are my reeling and floundering thoughts, my head feels as if 'tis being split apart by some cracking mallet. Papa is not my real father. From Goodman Glover my blood does derive. And I carry my father's child.

Behind me, now, the court refills. Achingly I hear the noise of the magistrates' chairs scraping across the floor. I hear the excited chatter of the audience, jabbering over a morn of unexpected surprises. And it is with a sick heart that I realize when I am returned to my jury, Mama shall not be present as witness.

Salem, 18 September 1692, eve

I write in haste, for Mama needs me. When I was returned to the court chamber, the last time to be stood before gaping eyes, the Chief Justice banged his gavel for order, then turned ferociously toward me and growled, "Rachel Ward. You are convicted of the crime of compacting with the Devil."

His words little affected me. Too severe was the evidence for anything else.

"Do you wish to confess?" he demanded.

"Nay, sir," I said, softly. Then I steadied myself, for if I am to go to my grave, it will be with the certainty that I have done nothing wrong. "I am not a witch," I said, clearly. "And neither is my mother."

At that, another uproar ensued, causing the Chief Justice to once more bang his gavel while bellowing:

"Rachel Ward! Your sentence is death! By hanging!"

So oft had I heard those words in my despondent envisionings, I did not think they would move me. But they did. They hit me with a jolt. And when I took a deep breath, I savored it, wondering if anyone in that chamber realized what miracle exists in such a simple thing as breathing.

Desperately my eyes searched for Jeremiah, grasping for strength, wondering if he realized the bond we now had in common, yearning for his comfort and understanding. Alas, his bench was vacant. He had not stayed for my conviction. The pain was too great, his new knowledge too close to experience, and I forgave him. In the bench behind, the weasely form of Goodman Glover had shrunk to be indiscernible within the gawking sea of faces, and his pinched pallor was ghostly and green. How much he learned that he had not known prior, I do not know. Were he to learn I carried his child, I was certain it would have destroyed him, and in that, I gained satisfaction.

All else in that sea of faces I do not remember. Too close to death was I to pick out individual gasps and gleams, for all I savored was the miracle of breathing.

I shall not, however, think of it any longer. I have more disturbing things to consider. When I was returned to my cell, I found Mama—proud, dignified Mama—chained, broken and weeping. My current mission must be to console her and to provide her with strength for what lies ahead.

Salem, 20 September 1692, aft

For two days I have not written due to all that has occurred.

Mama is so broken and dispirited, that it is as if she is the child and I the mother. How wretched am I for the past griefs I have caused her and for how I have misjudged her, all the while thinking her affection was nothing for me and all for Mercy. How much she has sacrificed in my cause, and what guilt it brings me.

The first eve we spoke but little, for Mama continually wept over all the mistakes she has made. I thought my own mistakes to hold even greater enormity, having been such an ungrateful daughter. But Mama maintained that, nay, she was the one at fault, that her misjudgements were horrendous, and that even the trial she handled badly. Not my salvation was she, she wept, but my hangman.

How it disturbed me to see her once composed, controlled demeanor fall to pieces, now a shattered old woman. The rock I had so long depended upon was no longer solid and firm, and as swiftly as if she had been taken in death, the Mama I had once known was gone from me. Erect shoulders now slumped and heaved with defeat. Clear, steady eyes were shot with pain and were red and swollen from tears. And capable, strong hands now trembled as if with palsy while they nervously clutched and unclutched at disheveled skirts. But the outward signs were not near so disturbing as her inward breaking and the knowledge that in spirit Mama was lost and changed forever.

At first her sudden deterioration was disorienting to me, and I knew not how to react, save for a fear that began to envelop me as well. With Mama's confidence went mine also. However, my own fears eventually subsided with a resurgence of the strength I have had to develop, and fortunately that strength began to serve me. Thus, God provideth where He also taketh away.

With my own spoon, I helped Mama to eat, ladling suppawn from the chamber's unappetizing bowl and holding it to Mama's lips, all the while encouraging—nay, pleading—her to take sustenance which I knew would be sorely needed. With my skirts, I wiped her despondent tears. With my hands, I held her trembling fingers to implore composure.

About her public confession, there was still so much I wanted to know yet feared to ask for dread of causing her further disquiet; but finally on the second afternoon, Mama's grief appeared more subdued, so I quietly began to venture my questions.

"Mama," I asked, gently. "Why did Daniel never mention that you were once a servant? I know why Papa didn't tell, for Papa would not have wanted to hurt you. But why did Daniel never say?"

Mama's face was the color of gray lye. Her eyes were dull, but she did not seem to mind talking about the past. In truth, I think it began to be a catharsis for her while we talked, such talk allowing her to emerge from the shadow which has always hung over her for the fear that her mistakes would someday be discovered. With tremulous voice, Mama said, "Daniel was so young then. And I was with him and your father as servant for such a short time before his mother died. I don't think Daniel really realized I was a servant. I don't think he realized it until morning last."

"But he knew about the debtor's prison."

"Aye. After your father and I wed, we journeyed to release my parents and took Daniel with us. 'Twas a mistake taking Daniel—I knew it even then. But your father was adamant, wanting his son to learn about the ways of the world. He said he wanted to teach Daniel responsibility by lesson. 'Twas then that Daniel learned how I, too, had once been in that prison, because my parents told him. And in the effusiveness of their gratitude for their release—release, which, of course, came through your father's charity—Daniel also learned of my lack of dowry and my spinsterhood. 'Twas impressionable information for a boy of five. Sadly, it was information never forgot."

Impulsively I squeezed her hand to reassure her of my own affection. "Why," I curiously asked, "does Daniel so resent you? Was the dowry really so important to him?"

"Nay. Not at first. At first his resentment was because he loved his own mother so much. You must understand it was quite a shock to Daniel when she died so suddenly. He had great difficulty accepting it, having so idolized his mother. Then, too, she was quite different than I. A very gentle, kindly woman, she was, and not only Daniel, but your father adored her. But she was also a frail, sickly woman, and—I don't mean this uncharitably—I think there were times when she was a burden to your father. Because of her delicate nature. In a second wife, I think your father wanted someone of sturdier stock. As was I. As for Daniel, he began to resent any affection your father showed for me, feeling such affection was a rejection of his own mother. And as the years passed, his resentment began to take other shapes and to search for other reasons. Reasons which had no foundation in fact. Such as my squandering your father's money. I never did as such, Rachel. Truly, I never intended so. But eventually, Daniel's resentment began to poison your father, driving a wedge between us. Daniel was always very close to your father, you see, and your father listened to him."

My next question I ventured with my heart in my throat, so important was it to me to be absolved of guilt. "So 'twas not I who tore the family apart?"

"Nay. At least not in ways you could control. You must understand how soon you came after the first wife's death. It was hard for both your father and Daniel to accept another family then. Much easier was it years later with Mercy. And Mercy was a more obedient temperament than you."

"Not as somber? Or unsociable?" I pressed.

"Aye," replied Mama, honestly, and though her honesty stung, I could not fault her for it.

Such a whole history of me that I have never learned before. Thirstily I wanted to know it all. "What about your parents?" I asked. "What happened to them?"

"We took them back to Dedham—which was my home. They lived with one of my uncles, but only for a short time. They died soon after from diseases they had contracted in prison."

"And . . . and Goodman Glover?" I ventured, tentatively. "What finally happened with him?"

"O Rachel, what a fool I was. 'Twas so unfair of me to never have told your father. All these years I've lived with the agony that he would learn. Yet if I *had* told him, he would never have married me. I was so desperate then. Our farm and every last wooden trencher was taken as result of my father's mismanagement. I found myself as spinster servant woman with no knowledge of how I would ever retrieve my parents from debtor's prison. And as such, I fell under the soothing spell of Isaac Glover. True, he is a vile man. But at first he did not appear so. So charming he can be—aye, Rachel, he truly can be. And so estranged was I from all that I knew that I clutched onto his soft charm like a helpless babe because he made me feel valuable and desired. If it had not been for your father's wife dying, I dread to think what would have become of me. But such events saved me. For a while afterward, Isaac Glover menaced me by threatening to tell of my horrendous transgression. But I did not fear him. I knew he wouldn't tell. The crime of inveigling affections would be his as well as mine. Besides, he was too proud to admit to dalliance with a servant girl. So he wed Sarah Walling, who was a scold and a nag and made his life miserable. But I always knew his revenge would come. And so it did, years later, at the trial of my daughter."

Nay, revenge came even before the trial, I thought; but I did not remind her. No purpose would be served by further suffering, nor by remembrance of how I had allowed myself to be so repulsively used. Yet through all this conversation Mama had continued to refer to Papa as my father, though now I knew he was not. I had to put my knowledge into words.

"Papa," I said softly, "is not my real father, Mama. Why do you still speak of him as such, now that I know the truth?"

My heart went out to her for the pain my statement caused, yet no longer could I hide behind a cloak of concealment. Too near is our end to take refuge in deceit.

Mama said staunchly, "I shall always think of my husband as your father." I knew she spoke the truth.

Was it not Papa who once told me some things are best left unsaid? Perhaps some are also best left unrecognized, else we shall destroy ourselves with our grief.

I had to ask of Mama, "Did Goodman Glover know? That he is my father by blood if not by name?"

"Nay," said Mama quietly, "not until today."

So that explained his sick reaction. He knew he had defiled his child, and with that knowledge he must live, to accept God's vengeance. I wished I could communicate to him that by his depravity he had begat yet another child, and I thought again of the life inside me. I wondered what twisted shape it would take, were it to survive. Perhaps 'tis best all our sordidness shall be snuffed out with the noose. God, in his infinite wisdom, has provided us our only escape.

Mama said, "I think his wife knew, though. I think 'tis why she tortured you. She came upon us once, in the woods, after we had exchanged . . . some intimacies. And from the guilt in my demeanor, I am certain she realized our assignation was more than just a chance encounter. Afterward, when they were wed, as was I, Sarah Glover was the only one to remark upon the swiftness of my birthing. Did she ever mention as such to you, Rachel, in her threats?"

I knew, then, why Mama had been so constant in her inquiry as to whether Goody Glover had spoken, and of what Goody Glover had said. And I knew, too, of the reason Goody Glover had fashioned me into a poppet so as to cast a spell, and why my eyes had been the last she had sought before she had died, at long last able to communicate her suspicions and her resentment which had run so deep and been so long harbored. How she must have hated me! Would she, I wondered, have become a scold and a rail had she not had cause for being so, had she acquired a husband who treated her with respect and affection. How queerly are we all fashioned by our circumstances.

"Nay, Mama," I replied. "She told me nothing. I am not even certain now how much I imagined and how much held truth. Sometimes I think the terror was of my own making, and the visions of my fancy. Perhaps I was merely the victim of my conscience and the fears of our neighbors."

Mama did not believe me. "You were possessed," she said. "Goody Glover found retaliation for my sins in you, her husband's daughter."

'Twas the first and only time Mama had openly spoken of my parentage, and I realize why even her mind refuses to acknowledge it. It is too sickening to speak.

Quietly, I asked, "What happened the day you went to see him, Mama? When you went to ask for my mercy?"

She paused for the slightest fraction of an instant before saying, "He threatened me. And he forced his way with me. Else he would expose you as a witch."

Her voice was dull and leaden, and whether it concealed emotion, or whether all emotion had already died, I do not know. As for me, I gasped. On my behalf, Goodman Glover had Mama as well as me ensnared in his vengeful net. Mama, poised, self-assured Mama, had fallen victim to a depraved man's lunacy. For the sake of her daughter.

Shuddering, I ventured, "And Goody White? Why did you allow Goody White to take over our home? And at a time when so much else was being lost?"

"'Twas another misguided attempt to save you," Mama replied, and so wretched did I feel for all the hatred I had once directed toward her, she all the while protecting me, that I did not think I could bear another word.

"How?" I asked, weakly.

"I feared she would use her child's mangled leg to accuse you of witching," Mama said. "Too little did I realize she would use an occurrence even more convincing. You see, Rachel, since the start of your visions, I feared all would come to this."

I wondered if Mama realized all the hate I had once communicated and what she thought of it. For a moment I thought of explaining that hatred, and begging forgiveness, but I did not; such explanation would be not a catharsis, but a wound, a wound which would fester and never heal were it to be opened and examined. Whatever Mama thinks of my past actions shall remain unspoken, therefore hopefully forgotten, and in our days remaining I shall try to make it up to her.

Two days now have thus seen Mama and me sitting side by side, bound by our mutual chains on the chill, damp earthen floor, and for all the disagreeableness of our circumstances, we have never been closer either in body or spirit. Sadly for these two nights that have passed, for these two morns, for these two noons, Papa has not been to visit, nor has Mercy. I do not pretend to understand their motives. I can only hope Mercy, Mama's beloved, is being prevented from her desperate desire by a brother filled with irrational hatred. I can only think that Papa is wracked by tormented knowledge of events which occurred before he was wed, and for that I am disappointed in him. I had thought Papa capable of greater understanding. To Mama, I do not speak of this. Yet too sharply do I feel her pain, for too well do I know the sting of desertion.

The mute girl becomes a salve for me, providing distraction from both Mama's and my sufferings, and gives me the opportunity to concentrate upon some subject which does not hurt. I offered her part of my bread this morn. Then I asked her her name, once more hoping she would enter into an utterance, but it did not surprise me that she did not respond.

Softly, I cajoled, "You have such pretty hair. Does she not have pretty hair, Mama? Even though 'tis matted, I see it still shine. Truly I can." I started to remark that "Someday soon, when I am in Heaven, I shall send you down a comb so your lovely hair can be soft and silky as it once was," but I stopped myself from such remark. By unspoken agreement, neither Mama nor I refer to the future, because it is too depressing. Instead, I said, "Pray, your name at least tell me. So I have something to call you by."

She did not reply. Her dark, vacant eyes never moved from the wall before her. No matter. I shall continue to speak to her, with me providing both sides of conversation, much like one does with a puppy.

I go now to another occurrence, which was Jeremiah's visit. But wait! The jailer comes now with our evening meal, and I must help Mama to eat.

Salem, 20 September 1692, eve

Of Jeremiah's visit, I shall now tell.

His appearance this aft was entirely without expectation and caught me by much surprise. Upon arriving in the antechamber, I discovered he had wheedled himself into the jailer's better graces by carrying some brandy as a gift, and though I was brought merely journey cake, I was soon appeased for my lesser present by the jailer's drunken good spirits which allowed Jeremiah and I to be alone without disturbance. And eventually, from beyond our antechamber door, we heard a wheezing snore, telling us Jeremiah's brandy had been aptly appreciated.

To my great relief, there was no awkwardness in Jeremiah's speech, and when he crossed the chamber to greet me, he smiled and held my two chained hands betwixt his own.

"How do you fare?" he asked, quickly, and while there was concern in his voice, there was no pity. Had there been pity, I think I would have broken.

"I do well," I lied. He knew I lied, yet he smiled reassuringly, which gave me strength.

"I've been a fool," he said. "I shall not even ask you to forgive me."

"Your apology came at my trial," I told him. "'Twas much more than I had ever hoped."

"Nay," he maintained, firmly. "You should have hoped for even more. Always I thought I had good judgement. Always I considered myself level-headed, conscientious, and acting with what was socially proper and justified. I was none of those things."

"Nay, Jeremiah. Pray, don't so chastise yourself. You were no different than anyone else. I . . . I just wanted you to be, that's all."

"And I shall be, Rachel! I shall! I promise you that!"

He put his arms around me then, and hugged me, my chains cutting across his chest as I returned his hug, but if the chains hurt him, he did not remark upon it.

"How I admire you," he said into my hair. "What strength you have shown."

"You have strength, too, Jeremiah. Strength to admit you were wrong. Not many are capable of that."

"But only after so much damage was done. Is it damage, Rachel? Do you still care for me? Pray, say you do! I always thought I had such a generous heart, but yours is enormous. Selfless. O that mine were so!"

"Jeremiah! Could I ever *not* care for you? I have since you helped me learn my letters. And *your* heart is generous, too. Merely in a different way than mine, that's all. How I always yearned for the trust you have in people, your openness. You shall always be a success in this world, Jeremiah, do you know that? You'll be a success because everyone likes you. Not as I am considered—always labelled peculiar."

"Peculiar only to those too narrow to see. Unique, Rachel. Unique and special is what you are."

I could not keep the bitterness from my tone as I replied, "Uniqueness is not acceptable in this world, Jeremiah. One must be harmonious with the herd. As you have witnessed two days past."

He pulled away from me then, staring down at me, his hands on my shoulders. And when he answered, his voice was as bitter as mine. "These witch trials have turned us all inside out."

"Aye, they have. Mama is so broken I do not even recognize her. 'Tis a malicious world indeed when a woman's life can be torn asunder by another woman's whim. I speak of Goody Bishop, Jeremiah. Goody Bishop who has positioned herself as judge, jury and executioner of us all."

"I know of whom you speak. But what of *you,* Rachel? What shall *you* do?"

"I?" I asked, confused.

"Aye, *you.* Shall you now confess?"

Stunned, I could scarce believe his question. "To witching?" I gasped. "Jeremiah! Pray don't say you still think me a witch!"

"Nay, never! You are no more a witch than I! But confessing as such can save you from the gallows."

"Confession to a lie?" I spat, contemptuously. "Tis what Goody Bishop and all the others would have me do! Me, and all others like me! They would wish to forever ostracize us so they might hold us up as visual examples of the power of the Devil! Aye, much more would they prefer *that* alternative than their precious example lost to the gallows!"

"But you could *live,* Rachel. You'd be alive!"

"For what living, pray tell? Nay, Jeremiah. Even I do not possess strength to exist under a label which is despised, feared and shunned. And even had I such strength, I would not do so out of principle. Rather would I meet the gibbet with honesty than escape through the weakness of a lie."

Gently Jeremiah's sunburnt hands ran down my arms, caressing them, and he said softly, "I did not think you would betray your principles."

Those soft words provided me all the courage I would ever need, not only for this lifetime, but my next, and with them I know I shall no longer fear my fate but shall go to meet it with the honor and dignity I have so desperately grappled to maintain. To do less would betray not only myself, but Jeremiah, and God.

Swiftly, I said, "Tell me about your parents, Jeremiah. What have you done with the locket? What has become of it all?"

The pain was evident in his face, and he again pulled me toward him, this time to conceal that pain. "I had to do nothing," he softly said, his voice breaking. "The Indian servant returned for her lost keepsake, and her burden was too great to carry. She told my mother everything."

Thus, I knew why his parents had not returned to the trial. Saddened, I asked, "What . . . what happened?"

"My mother's heart is broken. As is my father's. They lie in separate chambers, weeping. The old Indian tends to my mother but cannot console her. I know not what is to happen."

The desperateness of the situation overwhelmed me, so I buried my head deeper into his chest, asking nothing further, offering no words of consolation, for there was nothing I could say or do that would help. Compassion, by holding, was all that I could offer.

Jeremiah said, "I'm sorry, Rachel. Sorry I did not believe you."

"I know, Jeremiah."

"I shall never doubt you again."

Miserably, I thought, "You shan't have opportunity!" But I did not say so.

He pulled back from me then, gently, and smiled into my eyes. "I have good news," he said. "Goodman Glover is no longer with us."

'Twas the first he had spoken of my own private

tragedy, and the mere speaking gave me a jolt, much less the information. Surprised, I asked, "Where did he go?"

"To where the devil has taken him. He has flung himself from a tree, and the Lord's mercy snapped his neck, leaving him as Satan's fodder. I think not many shall weep."

Certainly not I, I thought, bitterly. I only regret his retribution was not slower and more painful, but I shall not dispute God's plan. Thank you, God, for allowing me to go to the gallows with a lighter heart, never doubting your justness in all things reverent.

Jeremiah held me again, tenderly, and I knew he was thinking of my child and how near my circumstances were to his own. His hand, as it ran through my hair, moved with sympathy, but sympathy merely increased my misery; suddenly I realized that if Jeremiah looked at me in pain that moment, I would not be able to endure it.

Swiftly I said, "I love you, Jeremiah. I have always loved you. I want you to remember that, and that in spirit I shall always be with you. And I want you to tell Ann, too, that I forgive her. Will you do that for me, Jeremiah? I shan't want Ann to live in sorrow, for I know she did what she felt was right and just. Pray, Jeremiah, tell all that I forgive. I shan't want to leave any bitterness behind. Too much bitterness have we all already tasted. And say a prayer, too, Jeremiah, that God shall soon remove this hatred and fear that have so divided us."

Fortunately my jailer returned then, having awakened from his wheezing slumber, for my voice broke, and the strain would have been too great had I remained. I could smell the brandy on the jailer's breath as he led me away, my chains clanging against the rutted floor.

It was with reluctance that Jeremiah forced himself to release me, and he called out—"Do not despair!"—as he watched me go.

"Aye," I murmured quietly, and could not bear to turn to see him one last time. I wish to remember him as I knew him best, not bidding me farewell in the antechamber of a prison, but with his easy smile as we raced across a pasture.

Thus it was with a heavy heart that I returned to Mama, the mute girl and my wretched cell, wondering what shall happen to them after I am gone.

Asea, 23 September 1692

Scarce do I know where to start.

Evening last, in the dead of night, while Mama slept with her head upon my shoulder, I suddenly heard the door creak open. So dark was the chamber, however, being lit only by the small shaft of moonlight coming from the tall, barred window, that at first I thought the creak to be due to a rat. Then I heard a frantic whisper.

"Rachel? Rachel, are you here?"

I thought I was dreaming! 'Twas Jeremiah! Surely it could not be so!

"Rachel?" it repeated, urgently. "Rachel, are you here?"

"Jeremiah?" I breathed. "Is it you?"

In seconds the door flew open, then closed. I could make out his tall dark form stumbling over sleeping heaps of rags. Sweet heavens! What was he doing?

"Over here!" I said in a whisper, throwing off Mama's head and jolting her confusedly awake. "What do you do, Jeremiah? Are you insane—"

"Hush!" he softly ordered, suddenly beside me. In his hands were the jailer's keys, and he was fumbling with them to find the one to my irons. Hurriedly he explained, "The brandy. I left another for the jailer early this eve. For hours I've waited, thinking he'd never fall into stupor! But I shall explain all later. We must hasten! We haven't much time!"

"Angels above, Jeremiah! You shall find yourself amongst us!"

"Of that, I have no intent!" he replied, still fumbling to find a key that fit. "Now pray, hush! Else you shall awaken the others."

So tight was my throat throughout this frantic search for keys, that while the search required no more than a minute, in the black darkness and with the panic of what could befall us all, it seemed to require an eternity. How thankful I was for Mama's disorientation. She seemed to realize not at all what was occurring. By the time Jeremiah at long last released my irons, and I finally heard that blessed small click, my heart was pounding so frantically, I thought the whole chamber should reverberate with its thunder. Swiftly, Jeremiah turned to Mama, releasing her as well.

Nearly hysterical, I said, "Where shall we go? What shall we do? They shall find us!"

"Nay," whispered Jeremiah, as he rapidly pulled me to my feet. "I have a ship. Now, make haste! No more questions!"

I thought I would never get Mama to the door, so confused was she and so feeble in spirit, and I am certain she wanted only to lie in that filthy spot to die, thinking life held nothing else for her. Thus, Jeremiah and I had to half support and half carry her over the sleeping heaps of our neighbors, and when in what seemed like eons we finally reached the door, I was ready to instantly bolt, Mama in tow, and would have, had I not suddenly heard a soft voice behind me.

"Susannah," it said.

Startled, I froze. 'Twas the same voice which had

before bid "God be with you." Who was it? Which woman had shown me her compassion? Was she now to reveal herself?

"My name is Susannah," it repeated.

Astonished, I realized it was the mute girl! She had spoken!

From the corner of a far bench, the girl's dark eyes were turned toward me, pleading. Hastily I made a decision.

"Jeremiah! We have to take her!"

"Nay! There's not time!"

"But we can't just leave her!"

"Would you have us take the others, as well?"

"Just her, Jeremiah! Please! She was my only friend! I can't go without her!"

I thought Jeremiah would strangle me on the spot—else swiftly shove me back inside and leave me to my insanity. But to his everlasting credit, Jeremiah swiftly stepped over two sleeping bodies, lifted the girl, threw her over his shoulder and was back in the corridor, fastening closed the door.

Between Mama and the mute girl, I feared we should never make it out of that prison, me tugging on Mama who kept resisting, while the mute girl, who was finally relieved of her chains in the antechamber, remained so dazed that her bones were like a limp pillow. Carefully Jeremiah dropped the ring of enormous keys upon the jailer's table, not daring to attempt to retie the severed rope around the jailer's waist (which is how, I learned, Jeremiah came to possess the keys in the first place, with the aid of a small knife), and I knew as soon as the jailer awoke, he would be after us. Never have I experienced or tasted such fear as at that moment, with the sleeping jailer before us and freedom so near; and never do I wish to taste such fear again.

Outside were tied two horses—one being Jeremiah's,

the other belonging to the jailer. We stole the jailer's, which I knew would make him more furious still. Jeremiah and the mute girl rode his. Mama and I took the jailer's. Blindly we rode like a fierce storm through the black night. I followed Jeremiah like a sheep, trusting him completely, but fearing every moment to hear the pounding of horses pursuing us.

When we reached the sea, Jeremiah knew exactly where to lead us, having made the arrangements, and once on board, a salty smelling seaman led us down into the ship's hold, which was small and dark and stacked with sacks of wheat and barley bound for England. And who was I to find alongside us as travelling companions? Jeremiah's mother (Jane) and her old Indian servant!

For the remainder of the evening and half into the following day, we were locked in that dark hold for safety until asea, and it was during that time that I learned all else that had occurred. Jeremiah was the one who told me. He sat beside me, his arm around me, applying salve to my bleeding ankles and wrists.

I learned that our ship is one belonging to an old friend of Captain Bradley, Jane's adoptive father, and through that friendship is how our passage came to be arranged. Jane, her pretty face wounded and weeping, has left Jeremiah's father. Nay, she did not desert him in his despair. Rather, she showed him the kindness of release, for without such release they would have remained locked forever in their situation of desperate tragedy. Kindness, I think, takes many forms, and I know Jane's was not easy. Often do I see her pretty dark head nestled upon the shoulder of her servant, and I know in her thoughts she relives all she has left behind.

So much do Jane and I have in common, and yet so much do we differ. She loved the father of her child; I despise mine. I thought much of that child during the day and a half when we were secretted within our hold, and at times it depressed me greatly, for sorely do I regret that I shall always have reminder of Goodman Glover and his sordid use of me. I wondered if ever I could find love for a child that represented such a painful memory, and with desperation I spoke of this to Jeremiah on the second day when finally we were able to go out on deck and smell the crisp, salty sea with its biting winds that reddened my cheeks and tousled my hair.

"You must forget the child's parentage," Jeremiah advised me. "Fatherhood is earned not from blood but from love and raising. You, yourself, should know as such. Was not your true father your mother's husband?"

Troubled, I sighed, saying, "I do try to think so. Aye, I shall always think of Papa as my father. Yet I wonder how I would have felt had I known the truth from the beginning."

"Forget that truth," he said. "Forget it now and forever after. Force it from your mind so it never occurs to you to tell the child. The child must never know! Truth," he added, forcefully, "sometimes holds the least compassion. When so, silence is the better."

The last, I knew was spoken from experience, and I cannot help but wonder how his own knowledge would shape him in the years to come. 'Twill add character, I think, and make him stronger. Thus, when I tremble for what form a child shall take whose father's blood runs twice through its veins, and when I dread for a babe born both grotesque and inferior for its genetic depravity, I have only to look at Jeremiah to be assuaged. Pray, God, may my child be even a fraction so admirable.

Jeremiah's arm rested upon my shoulder, and I

looked up into his face as he gazed out at the choppy sea. His thoughts were on the future, moved from our troublesome history. "Where we go now," he said, "we shall start a new life. I know not what England brings, but it shall be better than what we left."

Stung by the realization of what I shall never again see, I said, "We tried so hard, Jeremiah. All of us did. Can we ever go back do you think?"

"Nay," replied Jeremiah, bitterly. "Small minds await us behind. Small minds and perceptions of us that are not accurate. We would never be accepted."

"But *we* know who we are—and what we're like."

"Our own knowing means nothing. 'Tis not how we see ourselves, but how others see us, that makes us what we are. In England, we shall bear no burden of the past."

He kissed me then. He turned me toward him, cupped my face within his hands and lowered his lips to mine, firmly, and with emotion. Absent was the soft brushing of lips we had oft exchanged in the past, and absent, too was awkwardness and youth. Jeremiah kissed me as a man would kiss a woman, and I knew that I loved him.

When we broke, we stood at the railing, watching the swell of the waves beneath us, and I could not help but recall that never once had I seen Mama and Papa kiss, nor even hold hands. Perhaps such display is evil, as I have always been taught. But I do not think so. I think God intends us to love and to show that love. For it is the gentlest of all emotions, and yet the fiercest.

I sit now, writing upon our rolling deck, trying to imagine what is to become of us all. What a bizarre assortment we are: me, in my tattered filthy garb, so clearly just released from prison, always an outcast, and newly stirring with child; Mama, who is now more infant than mother, bereft of her dignity, and broken;

Jane, who has left behind both husband and father, and whose pretty face is too lovely for such grief; a wrinkled old Indian slave woman, whose coppery squareness has become Jane's solace; small, thin Susannah, once mute, but no longer so; and Jeremiah, with his father's blood twice in his veins, and who leads us all. We have not a pence amongst us, nor a destination to offer roof nor shelter. But we shall survive. God would not have taken us this far if He intended to cast us to the ocean winds. I do not believe Jeremiah, though, when he says we shall never return to Salem. I think someday we shall. And it shall be with a hope and a promise that we cannot now foresee.

Susannah spoke with me today. She told me a little of her history, which is quite surprising. But I shall write of that tomorrow.